12

VICTORIAN
GHOST
STORIES

MICHAEL COX is a senior commissioning editor with Oxford
University Press. He has edited *The Oxford Book of English
Ghost Stories* (1986), *Victorian Ghost Stories* (1991) (both with
R. A. Gilbert), *Victorian Detective Stories* (1992), *The Oxford Book of
Historical Stories* (with Jack Adrian, 1994), *The Oxford Book of Spy
Stories* (1996), and *The Oxford Book of Twentieth-Century Ghost
Stories* (1996).

12

VICTORIAN GHOST STORIES

Selected and introduced by

MICHAEL COX

Oxford   New York

OXFORD UNIVERSITY PRESS

Oxford University Press, Great Clarendon Street, Oxford OX2 6DP

Oxford New York

Athens Auckland Bangkok Bogota Bombay
Buenos Aires Calcutta Cape Town Dar es Salaam
Delhi Florence Hong Kong Istanbul Karachi
Kuala Lumpur Madras Madrid Melbourne
Mexico City Nairobi Paris Singapore
Taipei Tokyo Toronto

and associated companies in
Berlin Ibadan

Oxford is a trade mark of Oxford University Press

First published as an Oxford University Press Paperback 1997

British Library Cataloguing in Publication Data
Data available

Library of Congress Cataloging in Publication Data
Data available

ISBN 0–19–288026–8

3 5 7 9 10 8 6 4 2

Typeset by Jayvee, Trivandrum, India
Printed in Great Britain by
Caledonian International Book Manufacturing Ltd.
Glasgow

CONTENTS

Contents

INTRODUCTION

In the year 1670, that inveterate gossip John Aubrey recorded the appearance, not far from Cirencester, of an apparition: 'Being demanded, whether a good spirit or a bad? returned no answer, but disappeared with a curious perfume and a most melodious twang.' In one sense this is a ghost story; but it is not the kind of ghost story celebrated in this collection. Like Aubrey's apparition, 'real' ghosts—the entities that populate the usually dreary literature of psychical research—are typically fleeting, enigmatic, and motiveless. Their fictional counterparts, however, are of a very different order, often pursuing their ends with deadly persistence, and displaying both cunning and indiscriminate hostility. Others are gentler, but no less determined and purposeful. Whether malevolent or not, the ghosts of fiction forge relationships with the living: they become part of our world, within a continuum of life and death.

Our expectations of what a good ghost story should be, as well as how a ghost should behave, derive largely from the fictional ghosts of the nineteenth century, for it was during the high Victorian period, from about 1840 to 1890, that a body of fiction was created in which the certainties and assumptions of contemporary culture—driven by science and secularism—were challenged by narratives that proposed alternative readings of humanity's place in the scheme of things. In his *History of Witchcraft and Demonology* (1926), Montague Summers bemoaned—in typical fashion—the fact that the study of witchcraft had not received adequate attention from serious students of history. He pointed to the 'heavy and crass materialism' of the eighteenth and (especially) nineteenth centuries as a reason for this neglect. However, continued Summers, 'The cycle of time has had its revenge . . . The extraordinary vogue of an immense adherence to Spiritism would alone prove that, whilst the widespread interest that is taken in mysticism is a yet healthier sign that the world will no longer be content to be fed on dry husks and the chaff of straw. And these are only just two indications, and by no means the most significant, out of many.' Summers, being also a keen and discriminating connoisseur of supernatural fiction, and the editor of a pioneering anthology of Victorian ghost stories, would certainly have included the popular appeal of ghost stories amongst his indicators of time's revenge on materialism. The profusion of ghost stories published in the nineteenth century signifies, at the lowest level, nothing more than a taste for thrills amongst a literate but unsophisticated readership. Vicarious fear is a powerful attractant, and Victorian writers became skilled at manipulating primal sources of terror and revulsion. In J. S. Le Fanu's 'Narrative of the Ghost of a Hand' (incorporated into his novel *The House by the Churchyard*, 1863), Mrs Prosser is sitting in the twilight by her open back parlour window when she notices 'a hand stealthily placed upon the stone window-sill outside, as if by someone beneath the window . . . There was nothing but the hand, which was rather short, but handsomely formed, and white and plump, laid on the edge of the window-sill.' We never see more than this hand—this fat white hand without a body. How different from the Jacobean stage ghosts with their earth-stained shrouds and gaping wounds, or the spectral monks of Gothic fiction. No one is really frightened by the ghost of Hamlet's father; but Le Fanu's fat white hand remains a potent agent of discomfort:

There was a candle burning on a small table at the foot of the bed, besides the one he held in one hand . . . He drew the curtain at the side of the bed, and saw Mrs Prosser lying, as for a few seconds he mortally feared, dead, her face being motionless, white, and covered with a cold dew; and on the pillow, close beside her head, and just within the curtains, was the same white, fattish hand, the wrist resting on the pillow, and the fingers extended towards her temple with a slow, wavy motion.

Not all Victorian ghost stories depended on *Grand Guignol* excess for their effects; indeed, a high proportion—as this collection shows—appealed strongly to the age's taste for sentimentality. Yet even in tales that have no other purpose than to arouse pleasurable fear in their readers, Victorian ghost stories often reflected deeper concerns, and remain valuable social and cultural documents for this reason. Taken together they show the intransigence of immemorial beliefs, or what the rationalist calls superstition—all the more remarkable in a materially advancing age. In this sense, Victorian ghost fiction mirrored the contemporary intellectual debate between science and religion, and between science and art, and is suggestive of the cultural tensions caused by rapid material change.

The stories in this selection are typically Victorian in other ways, too. For instance, the presence of Amelia Edwards, Rhoda Broughton, Margaret Oliphant, and others reflects the important contributions made by women writers to the development of supernatural fiction throughout the nineteenth century. I have tried to select examples that show the variety of Victorian ghost fiction; they are also stories that work *as* stories, that function efficiently as self-contained narratives, regardless of the genre to which they belong. There are tales of vengeance from beyond the grave, but also of magnanimity and continuing love in those who, though dead, retain a compelling interest in the living. Here, certainly, is malevolence and terror; but there is tenderness and pathos, too, presented in language that is entirely of its time.

To savour these stories fully we must imagine ourselves in a slower, quieter world, lit by gas and tallow. The winter evenings are long; and as we sit by a crackling fire after a good dinner, with a magazine open before us, there is a cold wind rising outside. But we are snug and cosy, and disposed to be frightened a little. We read, not of places and characters remote from ourselves, but of people and situations that we recognize as being part of our own experience: railway stations, colonial postings, quiet suburban squares, city streets, country houses, all populated by people like us. We must picture ourselves sitting at the heart of a great and expanding empire, at a time when, on all sides, the light of science and reason is being shed on the dark corners of ignorance and superstition. But for the moment we are content to surrender to the old instincts as we suspend, not just our disbelief, but our trust in human self-sufficiency. For if there is a moral to these stories—which all, in their various ways, offer fascinating windows on to the Victorian world—it is that such a trust is illusory and is itself a fiction.

MICHAEL COX
December 1996

1

AMELIA B. EDWARDS

An Engineer's Story

His name was Matthew Price; mine is Benjamin Hardy. We were born within a few days of each other; bred up in the same village; taught at the same school. I cannot remember the time when we were not close friends. Even as boys, we never knew what it was to quarrel. We had not a thought, we had not a possession, that was not in common. We would have stood by each other fearlessly, to the death. It was such a friendship as one reads about sometimes in books—fast and firm as the great Tors upon our native moorlands, true as the sun in the heavens.

The name of our village was Chadleigh. Lifted high above the pasture-flats which stretched away at our feet like a measureless green lake and melted into mist on the furthest horizon, it nestled, a tiny stone-built hamlet, in a sheltered hollow about midway between the plain and the plateau.

Above us, rising ridge beyond ridge, slope beyond slope, spread the mountainous moor-country, bare and bleak for the most part, with here and there a patch of cultivated field or hardy plantation, and crowned highest of all with masses of huge grey crag, abrupt, isolated, hoary, and older than the deluge. These were the Tors—Druids' Tor, King's Tor, Castle Tor, and the like; sacred places, as I have heard, in the ancient time, where crownings, burnings, human sacrifices, and all kinds of bloody heathen rites were performed.

Bones, too, had been found there, and arrowheads, and ornaments of gold and glass. I had a vague awe of the Tors in those boyish days, and would not have gone near them after dark for the heaviest bribe.

I have said that we were born in the same village. He was the son of a small farmer, named William Price, and the eldest of a family of

1

seven; I was the only child of Ephraim Hardy, the Chadleigh black-smith—a well-known man in those parts, whose memory is not forgotten to this day.

Just so far as a farmer is supposed to be a bigger man than a black-smith, Mat's father might be said to have a better standing than mine; but William Price, with his smallholding and his seven boys, was, in fact, as poor as many a day-labourer; whilst the blacksmith, well-to-do, bustling, popular, and open-handed, was a person of some importance in the place.

All this, however, had nothing to do with Mat and myself. It never occurred to either of us that his jacket was out at elbows, or that our mutual funds came altogether from my pocket. It was enough for us that we sat on the same school-bench, conned our tasks from the same primer, fought each other's battles, screened each other's faults, fished, nutted, played truant, robbed orchards and birds' nests together, and spent every half-hour, authorized or stolen, in each other's society.

It was a happy time; but it could not go on for ever. My father, being prosperous, resolved to put me forward in the world. I must know more and do better than himself. The forge was not good enough, the little world of Chadleigh not wide enough, for me. Thus it happened that I was still swinging the satchel when Mat was whistling at the plough, and that at last, when my future course was shaped out, we were separated, as it then seemed to us, for life.

For, blacksmith's son as I was, furnace and forge, in some form or other, pleased me best. I chose to be a working engineer. So my father by-and-by apprenticed me to a Birmingham iron-master; and, having bidden farewell to Mat, and Chadleigh, and the grey old Tors in the shadow of which I had spent all the days of my life, I turned my face northward, and went over into 'the Black Country'.

I am not going to dwell on this part of my story. How I worked out the term of my apprenticeship; how, when I had served my full time and become a skilled workman, I took Mat from the plough and brought him over to the Black Country, sharing with him lodging, wages, experience—all, in short, that I had to give; how he, naturally quick to learn and brimful of quiet energy, worked his way up a step at a time, and came by-and-by to be a 'first hand' in his own department; how, during all these years of change, and trial, and effort, the old boyish affection never wavered or weakened, but went on growing with our growth and strengthening with our strength—are facts which I need do no more than outline in this place.

About this time—it will be remembered that I speak of the days when Mat and I were on the bright side of thirty—it happened that our firm contracted to supply six first-class locomotives to run on the new line, then in progress of construction, between Turin and Genoa. It was the first Italian order we had taken.

We had had dealings with France, Holland, Belgium, Germany; but never with Italy. The connection, therefore, was new and valuable—all the more valuable because our Transalpine neighbours had but lately begun to lay down the iron roads, and would be safe to need more of our good English work as they went on. So the Birmingham firm set themselves to the contract with a will, lengthened our working hours, increased our wages, took on fresh hands, and determined, if energy and promptitude could do it, to place themselves at the head of the Italian labour-market, and stay there. They deserved and achieved success.

The six locomotives were not only turned out to time, but were shipped, dispatched, and delivered with a promptitude that fairly amazed our Piedmontese consignee. I was not a little proud, you may be sure, when I found myself appointed to superintend the transport of the engines. Being allowed a couple of assistants, I contrived that Mat should be one of them; and thus we enjoyed together the first great holiday of our lives.

It was a wonderful change for two Birmingham operatives fresh from the Black Country. Genoa, that fairy city, with its crescent background of Alps; the port crowded with strange shipping; the marvellous blue sky and bluer sea; the painted houses on the quays; the quaint cathedral faced with black and white marble; the street of jewellers, like an Arabian Nights' bazaar; the street of palaces with its Moorish courtyards, its fountains and orange-trees; the women veiled like brides; the galley-slaves chained two and two; the processions of priests and friars; the everlasting clangour of bells; the babble of a strange tongue; the singular lightness and brightness of the climate—made, altogether, such a combination of wonders that we wandered

3

about the first day in a kind of bewildered dream, like children at a fair. Before that week was ended, being tempted by the beauty of the place and the liberality of the pay, we had agreed to take service with the Turin and Genoa Railway Company, and to turn our backs upon Birmingham for ever.

Then began a new life—a life so active and healthy, so steeped in fresh air and sunshine, that we sometimes marvelled how we could have endured the gloom of the Black Country. We were constantly up and down the line—now at Genoa, now at Turin, taking trial trips with the locomotives, and placing our old experience at the service of our new employers.

In the meanwhile we made Genoa our headquarters, and hired a couple of rooms over a small shop in a by-street sloping down to the quays. Such a busy little street—so steep and winding that no vehicles could pass through it, and so narrow that the sky looked like a mere strip of deep blue ribbon overhead! Every house in it, however, was a shop where the goods encroached on the footway, or were piled about the door, or hung like tapestry from the balconies; and all day long, from dawn to dusk, an incessant stream of passers-by poured up and down between the port and the upper quarter of the city.

Our landlady was the widow of a silver-worker, and lived by the sale of filigree ornaments, cheap jewellery, combs, fans, and toys in ivory and jet. She had an only daughter, named Gianetta, who served in the shop and was simply the most beautiful woman I ever beheld. Looking back across this weary chasm of years, and bringing her image before me (as I can and do) with all the vividness of life, I am unable, even now, to detect a flaw in her beauty. I do not attempt to describe her. I do not believe there is a poet living who could find the words to do it; but I once saw a picture that was somewhat like her (not half so lovely, but still like her), and, for aught I know, that picture is still hanging where I last looked at it—upon the walls of the Louvre.

It represented a woman with brown eyes and golden hair, looking over her shoulder into a circular mirror held by a bearded man in the background. In this man, as I then understood, the artist had painted his own portrait; in her, the portrait of the woman he loved. No picture that I ever saw was half so beautiful, and yet it was not worthy to be named in the same breath with Gianetta Coneglia.

You may be certain the widow's shop did not want for customers. All Genoa knew how fair a face was to be seen behind that dingy little counter; and Gianetta, flirt as she was, had more lovers than she cared to remember, even by name. Gentle and simple, rich and poor, from the red-capped sailor buying his earrings or his amulet, to the noble-man carelessly purchasing half the filigrees in the window, she treated them all alike—encouraged them, laughed at them, led them on and turned them off at her pleasure. She had no more heart than a marble statue; as Mat and I discovered by-and-by, to our bitter cost.

I cannot tell to this day how it came about, or what first led me to suspect how things were going with us both; but long before the wan-ing of that Autumn a coldness had sprung up between my friend and myself. It was nothing that could have been put into words. It was nothing that either of us could have explained or justified, to save his life. We lodged together, ate together, worked together, exactly as before; we even took our long evening's walk together, when the day's labour was ended; and except, perhaps, that we were more silent than of old, no mere looker-on could have detected a shadow of change. Yet there it was, silent and subtle, widening the gulf between us every day.

It was not his fault. He was too true and gentle-hearted to have willingly brought about such a state of things between us. Neither do I believe—fiery as my nature is—that it was mine. It was all hers—hers from first to last—the sin, and the shame, and the sorrow.

If she had shown a fair and open preference for either of us, no real harm could have come of it. I would have put any constraint upon myself, and, Heaven knows! have borne any suffering, to see Mat really happy. I know that he would have done the same, and more if he could, for me. But Gianetta cared not one bajocco for either. She never meant to choose between us.

It gratified her vanity to divide us; it amused her to play with us. It would pass my power to tell how, by a thousand imperceptible shades of coquetry—by the lingering of a glance, the substitution of a word, the flitting of a smile—she contrived to turn our heads, and torture our hearts, and lead us on to love her. She deceived us both. She buoyed us both up with hope; she maddened us with jealousy; she crushed us with despair. For my part, when I seemed now and then to wake to a sudden sense of the ruin that was about our path, and saw how the truest friendship that ever bound two lives together was drifting on to wreck and ruin, I asked myself whether any woman in the world was worth what Mat had been to me and I to him. But this was not often. I was readier to shut my eyes upon the truth than to face it; and so lived on, wilfully, in a dream.

Thus the Autumn passed away, and Winter came—the strange, treacherous Genoese Winter, green with olive and ilex, brilliant with sunshine, and bitter with storm. Still, rivals at heart and friends on the surface, Mat and I lingered on in our lodging in the Vicolo Balba. Still Gianetta held us with her fatal wiles and her still more fatal beauty. At length there came a day when I felt I could bear the horrible misery and suspense of it no longer. The sun, I vowed, should not go down before I knew my sentence. She must choose between us. She must either take me or let me go. I was reckless. I was desperate. I was determined to know the worst or the best. If the worst, I would at once turn my back upon Genoa, upon her, upon all the pursuits and purposes of my past life, and begin the world anew. This I told her, passionately and sternly, standing before her in the little parlour at the back of the shop, one bleak December morning.

'If it's Mat whom you care for most,' I said, 'tell me so in one word, and I will never trouble you again. He is better worth your love. I am jealous and exacting; he is as trusting and unselfish as a woman. Speak, Gianetta; am I to bid you goodbye for ever and ever, or am I to write home to my mother in England, bidding her pray to God to bless the woman who has promised to be my wife?'

'You plead your friend's cause well,' she replied haughtily. 'Matteo ought to be grateful. This is more than he ever did for you.'

'Give me an answer, for pity's sake,' I exclaimed, 'and let me go!'

'You are free to go or stay, Signor Inglese,' she replied, 'I am not your gaoler.'

'Do you bid me leave you?'

'Beata Madre! not I.'

'Will you marry me, if I stay?'

She laughed aloud—such a merry, mocking, musical laugh, like a chime of silver bells!

'You ask too much,' she said.

'Only what you have led me to hope these five or six months past.'

'That is just what Matteo says. How tiresome you both are!'

'Oh, Gianetta,' I said, passionately, 'be serious for one moment! I am a rough fellow, it is true—not half good enough or clever enough for you; but I love you with my whole heart, and an Emperor could do no more.'

'I am glad of it,' she replied; 'I do not want you to love me less.'

'Then you cannot wish to make me wretched! Will you promise me?'

'I promise nothing,' said she, with another burst of laughter; 'except that I will not marry Matteo!'

Except that she would not marry Matteo! Only that. Not a word of hope for myself. Nothing but my friend's condemnation. I might get comfort, and selfish triumph, and some sort of base assurance out of that, if I could. And so, to my shame, I did. I grasped at the vain encouragement, and, fool that I was! let her put me off again un-answered. From that day I gave up all effort at self-control, and let myself drift blindly on—to destruction.

At length things became so bad between Mat and myself that it seemed as if an open rupture must be at hand. We avoided each other, scarcely exchanged a dozen sentences in a day, and fell away from all our old familiar habits. At this time—I shudder to remember it!—there were moments when I felt that I hated him.

Thus, with the trouble deepening and widening between us day by day, another month or five weeks went by, and February came; and, with February, the Carnival. They said in Genoa that it was a particu-larly dull carnival; and so it must have been, for, save a flag or two hung out in some of the principal streets, and a sort of festa look about the women, there were no special indications of the season. It was, I think, the second day of the Carnival, when, having been on the line all the morning, I returned to Genoa at dusk, and to my surprise found Mat Price on the platform. He came up to me, and laid his hand on my arm.

'You are in late,' he said. 'I have been waiting for you three-quarters of an hour. Shall we dine together today?'

Impulsive as I am, this evidence of returning goodwill at once called up my better feelings.

'With all my heart, Mat,' I replied; 'shall we go to Gozzoli's?'

'No, no,' he said, hurriedly. 'Some quieter place—some place where we can talk. I have something to say to you.'

I noticed now that he looked pale and agitated, and an uneasy sense of apprehension stole upon me. We decided on the 'Pescatore', a little out-of-the-way trattoria, down near the Molo Vecchio. There, in a dingy salon frequented chiefly by seamen, and redolent of tobacco, we ordered our simple dinner. Mat scarcely swallowed a morsel, but, calling presently for a bottle of Sicilian wine, drank eagerly.

'Well, Mat,' I said, as the last dish was placed on the table, 'what news have you?'

'Bad.'

'I guessed that from your face.'

'Bad for you—bad for me. Gianetta . . .'

'What of Gianetta?'

He passed his hand nervously across his lips.

'Gianetta is false—worse than false,' he said, in a hoarse voice. 'She values an honest man's heart just as she values a flower for her hair—wears it for a day, then throws it aside for ever. She has cruelly wronged us both.'

'In what way? Good Heavens, speak out!'

'In the worst way that a woman can wrong those who love her. She has sold herself to the Marchese Loredano.'

The blood rushed to my head and face in a burning torrent. I could scarcely see, and dared not trust myself to speak.

'I saw her going towards the cathedral,' he went on, hurriedly. 'It was about three hours ago. I thought she might be going to confession, so I hung back and followed her at a distance. When she got inside, however, she went straight to the back of the pulpit, where this old man was waiting for her. You remember him—an old man who used to haunt the shop a month or two back. Well, seeing how deep in conversation they were, and how they stood close under the pulpit with their backs towards the church, I fell into a passion of anger and went straight up the aisle, intending to say or do something, I scarcely knew what; but, at all events, to draw her arm through mine, and take her home. When I came within a few feet, however, and found only a big pillar between myself and them, I paused. They could not see me, nor I them; but I could hear their voices distinctly, and—and I listened.'

'Well, and you heard. . . .'

'The terms of a shameful bargain—beauty on the one side, gold on the other; so many thousand francs a year; a villa near Naples—Pah! it makes me sick to repeat it.'

And with a shudder, he poured out another glass of wine and drank it at a draught.

'After that,' he said presently, 'I made no effort to bring her away. The whole thing was so cold-blooded, so deliberate, so shameful, that I felt I had only to wipe her out of my memory, and leave her to her fate. I stole out of the cathedral, and walked about here by the sea for ever so long, trying to get my thoughts straight. Then I remembered you, Ben; and the recollection of how this wanton had come between us and broken up our lives drove me wild. So I went up to the station and waited for you. I felt you ought to know it all; and—and I thought, perhaps, that we might go back to England together.'

'The Marchese Loredano!'

It was all that I could say; all that I could think. As Mat had just said of himself, I felt 'like one stunned'.

'There is one other thing I may as well tell you,' he added, reluctantly, 'if only to show you how false a woman can be. We—we were to have been married next month.'

'*We?* Who? What do you mean?'

'I mean that we were to have been married—Gianetta and I.'

A sudden storm of rage, of scorn, of incredulity swept over me at this, and seemed to carry my senses away.

'*You!*' I cried. 'Gianetta marry *you!* I don't believe it.'

'I wish I had not believed it,' he replied, looking up as if puzzled by my vehemence. 'But she promised me; and I thought when she promised it she meant it.'

'She told me weeks ago that she would never be your wife!'

His colour rose; his brow darkened; but when his answer came, it was as calm as the last.

'Indeed' he said. 'Then it is only one baseness more. She told me that she had refused you; and that was why we kept our engagement secret.'

'Tell the truth, Mat Price,' I said, well-nigh beside myself with suspicion. 'Confess that every word of this is false! Confess that Gianetta will not listen to you, and that you are afraid I may succeed where you have failed. As perhaps I shall—as perhaps I shall, after all!'

'Are you mad?' he exclaimed. 'What do you mean?'

'That I believe it's just a trick to get me away to England—that I don't credit a syllable of your story. You're a liar, and I hate you!'

He rose, and laying one hand on the back of his chair, looked me sternly in the face.

'If you were not Benjamin Hardy,' he said, deliberately, 'I would thrash you within an inch of your life.'

The words had no sooner passed his lips than I sprang at him. I have never been able distinctly to remember what followed. A curse—a blow—a struggle—a moment of blind fury—a cry—a confusion of tongues—a circle of strange faces. Then I see Mat lying back in the arms of a bystander; myself trembling and bewildered—the knife dropping from my grasp; blood upon the floor; blood upon my hands; blood upon his shirt. And then I hear those dreadful words:

'Oh, Ben, you have murdered me!'

He did not die—at least, not there and then. He was carried to the nearest hospital, and lay for some weeks between life and death. His case, they said, was difficult and dangerous. The knife had gone in just below the collar-bone, and pierced down into the lungs.

He was not allowed to speak or turn—scarcely to breathe with freedom. He might not even lift his head to drink. I sat by him day and night all through that sorrowful time. I gave up my situation on the railway; I quitted my lodging in the Vicolo Balba; I tried to forget that such a woman as Gianetta Coneglia had ever drawn breath.

I lived only for Mat; and he tried to live, more I believe for my sake than his own. Thus, in the bitter silent hours of pain and penitence, when no hand but mine approached his lips or smoothed his pillow, the old friendship came back with even more than its old trust and faithfulness. He forgave me fully and freely; and I would thankfully have given my life for him.

At length there came one bright Spring morning, when, dismissed as convalescent, he tottered out through the hospital gates, leaning on my arm and feeble as an infant. He was not cured; neither, as I then learned to my horror and anguish, was it possible that he ever could be cured.

He might, with care, live for some years; but the lungs were injured beyond hope of remedy, and a strong or healthy man he could never be again. These, spoken aside to me, were the parting words of the chief physician, who advised me to take him further south without delay.

I took him to a little coast-town called Rocca, some thirty miles beyond Genoa—a sheltered lonely place along the Riviera, where the sea was even bluer than the sky, and the cliffs were green with strange tropical plants, cacti, and aloes, and Egyptian palms.

Here we lodged in the house of a small tradesman; and Mat, to use his own words, 'set to work at getting well in good earnest'. But, alas! it was a work which no earnestness could forward. Day after day he went down to the beach, and sat for hours drinking the sea-air and watching the sails that came and went in the offing. By-and-by he could go no further than the garden of the house in which we lived.

A little later, and he spent his days on a couch beside the open window, waiting patiently for the end. Ay, for the end! It had come to that. He was fading fast—waning with the waning Summer, and conscious that the Reaper was at hand. His whole aim now was to soften the agony of my remorse and prepare me for what must shortly come.

'I would not live longer if I could,' he said, lying on his couch one Summer evening and looking up to the stars. 'If I had my choice at this moment, I would ask to go. I should like Gianetta to know that I forgave her.'

'She shall know it,' I said, trembling suddenly from head to foot.

He pressed my hand.

'And you'll write to father?'

'I will.'

I had drawn a little back, that he might not see the tears raining down my cheeks; but he raised himself on his elbow, and looked round.

'Don't fret, Ben,' he whispered; laid his head back wearily upon the pillow—and so died.

And this was the end of it. This was the end of all that made life life to me. I buried him there, in hearing of the wash of a strange sea on a strange shore. I stayed by the grave till the priest and the bystanders were gone. I saw the earth filled in to the last sod, and the gravedigger stamp it down with his feet.

Then, and not till then, I felt that I had lost him for ever—the friend I had loved, and hated, and slain. Then, and not till then, I knew that all rest and joy, and hope were over for me. From that moment my heart hardened within me, and my life was filled with loathing. Day and night, land and sea, labour and rest, food and sleep, were alike hateful to me.

It was the curse of Cain, and that my brother had pardoned me made it lie none the lighter. Peace on earth was for me no more, and goodwill towards men was dead in my heart for ever. Remorse softens some natures; but it poisoned mine. I hated all mankind, but above all mankind I hated the woman who had come between us two, and ruined both our lives.

He had bidden me seek her out, and be the messenger of his forgiveness. I had sooner have gone down to the port of Genoa and taken upon me the serge cap and shotted chain of any galley-slave at his toil in the public works; but for all that I did my best to obey him. I went back, alone and on foot. I went back, intending to say to her, 'Gianetta Coneglia, he forgave you—but God never will.' But she was gone.

The little shop was let to a fresh occupant. The neighbours only knew that mother and daughter had left the place quite suddenly, and that Gianetta was supposed to be under the 'protection' of the Marchese Loredano. How I made enquiries here and there—how I heard they had gone to Naples—and how, being restless and reckless of my time, I worked my passage in a French steamer, and followed her—how, having found the sumptuous villa that was now hers, I learned that she had left there some ten days and gone to Paris, where the Marchese was ambassador for the Two Sicilies—how, working my passage back again to Marseilles, and thence, in part by the river and in part by the rail, I made my way to Paris—how, day after day, I paced the streets and the parks, watched at the ambassador's gates, followed his carriage, and, at last, after weeks of waiting, discovered her address—how, having written to request an interview, her servants spurned me from her door and flung my letter in my face—how, looking up at her windows, I then, instead of forgiving, solemnly cursed her with the bitterest curses my tongue could devise—and how, this done, I shook the dust of Paris from my feet and became a wanderer upon the face of the earth, are facts which I have no space to tell.

The next six or eight years of my life were shifting and unsettled enough. A morose and restless man, I took employment here and there as opportunity offered, turning my hand to many things, and caring little what I earned, so long as the work was hard and the change incessant. First of all I engaged myself as chief engineer in one of the French steamers plying between Marseilles and Constantinople. At Constantinople I changed to one of the Austrian Lloyd's boats, and worked for some time to and from Alexandria, Jaffa, and those parts. After that, I fell in with a party of Mr Layard's men at Cairo, and so went up the Nile and took a turn at the excavations of the mound of Nimroud.

Then I became a working engineer on the new desert line between Alexandria and Suez; and by-and-by I worked my passage out to Bombay, and took service as an engine-fitter on one of the great Indian railways. I stayed a long time in India—that is to say, I stayed nearly two years, which was a long time for me; and I might not even have left so soon, but for the war that was declared just then with Russia. That tempted me. For I loved danger and hardship as other men love safety and ease; and as for my life, I had sooner have parted with it than kept it, any day. So I came straight back to England and betook myself to Portsmouth, where my testimonials at once procured me the sort of berth I wanted. I then went out to the Crimea in the engine-room of one of Her Majesty's war-steamers.

I served with the fleet, of course, while the war lasted; and when it was over, went wandering off again, rejoicing in my liberty. This time I went to Canada, and after working on a railway then in progress near the American frontier, I presently passed over into the States; journeyed from north to south; crossed the Rocky Mountains; tried a month or two of life in the gold country; and then, being seized with a sudden, aching, unaccountable longing to revisit that solitary grave so far away on the Italian coast, I turned my face once more towards Europe.

Poor little grave! I found it rank with weeds, the cross half shattered, the inscription half effaced. It was as if no one had loved him or remembered him. I went back to the house in which we had lodged together. The same people were still living there, and made me kindly welcome. I stayed with them for some weeks. I weeded, and planted, and trimmed the grave with my own hands, and set up a fresh cross in pure white marble. It was the first season of rest that I had known since I laid him there; and when at last I shouldered my knapsack and set forth again to battle with the world, I promised myself that, God willing, I would creep back to Rocca when my days drew near to ending, and be buried by his side.

From hence, being, perhaps, a little less inclined than formerly for very distant parts, and willing to keep within reach of that grave, I went no further than Mantua, where I engaged myself as an engine-driver on the line, then not long completed, between that city and Venice. Somehow, although I had been trained to the working engin-eering, I preferred in these days to earn my bread by driving. I liked the excitement of it, the sense of power, the rush of the air, the roar of the fire, the flitting of the landscape. Above all, I enjoyed to drive a night-express. The worse the weather, the better it suited with my sullen temper. For I was as hard, and harder than ever. The years had done nothing to soften me. They had only confirmed all that was blackest and bitterest in my heart.

I continued pretty faithful to the Mantua line, and had been work-ing on it steadily for more than seven months when that which I am now about to relate took place.

It was in the month of March. The weather had been unsettled for some days past, and the nights stormy; and at one point along the line, near Ponte di Brenta, the waters had risen and swept away some sev-enty yards of embankment. Since this accident, the trains had all been obliged to stop at a certain spot between Padua and Ponte di Brenta, and the passengers, with their luggage, had thence to be transported in all kinds of vehicles, by a circuitous country-road, to the nearest sta-tion on the other side of the gap, where another train and engine awaited them. This, of course, caused great confusion and annoy-ance, put all our timetables wrong, and subjected the public to a large amount of inconvenience.

In the meanwhile an army of navvies was drafted to the spot, and worked day and night to repair the damage. At this time I was driving

14

two through-trains each day; namely, one from Mantua to Venice in the early morning, and a return-train from Venice to Mantua in the afternoon—a tolerably full day's work, covering about one hundred and ninety miles of ground, and occupying between ten and eleven hours.

I was therefore not best pleased when, on the third or fourth day after the accident, I was informed that, in addition to my regular allowance of work, I should that evening be required to drive a special train to Venice. This special train, consisting of an engine, a single carriage, and a break-van, was to leave the Mantua platform at eleven; at Padua the passengers were to alight and find post-chaises waiting to convey them to Ponte di Brenta; at Ponte di Brenta another engine, carriage, and break-van were to be in readiness. I was charged to accompany them throughout.

'Corpo di Bacco,' said the clerk who gave me my orders, 'you need not look so black, man. You are certain of a handsome gratuity. Do you know who goes with you?'

'Not I.'

'Not you, indeed! Why, it's the Duca Loredano, the Neapolitan ambassador.'

'Loredano!' I stammered. 'What Loredano? There was a Marchese. . . .'

'Certo. He was the Marchese Loredano some years ago; but he has come into his dukedom since then.'

'He must be a very old man by this time.'

'Yes, he is old; but what of that? He is as hale, and bright, and stately as ever. You have seen him before?'

'Yes,' I said, turning away; 'I have seen him—years ago.'

'You have heard of his marriage?'

I shook my head.

The clerk chuckled, rubbed his hands, and shrugged his shoulders.

'An extraordinary affair,' he said. 'Made a tremendous *esclandre* at the time. He married his mistress—quite a common, vulgar girl—a Genoese—very handsome; but not received of course. Nobody visits her.'

'Married her!' I exclaimed. 'Impossible.'

'True, I assure you.'

I put my hand to my head. I felt as if I had had a fall or a blow.

'Does she—does she go tonight?' I faltered.

'Oh dear, yes—goes everywhere with him—never lets him out of her sight. You'll see her—la bella Duchessa!'

With this my informant laughed and rubbed his hands again, and went back to his office.

The day went by, I scarcely know how, except that my whole soul was in a tumult of rage and bitterness. I returned from my afternoon's work about 7.25, and at 10.30 I was once again at the station. I had examined the engine, given instructions to the Fochista, or stoker, about the fire, seen to the supply of oil and got all in readiness, when, just as I was about to compare my watch with the clock in the ticket-office, a hand was laid upon my arm, and a voice in my ear said:

'Are you the engine-driver who is going on with this special train?'

I had never seen the speaker before. He was a small, dark man, muffled up about the throat, with blue glasses, a large black beard, and his hat drawn low upon his eyes.

'You are a poor man, I suppose,' he said, in a quick, eager whisper, 'and, like other poor men, would not object to be better off. Would you like to earn a couple of thousand florins?'

'In what way?'

'Hush! You are to stop at Padua, are you not, and to go on again at Ponte di Brenta?'

I nodded.

'Suppose you did nothing of the kind. Suppose, instead of turning off the steam, you jump off the engine, and let the train run on?'

'Impossible. There are seventy yards of embankment gone, and . . .'

'Basta! I know that. Save yourself, and let the train run on. It would be nothing but an accident.'

I turned hot and cold; I trembled; my heart beat fast, and my breath failed.

'Why do you tempt me?' I faltered.

'For Italy's sake,' he whispered; 'for liberty's sake. I know you are no Italian; but for all that you may be a friend. This Loredano is one of his country's bitterest enemies. Stay, here are the two thousand florins.'

I thrust his hand back fiercely.

'No—no,' I said. 'No blood-money. If I do it, I do it neither for Italy nor for money; but for vengeance.'

'For vengeance!' he repeated.

At this moment the signal was given for backing up to the platform. I sprang to my place upon the engine without another word. When I again looked towards the spot where he had been standing, the stranger was gone.

I saw them take their places—Duke and Duchess, secretary and priest, valet and maid. I saw the station-master bow them into the carriage, and stand, bare-headed, beside the door. I could not distinguish their faces; the platform was too dusk, and the glare from the engine-fire too strong; but I recognized her stately figure, and the poise of her head. Had I not been told who she was, I should have known her by those traits alone. Then the guard's whistle shrilled out, and the station-master made his last bow; I turned the steam on, and we started.

My blood was on fire. I no longer trembled or hesitated. I felt as if every nerve was iron, and every pulse instinct with deadly purpose. She was in my power, and I would be revenged. She should die—she for whom I had stained my soul with my friend's blood! She should die in the plenitude of her wealth and her beauty, and no power on earth should save her!

The stations flew past. I put on more steam; I bade the fireman heap in the coke, and stir the blazing mass. I would have outstripped the wind, had it been possible. Faster and faster—hedges and trees, bridges and stations, flashing past—villages no sooner seen than gone—telegraph wires twisting, and dipping, and twining themselves in one, with the awful swiftness of our pace! Faster and faster, till the fireman at my side looks white and scared, and refuses to add more fuel to the furnace! Faster and faster, till the wind rushes in our faces and drives the breath back upon our lips!

I would have scorned to save myself. I meant to die with the rest. Mad as I was—and I believe from my soul that I was utterly mad for the time—I felt a passing pang of pity for the old man and his suite. I would have spared the poor fellow at my side, too, if I could; but the pace at which we were going made escape impossible.

Vicenza was passed—a mere confused vision of lights. Pojana flew by. At Padua, but nine miles distant, our passengers were to alight. I saw the fireman's face turned upon me in remonstrance; I saw his lips move, though I could not hear a word; I saw his expression change suddenly from remonstrance to a deadly terror; and then—merciful Heaven! then for the first time I saw that he and I were no longer alone upon the engine.

There was a third man—a third man standing on my right hand, as the fireman was standing on my left—a tall, stalwart man, with short curling hair, and a flat Scotch cap upon his head. As I fell back in the first shock of surprise, he stepped forward, took my place at the engine, and turned the steam off. I opened my lips to speak to him. He turned his head slowly, and looked me in the face.

Matthew Price!

I uttered one long wild cry, flung my arms wildly up above my head, and fell as if I had been smitten with an axe.

I am prepared for the objections that may be made to my story. I expect, as a matter of course, to be told that this was an optical illusion; or that I was suffering from pressure on the brain; or even that I laboured under an attack of temporary insanity. I have heard all these arguments before, and, if I may be forgiven for saying so, I have no desire to hear them again. My own mind has been made up on the subject for many a year. All that I can say—all that I *know* is—that Matthew Price came back from the dead to save my soul and the lives of those whom I, in my guilty rage, would have hurried to destruction. I believe this as I believe in the mercy of Heaven and the forgiveness of repentant sinners.

2

J. S. LE FANU

Madam Crowl's Ghost

I'm an old woman now; and I was but thirteen my last birthday, the night I came to Applewale House. My aunt was the housekeeper there, and a sort o' one-horse carriage was down at Lexhoe to take me and my box up to Applewale.

I was a bit frightened by the time I got to Lexhoe, and when I saw the carriage and horse, I wished myself back again with my mother at Hazelden. I was crying when I got into the 'shay'—that's what we used to call it—and old John Mulbery that drove it, and was a good-natured fellow, bought me a handful of apples at the Golden Lion, to cheer me up a bit; and he told me that there was a currant-cake, and tea, and pork-chops, waiting for me, all hot, in my aunt's room at the great house. It was a fine moonlight night and I eat the apples, lookin' out o' the shay winda.

It is a shame for gentlemen to frighten a poor foolish child like I was. I sometimes think it might be tricks. There was two on 'em on the tap o' the coach beside me. And they began to question me after nightfall, when the moon rose, where I was going to. Well, I told them it was to wait on Dame Arabella Crowl, of Applewale House, near by Lexhoe.

'Ho, then,' says one of them, 'you'll not be long there!'

And I looked at him as much as to say, 'Why not?' for I had spoke out when I told them where I was goin', as if 'twas something clever I had to say.

'Because,' says he—'and don't you for your life tell no one, only watch her and see—she's possessed by the devil, and more an half a ghost. Have you got a Bible?'

19

'Yes, sir,' says I. For my mother put my little Bible in my box, and I knew it was there: and by the same token, though the print's too small for my ald eyes, I have it in my press to this hour.

As I looked up at him, saying 'Yes, sir,' I thought I saw him winkin' at his friend; but I could not be sure.

'Well,' says he, 'be sure you put it under your bolster every night, it will keep the ald girl's claws aff ye.'

And I got such a fright when he said that, you wouldn't fancy! And I'd a liked to ask him a lot about the ald lady, but I was too shy, and he and his friend began talkin' together about their own consarns, and dowly enough I got down, as I told ye, at Lexhoe. My heart sank as I drove into the dark avenue. The trees stands very thick and big, as ald as the ald house almost, and four people, with their arms out and finger-tips touchin', barely girds round some of them.

Well, my neck was stretched out o' the winda, looking for the first view o' the great house; and, all at once we pulled up in front of it.

A great white-and-black house it is, wi' great black beams across and right up it, and gables lookin' out, as white as a sheet, to the moon, and the shadows o' the trees, two or three up and down upon the front, you could count the leaves on them, and all the little diamond-shaped winda-panes, glimmering on the great hall winda, and great shutters, in the old fashion, hinged on the wall outside, boulted across all the rest o' the windas in front, for there was but three or four servants, and the old lady in the house, and most o' t'rooms was locked up.

My heart was in my mouth when I sid the journey was over, and this, the great house afore me, and I sa near my aunt that I never sid till noo, and Dame Crowl, that I was come to wait upon, and was afeard on already.

My aunt kissed me in the hall, and brought me to her room. She was tall and thin, wi' a pale face and black eyes, and long thin hands wi' black mittins on. She was past fifty, and her word was short; but her word was law. I hev no complaints to make of her; but she was a hard woman, and I think she would hev bin kinder to me if I had bin her sister's child in place of her brother's. But all that's o' no consequence noo.

The squire—his name was Mr Chevenix Crowl, he was Dame Crowl's grandson—came down there, by way of seeing that the old lady was well treated, about twice or thrice in the year. I sid him but twice all the time I was at Applewale House.

I can't say but she was well taken care of, notwithstandin', but that was because my aunt and Meg Wyvern, that was her maid, had a conscience, and did their duty by her.

Mrs Wyvern—Meg Wyvern my aunt called her to herself, and Mrs Wyvern to me—was a fat, jolly lass of fifty, a good height and a good breadth, always good-humoured, and walked slow. She had fine wages, but she was a bit stingy, and kept all her fine clothes under lock and key, and wore, mostly, a twilled chocolate cotton, wi' red, and yellow, and green sprigs and balls on it, and it lasted wonderful.

She never gave me nout, not the vally o' a brass thimble, all the time I was there; but she was good-humoured, and always laughin', and she talked no end o' proas over her tea; and, seeing me sa sackless and dowly, she roused me up wi' her laughin' and stories; and I think I liked her better than my aunt—children is so taken wi' a bit o' fun or a story—though my aunt was very good to me, but a hard woman about some things, and silent always.

My aunt took me into her bed-chamber, that I might rest myself a bit while she was settin' the tea in her room. But first she patted me on the shouther, and said I was a tall lass o' my years, and had spired up well, and asked me if I could do plain work and stitchin'; and she looked in my face, and said I was like my father, her brother, that was dead and gone, and she hoped I was a better Christian, and wad na du a' that lids.

It was a hard sayin' the first time I set my foot in her room, I thought.

When I went into the next room, the housekeeper's room—very comfortable, yak (oak) all round—there was a fine fire blazin' away, wi' coal, and peat, and wood, all in a low together, and tea on the table, and hot cake, and smokin' meat; and there was Mrs Wyvern, fat, jolly, and talkin' away, more in an hour than my aunt would in a year.

While I was still at my tea my aunt went upstairs to see Madam Crowl.

'She's agone up to see that old Judith Squailes is awake,' says Mrs Wyvern. 'Judith sits with Madam Crowl when me an Mrs Shutters'— that was my aunt's name—'is away. She's a troublesome old lady. Ye'll hev to be sharp wi' her, or she'll be into the fire, or out o' t' winda. She goes on wires, she does, old though she be.'

'How old, ma'am?' says I.

'Ninety-three her last birthday, and that's eight months gone,' says she; and she laughed. 'And don't be askin' questions about her before your aunt—mind, I tell ye; just take her as you find her, and that's all.'

'And what's to be my business about her, please ma'am?' says I.

'About the old lady? Well,' says she, 'your aunt, Mrs Shutters, will tell you that; but I suppose you'll hev to sit in the room with your work, and see she's at no mischief, and let her amuse herself with her things on the table, and get her her food or drink as she calls for it, and keep her out o' mischief, and ring the bell hard if she's troublesome.'

'Is she deaf, ma'am?'

'No, nor blind,' says she; 'as sharp as a needle, but she's gone quite aupy, and can't remember nout rightly; and Jack the Giant Killer, or Goody Twoshoes will please her as well as the King's court, or the affairs of the nation.'

'And what did the little girl go away for, ma'am, that went on Friday last? My aunt wrote to my mother she was to go.'

'Yes; she's gone.'

'What for?' says I again.

'She didn't answer Mrs Shutters, I do suppose,' says she. 'I don't know. Don't be talkin'; your aunt can't abide a talkin' child.'

'And please, ma'am, is the old lady well in health?' says I.

'It ain't no harm to ask that,' says she. 'She's torflin' a bit lately, but better this week past, and I dare say she'll last out her hundred years yet. Hish! Here's your aunt coming down the passage.'

In comes my aunt, and begins talkin' to Mrs Wyvern, and I, beginnin' to feel more comfortable and at home like, was walkin' about the room lookin' at this thing and at that. There was pretty old china things on the cupboard, and pictures again the wall; and there was a door open in the wainscot, and I sees a queer old leathern jacket, wi' straps and buckles to it, and sleeves as long as the bed-post, hangin' up inside.

'What's that you're at, child?' says my aunt, sharp enough, turning about when I thought she least minded. 'What's that in your hand?'

'This, ma'am?' says I, turning about with the leathern jacket. 'I don't know what it is, ma'am.'

Pale as she was, the red came up in her cheeks, and her eyes flashed wi' anger, and I think only she had half a dozen steps to take, between her and me, she'd a gov me a sizzup. But she did give me a shake by the shouther, and she plucked the thing out o' my hand, and says she, 'While ever you stay here, don't ye meddle wi' nout that don't belong to ye,' and she hung it up on the pin that was there, and shut the door wi' a bang and locked it fast.

Mrs Wyvern was liftin' up her hands and laughin' all this time, quietly in her chair, rolling herself a bit in it, as she used when she was kinkin'.

The tears was in my eyes, and she winked at my aunt, and says she, dryin' her own eyes that was wet wi' the laughin', 'Tut, the child meant no harm—come here to me, child. It's only a pair o' crutches for lame ducks, and ask us no questions mind, and we'll tell ye no lies; and come here and sit down, and drink a mug o' beer before ye go to your bed.'

My room, mind ye, was upstairs, next to the old lady's, and Mrs Wyvern's bed was near hers in her room and I was to be ready at call, if need should be.

The old lady was in one of her tantrums that night and part of the day before. She used to take fits o' the sulks. Sometimes she would not let them dress her, and other times she would not let them take her clothes off. She was a great beauty, they said, in her day. But there was no one about Applewale that remembered her in her prime. And she was dreadful fond o' dress, and had thick silks, and stiff satins, and velvets, and laces, and all sorts, enough to set up seven shops at the least. All her dresses was old-fashioned and queer, but worth a fortune.

Well, I went to my bed. I lay for a while awake; for a' things was new to me; and I think the tea was in my nerves, too, for I wasn't used to it, except now and then on a holiday, or the like. And I heard Mrs Wyvern talkin', and I listened with my hand to my ear; but I could not hear Mrs Crowl, and I don't think she said a word.

There was great care took of her. The people at Applewale knew that when she died they would every one get the sack; and their situations was well paid and easy.

The doctor come twice a week to see the old lady, and you may be sure they all did as he bid them. One thing was the same every time; they were never to cross or frump her, any way, but to humour and please her in everything.

So she lay in her clothes all that night, and next day, not a word she said, and I was at my needlework all that day, in my own room, except when I went down to my dinner.

I would a liked to see the ald lady, and even to hear her speak. But she might as well a'bin in Lunnon a' the time for me.

When I had my dinner my aunt sent me out for a walk for an hour. I was glad when I came back, the trees was so big, and the place so dark and lonesome, and 'twas a cloudy day, and I cried a deal, thinkin' of home, while I was walkin' alone there. That evening, the candles bein' alight, I was sittin' in my room, and the door was open into Madam Crowl's chamber, where my aunt was. It was, then, for the first time I heard what I suppose was the ald lady talking.

It was a queer noise like, I couldn't well say which, a bird, or a beast, only it had a bleatin' sound in it, and was very small.

I pricked my ears to hear all I could. But I could not make out one word she said. And my aunt answered:

'The evil one can't hurt no one, ma'am, bout the Lord permits.'

Then the same queer voice from the bed says something more that I couldn't make head nor tail on.

And my aunt med answer again: 'Let them pull faces, ma'am, and say what they will; if the Lord be for us, who can be against us?'

I kept listenin' with my ear turned to the door, holdin' my breath, but not another word or sound came in from the room. In about twenty minutes, as I was sittin' by the table, lookin' at the pictures in the old Æsop's Fables, I was aware o' something moving at the door, and lookin' up I sid my aunt's face lookin' in at the door, and her hand raised.

'Hish!' says she, very soft, and comes over to me on tiptoe, and she says in a whisper: 'Thank God, she's asleep at last, and don't ye make no noise till I come back, for I'm goin' down to take my cup o' tea, and I'll be back i' noo—me and Mrs Wyvern, and she'll be sleepin' in the room, and you can run down when we come up, and Judith will gie ye yaur supper in my room.'

24

And with that away she goes.

I kep' looking at the picture-book, as before, listenin' every noo and then, but there was no sound, not a breath, that I could hear; an' I began whisperin' to the pictures and talkin' to myself to keep my heart up, for I was growin' feared in that big room.

And at last up I got, and began walkin' about the room, lookin' at this and peepin' at that, to amuse my mind, ye'll understand. And at last what sud I do but peeps into Madame Crowl's bed-chamber.

A grand chamber it was, wi' a great four-poster, wi' flowered silk curtains as tall as the ceilin', and foldin' down on the floor, and drawn close all round. There was a lookin'-glass, the biggest I ever sid before, and the room was a blaze o' light. I counted twenty-two wax-candles, all alight. Such was her fancy, and no one dared say her nay.

I listened at the door, and gaped and wondered all round. When I heard there was not a breath, and did not see so much as a stir in the curtains, I took heart, and I walked into the room on tiptoe, and looked round again. Then I takes a keek at myself in the big glass; and at last it came in my head, 'Why couldn't I ha' a keek at the ald lady herself in the bed?'

Ye'd think me a fule if ye knew half how I longed to see Dame Crowl, and I thought to myself if I didn't peep now I might wait many a day before I got so gude a chance again.

Well, my dear, I came to the side o' the bed, the curtains bein' close, and my heart a'most failed me. But I took courage, and I slips my finger in between the thick curtains, and then my hand. So I waits a bit, but all was still as death. So, softly, softly I draws the curtain, and there, sure enough, I sid before me, stretched out like the painted lady on the tomb-stean in Lexhoe Church, the famous Dame Crowl, of Applewale House. There she was, dressed out. You never sid the like in they days. Satin and silk, and scarlet and green, and gold and pink lace; by Jen! 'twas a sight! A big powdered wig, half as high as herself, was a-top o' her head, and, wow!—was ever such wrinkles?—and her old baggy throat all powdered white, and her cheeks rouged, and mouse-skin eyebrows, that Mrs Wyvern used to stick on, and there she lay grand and stark, wi' a pair o' clocked silk hose on, and heels to her shoon as tall as nine-pins. Lawk! But her nose was crooked and thin, and half the whites o' her eyes was open. She used to stand, dressed as she was, gigglin' and dribblin' before the lookin'-glass, wi' a fan in her hand, and a big nosegay in her bodice. Her wrinkled little hands was stretched down by her sides, and such long nails, all cut into points, I never sid in my days. Could it ever a bin the fashion for grit fowk to wear their finger-nails so?

Well, I think ye'd a-bin frightened yourself if ye'd a sid such a sight. I couldn't let go the curtain, nor move an inch, nor take my eyes off her; my very heart stood still. And in an instant she opens her eyes, and up she sits, and spins herself round, and down wi' her, wi' a clack on her two tall heels on the floor, facin' me, ogglin' in my face wi' her two great glassy eyes, and a wicked simper wi' her old wrinkled lips, and lang fause teeth.

Well, a corpse is a natural thing; but this was the dreadfullest sight I ever sid. She had her fingers straight out pointin' at me, and her back was crooked, round again wi' age. Says she:

'Ye little limb! What for did ye say I killed the boy? I'll tickle ye till ye're stiff!'

If I'd a thought an instant, I'd a turned about and run. But I couldn't take my eyes off her, and I backed from her as soon as I could; and she came clatterin' after, like a thing on wires, with her fingers pointing to my throat, and she makin' all the time a sound with her tongue like zizz-zizz-zizz.

I kept backin' and backin' as quick as I could, and her fingers was only a few inches away from my throat, and I felt I'd lose my wits if she touched me.

I went back this way, right into the corner, and I gev a yellock, ye'd think saul and body was partin', and that minute my aunt, from the door, calls out wi' a blare, and the ald lady turns round on her, and I turns about, and ran through my room, and down the back stairs, as hard as my legs could carry me.

I cried hearty, I can tell you, when I got down to the housekeeper's room. Mrs Wyvern laughed a deal when I told her what happened. But she changed her key when she heard the ald lady's words.

'Say them again,' says she.

So I told her.

'Ye little limb! What for did ye say I killed the boy? I'll tickle ye till ye're stiff.'

'And did ye say she killed a boy?' says she.

'Not I, ma'am,' says I.

Judith was always up with me, after that, when the two elder women was away from her. I would a jumped out at winda, rather than stay alone in the same room wi' her.

It was about a week after, as well as I can remember, Mrs Wyvern, one day when me and her was alone, told me a thing about Madam Crowl that I did not know before.

She being young, and a great beauty, full seventy years before, had married Squire Crowl of Applewale. But he was a widower, and had a son about nine year old.

There never was tale or tidings of this boy after one mornin'. No one could say where he went to. He was allowed too much liberty, and used to be off in the morning, one day, to the keeper's cottage, and breakfast wi' him, and away to the warren, and not home, mayhap, till evening, and another time down to the lake, and bathe there, and spend the day fishin' there, or paddlin' about in the boat. Well, no one could say what was gone wi' him; only this, that his hat was found by the lake, under a haathorn that grows thar to this day, and 'twas thought he was drowned bathin'. And the squire's son, by his second marriage, by this Madam Crowl that lived sa dreadful lang, came in for the estates. It was his son, the ald lady's grandson, Squire Chevenix Crowl, that owned the estates at the time I came to Applewale.

There was a deal o' talk lang before my aunt's time about it; and 'twas said the step-mother knew more than she was like to let out. And she managed her husband, the ald squire, wi' her whiteheft and flatteries. And as the boy was never seen more, in course of time the thing died out of fowks' minds.

I'm goin' to tell ye noo about what I sid wi' my own een.

I was not there six months, and it was winter time, when the ald lady took her last sickness.

The doctor was afeard she might a took a fit o' madness, as she did, fifteen years befoore, and was buckled up, many a time, in a strait-waistcoat, which was the very leathern jerkin' I sid in the closet, off my aunt's room.

Well, she didn't. She pined, and windered, and went off, torflin', torflin', quiet enough, till a day or two before her flittin', and then she took to rabblin', and sometimes skirlin' in the bed, ye'd think a robber had a knife to her throat, and she used to work out o' the bed, and not being strong enough, then, to walk or stand, she'd fall on the flure, wi' her ald wizened hands stretched before her face, and skirlin' still for mercy.

Ye may guess I didn't go into the room, and I used to be shiverin' in my bed wi' fear, at her skirlin' and scrafflin' on the flure, and blarin' out words that id make your skin turn blue.

My aunt, and Mrs Wyvern, and Judith Squailes, and a woman from Lexhoe, was always about her. At last she took fits, and they wore her out.

T" sir (parson) was there, and prayed for her; but she was past praying with. I suppose it was right, but none could think there was much good in it, and sa at lang last she made her flittin', and a' was over, and old Dame Crowl was shrouded and coffined and Squire Chevenix was wrote for. But he was away in France, and the delay was sa lang, that t' sir and doctor both agreed it would not du to keep her langer out o' her place, and no one cared but just them two, and my aunt and the rest o' us, from Applewale, to go to the buryin'. So the old lady of Applewale was laid in the vault under Lexhoe Church; and we lived up at the great house till such time as the squire should come to tell his will about us, and pay off such as he chose to discharge.

I was put into another room, two doors away from what was Dame Crowl's chamber, after her death, and this thing happened the night before Squire Chevenix came to Applewale.

The room I was in now was a large square chamber, covered wi' yak pannels, but unfurnished except for my bed, which had no curtains to it, and a chair and a table, or so, that looked nothing at all in such a big room. And the big looking-glass, that the old lady used to keek into and admire herself from head to heel, now that there was na mair o' that wark, was put out of the way, and stood against the wall in my room, for there was shiftin' o' many things in her chambers ye may suppose, when she came to be coffined.

The news had come that day that the squire was to be down next morning at Applewale; and not sorry was I, for I thought I was sure to be sent home again to my mother. And right glad was I, and I was thinkin' of a' at hame, and my sister, Janet, and the kitten and the pymag, and Trimmer the tike, and all the rest, and I got sa fidgetty, I couldn't sleep, and the clock struck twelve, and me wide awake, and the room as dark as pick. My back was turned to the door, and my eyes toward the wall opposite.

Well, it could na be a full quarter past twelve, when I sees a lightin' on the wall befoore me, as if something took fire behind, and the shadas o' the bed, and the chair, and my gown, that was hangin' from the wall, was dancin' up and down, on the ceilin' beams and the yak pannels; and I turns my head ower my shouther quick, thinkin' something must a gone a' fire.

And what sud I see, by Jen! but the likeness o' the ald beldame, bedizened out in her satins and velvets, on her dead body, simperin', wi' her eyes as wide as saucers, and her face like the fiend himself. 'Twas a red light that rose about her in a fuffin low, as if her dress round her feet was blazin'. She was drivin' on right for me, wi' her ald shrivelled hands crooked as if she was goin' to claw me. I could not stir, but she passed me straight by, wi' a blast o' cald air, and I sid her, at the wall, in the alcove as my aunt used to call it, which was a recess where the state bed used to stand in ald times, wi' a door open wide, and her hands gropin' in at somethin' was there. I never sid that door befoore. And she turned round to me, like a thing on a pivot, flyrin' (grinning), and all at once the room was dark, and I standin' at the far side o' the bed; I don't know how I got there, and I found my tongue at last, and if I did na blare a yellock, rennin' down the gallery and almost pulled Mrs Wyvern's door, off t'hooks, and frightened her half out o' her wits.

Ye may guess I did na sleep that night; and wi' the first light, down wi' me to my aunt, as fast as my two legs cud carry me.

Well, my aunt did na frump or flite me, as I thought she would, but she held me by the hand, and looked hard in my face all the time. And she telt me not to be feared; and says she:

'Hed the appearance a key in its hand?'

'Yes,' says I, bringin' it to mind, 'a big key in a queer brass handle.'

'Stop a bit,' says she, lettin' go ma hand, and openin' the cupboard-door. 'Was it like this?' says she, takin' one out in her fingers and showing it to me, with a dark look in my face.

'That was it,' says I, quick enough.

29

'Are ye sure?' she says, turnin' it round.

'Sart,' says I, and I felt like I was gain' to faint when I sid it.

'Well, that will do, child,' says she, saftly thinkin', and she locked it up again.

'The squire himself will be here today, before twelve o'clock, and ye must tell him all about it,' says she, thinkin', 'and I suppose I'll be leavin' soon, and so the best thing for the present is, that ye should go home this afternoon, and I'll look out another place for you when I can.'

Fain was I, ye may guess, at that word.

My aunt packed up my things for me, and the three pounds that was due to me, to bring home, and Squire Crowl himself came down to Applewale that day, a handsome man, about thirty years ald. It was the second time I sid him. But this was the first time he spoke to me.

My aunt talked wi' him in the housekeeper's room, and I don't know what they said. I was a bit feared on the squire, he bein' a great gentleman down in Lexhoe, and I darn't go near till I was called. And says he, smilin':

'What's a' this ye a sen, child? it mun be a dream, for ye know there's na sic a thing as a bo or a freet in a' the world. But whatever it was, ma little maid, sit ye down and tell us all about it from first to last.'

Well, so soon as I med an end, he thought a bit, and says he to my aunt:

'I mind the place well. In old Sir Oliver's time lame Wyndel told me there was a door in that recess, to the left, where the lassie dreamed she saw my grandmother open it. He was past eighty when he telt me that, and I but a boy. It's twenty year sen. The plate and jewels used to be kept there, long ago, before the iron closet was made in the arras chamber, and he told me the key had a brass handle, and this ye say was found in the bottom o' the kist where she kept her old fans. Now, would not it be a queer thing if we found some spoons or diamonds forgot there? Ye mun come up wi' us, lassie, and point to the very spot.'

Loth was I, and my heart in my mouth, and fast I held by my aunt's hand as I stept into that awsome room, and showed them both how she came and passed me by, and le spot where she stood, and where the door seemed to open.

There was an ald empty press against the wall then, and shoving it aside, sure enough there was the tracing of a door in the wainscot, and a keyhole stopped with wood, and planed across as smooth as the rest, and the joining of the door all stopped wi' putty the colour o' yak, and, but for the hinges that showed a bit when the press was shoved aside, ye would not consayt there was a door there at all.

'Ha!' says he, wi' a queer smile, 'this looks like it.'

It took some minutes wi' a small chisel and hammer to pick the bit o' wood out o' the keyhole. The key fitted, sure enough, and, wi' a strang twist and a lang skreeak, the boult went back and he pulled the door open.

There was another door inside, stranger than the first, but the lacks was gone, and it opened easy. Inside was a narrow floor and walls and vault o' brick; we could not see what was in it, for 'twas dark as pick.

When my aunt had lighted the candle the squire held it up and stept in.

My aunt stood on tiptoe tryin' to look over his shouther, and I did na see nout.

'Ha! ha!' says the squire, steppin' backward. 'What's that? Gi'ma the poker—quick!' says he to my aunt. And as she went to the hearth I peeps beside his arm, and I sid squat down in the far corner a monkey or a flayin' on the chest, or else the maist shrivelled up, wizzened ald wife that ever was sen on yearth.

'By Jen!' says my aunt, as, puttin' the poker in his hand, she keeked by his shouther, and sid the ill-favoured thing, 'hae a care sir, what ye're doin'. Back wi' ye, and shut to the door!'

But in place o' that he steps in saftly, wi' the poker pointed like a swoord, and he gies it a poke, and down it a' tumbles together, head and a', in a heap o' bayans and dust, little meyar an' a hatful.

'Twas the bayans o' a child; a' the rest went to dust at a touch. They said nout for a while, but he turns round the skull as it lay on the floor.

Young as I was I consayted I knew well enough what they was thinkin' on.

'A dead cat!' says he, pushin' back and blowin' out the can'le, and shuttin' to the door. 'We'll come back, you and me, Mrs Shutters, and look on the shelves by-and-bye. I've other matters first to speak to ye about; and this little girl's goin' hame, ye say. She has her wages, and I mun mak' her a present,' says he, pattin' my shoulder wi' his hand.

And he did gimma a goud pound, and I went aff to Lexhoe about an hour after, and sa hame by the stagecoach, and fain was I to be at hame again; and I never saa ald Dame Crowl o' Applewale, God be thanked, either in appearance or in dream, at-efter. But when I was grown to be a woman my aunt spent a day and night wi' me at Littleham, and she telt me there was na doubt it was the poor little boy that was missing sa lang sen that was shut up to die thar in the dark by that wicked beldame, whar his skirls, or his prayers, or his thumpin' cud na be heard, and his hat was left by the water's edge, whoever did it, to mak' belief he was drowned. The clothes, at the first touch, a' ran into a snuff o' dust in the cell whar the bayans was found. But there was a handful o' jet buttons, and a knife with a green handle, together wi' a couple o' pennies the poor little fella had in his pocket, I suppose, when he was decoyed in thar, and sid his last o' the light. And there was, amang the squire's papers, a copy o' the notice that was prented after he was lost, when the old squire thought he might 'a run away, or bin took by gipsies, and it said he had a green-hefted knife wi' him, and that his buttons were o' cut jet. Sa that is a' I hev to say consarnin' ald Dame Crowl, o' Applewale House.

3

RHODA BROUGHTON

Poor Pretty Bobby

I

'Yes, my dear, you may not believe me, but I can assure you that you cannot dislike old women more, nor think them more contemptible supernumeraries, than I did when I was your age.'

This is what old Mrs Hamilton says—the old lady so incredibly tenacious of life (incredibly as it seems to me at eighteen) as to have buried a husband and five strong sons, and yet still to eat her dinner with hearty relish, and laugh at any such jokes as are spoken loudly enough to reach her dulled ears. This is what she says, shaking the while her head, which—poor old soul—is already shaking a good deal involuntarily. I am sitting close beside her armchair, and have been reading aloud to her; but as I cannot succeed in pitching my voice so as to make her hear satisfactorily, by mutual consent the book has been dropped in my lap, and we have betaken ourselves to conversation.

'I never said I disliked old women, did I?' reply I evasively, being too truthful altogether to deny the soft impeachment. 'What makes you think I do? They are infinitely preferable to old men; I do distinctly dislike *them*.'

'A fat, bald, deaf old woman,' continues she, not heeding me, and speaking with slow emphasis, while she raises one trembling hand to mark each unpleasant adjective: 'if in the year '2 any one had told me that I should have lived to be that, I think I should have killed them or myself! and yet now I am all three.'

'You are not *very* deaf,' say I politely—(the fatness and baldness admit of no civilities consistent with veracity)—but I raise my voice to pay the compliment.

'In the year '2 I was seventeen,' she says, wandering off into memory. 'Yes, my dear, I am just fifteen years older than the century, and *it* is getting into its dotage, is not it? The year '2—ah! that was just about the time that I first saw my poor Bobby! Poor pretty Bobby.'

'And who *was* Bobby?' ask I, pricking up my ears, and scenting, with the keen nose of youth, a dead-love idyll; an idyll of which this poor old hill of unsteady flesh was the heroine.

'I must have told you the tale a hundred times, have not I?' she asks, turning her old dim eyes towards me. 'A curious tale, say what you will; and explain it how you will. I think I *must* have told you; but indeed I forget to whom I tell my old stories and to whom I do not. Well, my love, you must promise to stop me if you have heard it before, but to me, you know, these old things are so much clearer than the things of yesterday.'

'You never told me, Mrs Hamilton,' I say, and say truthfully; for being a new acquaintance, I really have not been made acquainted with Bobby's history. 'Would you mind telling it me now, if you are sure that it would not bore you?'

'Bobby,' she repeats softly to herself, 'Bobby. I dare say you do not think it a very pretty name?'

'N—not particularly,' reply I honestly. 'To tell you the truth, it rather reminds me of a policeman.'

'I dare say,' she answers quietly; 'and yet in the year '2 I grew to think it the handsomest, dearest name on earth. Well, if you like, I will begin at the beginning and tell you how that came about.'

'Do,' say I, drawing a stocking out of my pocket, and thriftily beginning to knit to assist me in the process of listening.

'In the year '2 we were at war with France—you know that, of course. It seemed then as if war were our normal state; I could hardly remember a time when Europe had been at peace. In these days of stagnant quiet it appears as if people's kith and kin always lived out their full time and died in their beds. *Then* there was hardly a house where there was not one dead, either in battle, or of his wounds after battle, or of some dysentery or ugly parching fever. As for us, we had always been a soldier family—always; there was not one of us that had ever worn a black gown or sat upon a high stool with a pen behind his ear. I had lost uncles and cousins by the half-dozen and dozen, but, for my part, I did not much mind, as I knew very little about them, and black was more becoming wear to a person with my bright colour than anything else.'

At the mention of her bright colour I unintentionally lift my eyes from my knitting, and contemplate the yellow bagginess of the poor old cheek nearest me. Oh, Time! Time! what absurd and dirty turns you play us! What do you do with all our fair and goodly things when you have stolen them from us? In what far and hidden treasure-house do you store them?

'But I did care very much—very exceedingly—for my dear old father—not so old either—younger than my eldest boy was when he went; he would have been forty-two if he had lived three days longer. Well, well, child, you must not let me wander; you must keep me to it. He was not a soldier, was not my father; he was a sailor, a post-captain in His Majesty's navy, and commanded the ship *Thunderer* in the Channel fleet.

'I had struck seventeen in the year '2, as I said before, and had just come home from being finished at a boarding-school of repute in those days, where I had learnt to talk the prettiest *ancien régime* French, and to hate Bonaparte with unchristian violence, from a little ruined *émigre maréchale*; had also, with infinite expenditure of time, labour, and Berlin wool, wrought out "Abraham's Sacrifice of Isaac", and "Jacob's First Kiss to Rachel", in finest cross-stitch. Now I had bidden adieu to learning; had inly resolved never to disinter "Télémaque" and Thomson's "Seasons" from the bottom of my trunk; had taken a holiday from all my accomplishments, with the exception of cross-stitch, to which I still faithfully adhered—and, indeed, on the day I am going to mention, I recollect that I was hard at work on Judas Iscariot's face in Leonardo da Vinci's "Last Supper"— hard at work at it, sitting in the morning sunshine, on a straight-backed chair. We had flatter backs in those days; our shoulders were not made round by lolling in easy-chairs; indeed, no *then* upholsterer made a chair that it was possible to loll in. My father rented a house near Plymouth at that time, an in-and-out *nooky* kind of old house— no doubt it has fallen to pieces long years ago—a house all set round with unnumbered flowers, and about which the rooks clamoured all together from the windy elm tops. I was labouring in flesh-coloured

35

wool on Judas's left cheek, when the door opened and my mother entered. She looked as if something had freshly pleased her, and her eyes were smiling. In her hand she held an open and evidently just-read letter.

' "A messenger has come from Plymouth," she says, advancing quickly and joyfully towards me. "Your father will be here this afternoon."

' *"This afternoon!"* cry I, at the top of my voice, pushing away my heavy work-frame. "How delightful! But how—how can that happen?"

' "They have had a brush with a French privateer," she answers, sitting down on another straight-backed chair, and looking again over the large square letter, destitute of envelope, for such things were not in those days, "and then they succeeded in taking her. Yet they were a good deal knocked about in the process, and have had to put into Plymouth to refit; so he will be here this afternoon for a few hours."

' "Hurrah!" cry I, rising, holding out my scanty skirts, and beginning to dance.

' "Bobby Gerard is coming with him," continues my mother, again glancing at her dispatch. "Poor boy, he has had a shot through his right arm, which has broken the bone! So your father is bringing him here for us to nurse him well again."

'I stop in my dancing.

' "Hurrah again!" I say brutally. "I do not mean about his arm; of course, I am very sorry for that; but, at all events, I shall see him at last. I shall see whether he is like his picture, and whether it is not as egregiously flattered as I have always suspected."

'There were no photographs you know in those days—not even hazy daguerreotypes—it was fifty good years too soon for them. The picture to which I allude is a miniature, at which I had stolen many a deeply longing admiring glance in its velvet case. It is almost impossible for a miniature not to flatter. To the most coarse-skinned and mealy-potato-faced people it cannot help giving cheeks of the texture of a rose-leaf, and brows of the grain of finest marble.

' "Yes," replies my mother, absently, "so you will. Well, I must be going to give orders about his room. He would like one looking on the garden best, do not you think, Phœbe?—one where he could smell the flowers and hear the birds?"

'Mother goes, and I fall into a meditation. Bobby Gerard is an orphan. A few years ago his mother, who was an old friend of my father's—who knows! perhaps an old love—feeling her end drawing nigh, had sent for father, and had asked him, with eager dying tears, to take as much care of her pretty forlorn boy as he could, and to shield him a little in his tender years from the evils of this wicked world, and to be to him a wise and kindly guardian, in the place of those natural ones that God had taken. And father had promised, and when he promised there was small fear of his not keeping his word.

'This was some years ago, and yet I had never seen him nor he me; he had been almost always at sea and I at school. I had heard plenty about him—about his sayings, his waggeries, his mischievousness, his soft-heartedness, and his great and unusual comeliness; but his outward man, save as represented in that stealthily peeped-at miniature, had I never seen. They were to arrive in the afternoon; but long before the hour at which they were due I was waiting with expectant impatience to receive them. I had changed my dress, and had (though rather ashamed of myself) put on everything of most becoming that my wardrobe afforded. If you were to see me as I stood before the glass on that summer afternoon, you would not be able to contain your laughter; the little boys in the street would run after me throwing stones and hooting; but *then*—according to the *then* fashion and standard of gentility—I was all that was most elegant and *comme il faut*. Lately it has been the mode to puff one's self out with unnatural and improbable protuberances; *then* one's great life-object was to make one's self appear as scrimping as possible—to make one's self look as flat as if one had been ironed. Many people *damped* their clothes to make them stick more closely to them, and to make them define more distinctly the outline of form and limbs. One's waist was under one's arms; the sole object of which seemed to be to outrage nature by pushing one's bust up into one's chin, and one's legs were revealed through one's scanty drapery with startling candour as one walked or sat. I remember once standing with my back to a bright fire in our long drawing-room, and seeing myself reflected in a big mirror at the other end. I was so thinly clad that I was transparent, and could see through myself. Well, in the afternoon in question I was dressed quite an hour and a half too soon. I had a narrow little white gown, which clung successfully tight and close to my figure, and which was of so moderate a length as to leave visible my ankles and my neatly shod and cross-sandalled feet. I had long mittens on my arms, black, and embroidered on the backs in coloured silks; and above my hair, which at the back was scratched up to the top of my crown, towered a tremendous tortoiseshell comb; while on each side of my face modestly dropped a bunch of curls, nearly meeting over my nose.

'My figure was full—ah! my dear, I have always had a tendency to fat, and you see what it has come to—and my pink cheeks were more deeply brightly rosy than usual. I had looked out at every upper window, so as to have the furthest possible view of the road.

'I had walked in my thin shoes half way down the drive, so as to command a turn, which, from the house, impeded my vision, when, at last, after many tantalizing false alarms, and just five minutes later than the time mentioned in the letter, the high-swung, yellow-bodied, post-chaise hove in sight, dragged—briskly jingling—along by a pair of galloping horses. Then, suddenly, shyness overcame me—much as I loved my father, it was more as my personification of all knightly and noble qualities than from much personal acquaintance with him— and I fled.

'I remained in my room until I thought I had given them ample time to get through the first greetings and settle down into quiet talk. Then, having for one last time run my fingers through each ringlet of my two curl bunches, I stole diffidently downstairs.

'There was a noise of loud and gay voices issuing from the parlour, but, as I entered, they all stopped talking and turned to look at me.

' "And so this is Phœbe!" cries my father's jovial voice, as he comes towards me, and heartily kisses me. "Good Lord, how time flies! It does not seem more than three months since I saw the child, and yet then she was a bit of a brat in trousers, and long bare legs!'

'At this allusion to my late mode of attire, I laugh, but I also feel myself growing scarlet.

' "Here, Bobby!" continues my father, taking me by the hand, and leading me towards a sofa on which a young man is sitting beside my mother; "this is my little lass that you have so often heard of. Not such

a very little one, after all, is she? Do not be shy, my boy; you will not
see such a pretty girl every day of your life—give her a kiss."

'My eyes are on the ground, but I am aware that the young man
rises, advances (not unwillingly, as it seems to me), and bestows a kiss
somewhere or other on my face. I am not quite clear *where*, as I think
the curls impede him a good deal.

'Thus, before ever I saw Bobby, before ever I knew what manner of
man he was, I was kissed by him. That was a good beginning, was not it?

'After these salutations are over, we subside again into conversation—I sitting beside my father, with his arm round my waist, sitting
modestly silent, and peeping every now and then under my eyes, as
often as I think I may do so safely unobserved, at the young fellow
opposite me. I am instituting an inward comparison between nature
and art: between the real live man and the miniature that undertakes
to represent him. The first result of this inspection is disappointment,
for where are the lovely smooth roses and lilies that I have been wont
to connect with Bobby Gerard's name? There are no roses in his
cheek, certainly; they are paleish—from his wound, as I conjecture;
but even before that accident, if there were roses at all, they must have
been mahogany-coloured ones, for the salt sea winds and the high
summer sun have tanned his fair face to a rich reddish, brownish,
copperish hue. But in some things the picture lied not. There is the
brow more broad than high; the straight fine nose; the brave and
joyful blue eyes, and the mouth with its pretty curling smile. On the
whole, perhaps, I am not disappointed.

'By-and-by father rises, and steps out into the verandah, where the
canary birds hung out in their cages are noisily praising God after their
manner. Mother follows him. I should like to do the same; but a sense
of good manners, and a conjecture that possibly my parents may have
some subjects to discuss, on which they would prefer to be without
the help of my advice, restrain me. I therefore remain, and so does the
invalid.

II

'For some moments the silence threatens to remain unbroken
between us; for some moments the subdued sound of father's and

mother's talk from among the rosebeds and the piercing clamour of the canaries—fishwives among birds—are the only noises that salute our ears. Noise we make none ourselves. My eyes are reading the muddled pattern of the Turkey carpet; I do not know what his are doing. Small knowledge have I had of men, saving the dancing master at our school; a beautiful new youth is almost as great a novelty to me as to Miranda, and I am a good deal gawkier than she was under the new experience. I think he must have made a vow that he would not speak first. I feel myself swelling to double my normal size with confusion and heat; at last, in desperation, I look up, and say sententiously, "You have been wounded, I believe?"

' "Yes, I have."

'He might have helped me by answering more at large, might not he? But now that I am having a good look at him, I see that he is rather red too. Perhaps he also feels gawky and swollen; the idea encourages me.

' "Did it hurt very badly?"

' "N—not so very much."

' "I should have thought that you ought to have been in bed," say I, with a motherly air of solicitude.

' "Should you, why?"

' "I thought that when people broke their limbs they had to stay in bed till they were mended again."

' "But mine was broken a week ago," he answers, smiling and showing his straight white teeth—ah the miniature was silent about *them!* "You would not have had me stay in bed a whole week, like an old woman?"

' "I expected to have seen you much *iller*," say I, beginning to feel more at my ease, and with a sensible diminution of that unpleasant swelling sensation. "Father said in his note that we were to nurse you well again; that sounded as if you were *quite* ill."

' "Your father always takes a great deal too much care of me," he says, with a slight frown and darkening of his whole bright face. "I might be sugar or salt."

' "And very kind of him, too," I cry, firing up. "What motive beside your own good can he have for looking after you? I call you rather ungrateful."

' "Do you?" he says calmly, and without apparent resentment. "But you are mistaken. I am not ungrateful. However, naturally, you do not understand."

' "Oh, indeed!" reply I, speaking rather shortly, and feeling a little offended, "I dare say not."

'Our talk is taking a somewhat hostile tone; to what further amenities we might have proceeded is unknown; for at this point father and mother reappear through the window, and the necessity of conversing with each other at all ceases.

'Father stayed till evening, and we all supped together, and I was called upon to sit by Bobby, and cut up his food for him, as he was disabled from doing it for himself. Then, later still, when the sun had set, and all his evening reds and purples had followed him, when the night flowers were scenting all the garden, and the shadows lay about, enormously long in the summer moonlight, father got into the post-chaise again, and drove away through the black shadows and the faint clear shine, and Bobby stood at the hall door watching him, with his arm in a sling and a wistful smile on lips and eyes.

' "Well, we are not left *quite* desolate this time," says mother, turning with rather tearful laughter to the young man. "You wish that we were, do not you, Bobby?"

' "You would not believe me, if I answered 'No,' would you?" he asks, with the same still smile.

' "He is not very polite to us, is he, Phœbe?"

' "You would not wish me to be polite in such a case," he replies, flushing. "You would not wish me to be *glad* at missing the chance of seeing any of the fun?"

'But Mr Gerard's eagerness to be back at his post delays the probability of his being able to return thither. The next day he has a feverish attack, the day after he is worse; the day after that worse still, and in fine, it is between a fortnight and three weeks before he also is able to get into a post-chaise and drive away to Plymouth. And meanwhile mother and I nurse him and cosset him, and make him odd and cool drinks out of herbs and field-flowers, whose uses are now disdained or forgotten. I do not mean any offence to you, my dear, but I think that young girls in those days were less squeamish and more truly delicate than they are nowadays. I remember once I read *Humphrey Clinker*

41

aloud to my father, and we both highly relished and laughed over its jokes; but I should not have understood one of the darkly unclean allusions in that French book your brother left here one day. *You* would think it very unseemly to enter the bedroom of a strange young man, sick or well; but as for me, I spent whole nights in Bobby's, watching him and tending him with as little false shame as if he had been my brother. I can hear *now*, more plainly than the song you sang me an hour ago, the slumberous buzzing of the great brown-coated summer bees in his still room, as I sat by his bedside watching his sleeping face, as he dreamt unquietly, and clenched, and again unclenched, his nervous hands. I think he was back in the *Thunderer*. I can see *now* the little close curls of his sunshiny hair straggling over the white pillow. And then there came a good and blessed day, when he was out of danger, and then another, a little further on, when he was up and dressed, and he and I walked forth into the hayfield beyond the garden—reversing the order of things—*he*, leaning on *my* arm; and a good plump solid arm it was. We walked out under the heavy-leaved horse-chestnut trees, and the old and rough-barked elms. The sun was shining all this time, as it seems to me. I do not believe that in those days there were the same cold unseasonable rains as now; there were soft showers enough to keep the grass green and the flowers undrooped; but I have no association of overcast skies and untimely deluges with those long and azure days. We sat under a haycock, on the shady side, and indolently watched the hot haymakers—the shirt-sleeved men, and burnt and bare-armed women, tossing and raking; while we breathed the blessed country air, full of adorable scents, and crowded with little happy and pretty-winged insects.

' "In three days," says Bobby, leaning his elbow in the hay, and speaking with an eager smile, "three days at the furthest, I may go back again, may not I, Phœbe?"

' "Without doubt," reply I, stiffly, pulling a dry and faded ox-eye flower out of the odorous mound beside me; "for my part, I do not see why you should not go tomorrow, or indeed—if we could send into Plymouth for a chaise—this afternoon; you are so thin that you look all mouth and eyes, and you can hardly stand, without assistance, but these, of course, are trifling drawbacks, and I daresay would be rather an advantage on board ship than otherwise."

' "You are angry!" he says, with a sort of laugh in his deep eyes. "You look even prettier when you are angry than when you are pleased."

' "It is no question of my looks," I say, still in some heat, though mollified by the irrelevant compliment.

' "For the second time you are thinking me ungrateful," he says, gravely; "you do not tell me so in so many words, because it is towards yourself that my ingratitude is shown. The first time you told me of it, it was almost the first thing that you ever said to me."

' "So it was," I answer quickly; "and if the occasion were to come over again, I should say it again. I daresay you did not mean it, but it sounded exactly as if you were complaining of my father for being too careful of you."

' "He *is* too careful of me!" cries the young man, with a hot flushing of cheek and brow. "I cannot help it if it make you angry again; I *must* say it, he is more careful of me than he would be of his own son, if he had one."

' "Did he not promise your mother that he would look after you?" ask I, eagerly. "When people make promises to people on their deathbeds, they are in no hurry to break them; at least such people as father are not."

' "You do not understand," he says, a little impatiently, while that hot flush still dwells on his pale cheek. "My mother was the last person in the world to wish him to take care of my body at the expense of my honour."

' "What are you talking about?" I say, looking at him, with a lurking suspicion that, despite the steady light of reason in his blue eyes, he is still labouring under some form of delirium.

' "Unless I tell you all my grievance, I see that you will never comprehend," he says, sighing. "Well, listen to me, and you shall hear it; and if you do not agree with me when I have done, you are not the kind of girl I take you for."

' "Then I am sure I am not the kind of girl you take me for," reply I, with a laugh; "for I am fully determined to disagree with you entirely."

' "You know," he says, raising himself a little from his hay couch, and speaking with clear rapidity, "that, whenever we take a French prize a lot of the French sailors are ironed, and the vessel is sent into

43

port, in the charge of one officer and several men. There is some slight risk attending it—for my part, I think *very* slight—but I suppose that your father looks at it differently, for—*I have never been sent.*"

' "It is accident," say I, reassuringly. "Your turn will come in good time."

' "It is *not* accident!" he answers firmly. "Boys younger than I am—much less trustworthy, and of whom he has not half the opinion that he has of me—have been sent, but I, *never.* I bore it as well as I could for a long time, but now I can bear it no longer; it is not, I assure you, my fancy; but I can see that my brother officers, knowing how partial your father is to me—what influence I have with him in many things—conclude that my not being sent is my own choice; in short, that I am—*afraid.*" (His voice sinks with a disgusted and shamed intonation at the last word.) "Now—I have told you the sober facts—look me in the face" (putting his hand, with boyish familiarity, under my chin, and, turning round my curls, my features, and the front view of my big comb towards him), "and tell me whether you agree with me, as I said you would, or not—whether it is not cruel kindness on his part to make me keep a whole skin on such terms?"

'I look him in the face for a moment, trying to say that I do not agree with him, but it is more than I can manage.

"You were right," I say, turning my head away. "I *do* agree with you; I wish to heaven that I could honestly say that I did not."

' "Since you do, then," he cries excitedly—"Phœbe! I knew you would; I knew you better than you knew yourself—I have a favour to ask of you, a *great* favour, and one that will keep me all my life in debt to you."

' "What is it?" ask I, with a sinking heart.

' "Your father is very fond of you——"

' "I know it," I answer curtly.

' "Anything that you asked, and that was within the bounds of possibility, he would do," he continues, with eager gravity. "Well, this is what I ask of you: to write him a line, and let me take it when I go, asking him to send me home in the next prize."

'Silence for a moment, only the haymakers laughing over their rakes.

' "And if," say I, with a trembling voice, "you lose your life in this

44

Poor Pretty Bobby

service, you will have to thank me for it; I shall have your death on my head all through my life."

' "The danger is infinitesimal, as I told you before," he says, impatiently; "and even if it were greater than it is—well, life is a good thing, very good, but there are better things; and even if I come to grief, which is most unlikely, there are plenty of men as good as—better than—I, to step into my place."

' "It will be small consolation to the people who are fond of you that some one better than you is alive, though you are dead," I say, tearfully.

' "But I do not mean to be dead," he says, with a cheery laugh. "Why are you so determined on killing me? I mean to live to be an admiral. Why should not I?"

' "Why indeed?" say I, with a feeble echo of his cheerful mirth, and feeling rather ashamed of my tears.

' "And meanwhile you will write?" he says with an eager return to the charge; "and *soon*? Do not look angry and pouting, as you did just now, but I *must* go! What is there to hinder me? I am getting up my strength as fast as it is possible for any human creature to do, and just think how I should feel if they were to come in for something really good while I am away."

'So I wrote.

III

'I often wished afterwards that my right hand had been cut off before its fingers had held the pen that wrote that letter. You wonder to see me moved at what happened so long ago—before your parents were born—and certainly it makes not much difference now; for even if he had prospered then, and come happily home to me, yet, in the course of nature he would have gone long before now. I should not have been so cruel as to have wished him to have lasted to be as I am. I did not mean to hint at the end of my story before I have reached the middle. Well—and so he went, with the letter, in his pocket, and I felt something like the king in the tale, who sent a messenger with a letter, and wrote in the letter, "Slay the bearer of this as soon as he arrives!" But before he went—the evening before, as we walked in the garden after

45

supper, with our monstrously long shadows stretching before us in the moonlight—I do not think he said in so many words, "Will you marry me?" but somehow, by some signs or words on both our parts, it became clear to us that, by-and-by, if God left him alive, and if the war ever came to an end, he and I should belong to one another. And so, having understood this, when he went he kissed me, as he had done when he came, only this time no one bade him; he did it of his own accord, and a hundred times instead of one; and for my part, this time, instead of standing passive like a log or a post, I kissed him back again, most lovingly, with many tears.

'Ah! parting in those days, when the last kiss to one's beloved ones was not unlikely to be an adieu until the great Day of Judgement, was a different thing to the listless, unemotional goodbyes of these stagnant times of peace!

'And so Bobby also got into a post-chaise and drove away, and we watched him too, till he turned the corner out of our sight, as we had watched father; and then I hid my face among the jessamine flowers that clothed the wall of the house, and wept as one that would not be comforted. However, one cannot weep for ever, or, if one does, it makes one blind and blear, and I did not wish Bobby to have a wife with such defects; so in process of time I dried my tears.

'And the days passed by, and nature went slowly and evenly through her lovely changes. The hay was gathered in, and the fine new grass and clover sprang up among the stalks of the grass that had gone; and the wild roses struggled into odorous bloom, and crowned the hedges, and then *their* time came, and they shook down their faint petals, and went.

'And now the corn harvest had come, and we had heard once or twice from our beloveds, but not often. And the sun still shone with broad power, and kept the rain in subjection. And all morning I sat at my big frame, and toiled on at the "Last Supper". I had finished Judas Iscariot's face and the other Apostles. I was engaged now upon the table-cloth, which was not interesting and required not much exercise of thought. And mother sat near me, either working too or reading a good book, and taking snuff—every lady snuffed in those days: at least in trifles, if not in great things, the world mends. And at night, when ten o'clock struck, I covered up my frame and stole listlessly upstairs to my room. There, I knelt at the open window, facing Plymouth and the sea, and asked God to take good care of father and Bobby. I do not know that I asked for any spiritual blessings for them, I only begged that they might be alive.

'One night, one hot night, having prayed even more heartily and tearfully than my wont for them both, I had lain down to sleep. The windows were left open, and the blinds up, that all possible air might reach me from the still and scented garden below. Thinking of Bobby, I had fallen asleep, and he is still mistily in my head, when I seem to wake. The room is full of clear light, but it is not morning: it is only the moon looking right in and flooding every object. I can see my own ghostly figure sitting up in bed, reflected in the looking-glass opposite. I listen: surely I heard some noise: yes—certainly, there can be no doubt of it—someone is knocking loudly and perseveringly at the hall-door. At first I fall into a deadly fear; then my reason comes to my aid. If it were a robber, or person with any evil intent, would he knock so openly and clamorously as to arouse the inmates? Would not he rather go stealthily to work, to force a *silent* entrance for himself? At worst it is some drunken sailor from Plymouth; at best it is a messenger with news of our dear ones. At this thought I instantly spring out of bed, and hurrying on my stockings and shoes and whatever garments come most quickly to hand—with my hair spread all over my back, and utterly forgetful of my big comb, I open my door, and fly down the passages, into which the moon is looking with her ghostly smile, and down the broad and shallow stairs.

'As I near the hall-door I meet our old butler also rather dishevelled, and evidently on the same errand as myself.

' "Who *can* it be, Stephens?" I ask, trembling with excitement and fear.

' "Indeed, ma'am, I cannot tell you," replies the old man, shaking his head, "it is a very odd time of night to choose for making such a noise. We will ask them their business, whoever they are, before we unchain the door."

'It seems to me as if the endless bolts would never be drawn—the key never be turned in the stiff lock; but at last the door opens slowly and cautiously, only to the width of a few inches, as it is still confined by the strong chain. I peep out eagerly, expecting I know not what.

'Good heavens! What do I see? No drunken sailor, no messenger, but, oh joy! oh blessedness! my Bobby himself—my beautiful boy-lover! Even *now*, even after all these weary years, even after the long bitterness that followed, I cannot forget the unutterable happiness of that moment.

' "Open the door, Stephens, quick!" I cry, stammering with eagerness. "Draw the chain; it is Mr Gerard; do not keep him waiting."

'The chain rattles down, the door opens wide and there he stands before me. At once, ere any one has said anything, ere anything has happened, a feeling of cold disappointment steals unaccountably over me—a nameless sensation, whose nearest kin is chilly awe. He makes no movement towards me; he does not catch me in his arms, nor even hold out his right hand to me. He stands there still and silent, and though the night is dry, equally free from rain and dew, I see that he is dripping wet; the water is running down from his clothes, from his drenched hair, and even from his eyelashes, on to the dry ground at his feet.

' "What has happened?" I cry, hurriedly, "How wet you are!" and as I speak I stretch out my hand and lay it on his coat sleeve. But even as I do it a sensation of intense cold runs up my fingers and my arm, even to the elbow. How is it that he is so chilled to the marrow of his bones on this sultry, breathless, August night? To my extreme surprise he does not answer; he still stands there, dumb and dripping. "Where have you come from?" I ask, with that sense of awe deepening. "Have you fallen into the river? How is it that you are so wet?"

' "It was cold," he says, shivering, and speaking in a slow and strangely altered voice, "bitter cold. I could not stay there."

' "Stay where?" I say, looking in amazement at his face, which, whether owing to the ghastly effect of moonlight or not, seems to me ash white. "Where have you been? What is it you are talking about?"

'But he does not reply.

' "He is really ill, I am afraid, Stephens," I say, turning with a forlorn feeling towards the old butler. "He does not seem to hear what I say to him. I am afraid he has had a thorough chill. What water can he have fallen into? You had better help him up to bed, and get him warm between the blankets. His room is quite ready for him, you know—come in;" I say, stretching out my hand to him, "you will be better after a night's rest."

'He does not take my offered hand, but he follows me across the threshold and across the hall. I hear the water drops falling drip, drip, on the echoing stone floor as he passes; then upstairs, and along the gallery to the door of his room, where I leave him with Stephens. Then everything becomes blank and nil to me.

'I am awoke as usual in the morning by the entrance of my maid with hot water.

' "Well, how is Mr Gerard this morning?" I ask, springing into a sitting posture.

'She puts down the hot water tin and stares at her leisure at me.

' "My dear Miss Phœbe, how should *I* know? Please God he is in good health and safe, and that we shall have good news of him before long."

' "Have not you asked how he is?" I ask impatiently. "He did not seem quite himself last night; there was something odd about him. I was afraid he was in for another touch of fever."

' "Last night—fever," repeats she, slowly and disconnectedly echoing some of my words. "I beg your pardon, ma'am, I am sure, but I have not the least idea in life what you are talking about."

' "How stupid you are!" I say, quite at the end of my patience. "Did not Mr Gerard come back unexpectedly last night, and did not I hear him knocking, and run down to open the door, and did not Stephens come too, and afterwards take him up to bed?"

'The stare of bewilderment gives way to a laugh.

' "You have been dreaming, ma'am. Of course I cannot answer for what you did last night, but I am sure that Stephens knows no more of the young gentleman than I do, for only just now, at breakfast, he was saying that he thought it was about time for us to have some tidings of him and master."

' "A dream!" cry I indignantly. "Impossible! I was no more dreaming then than I am now."

But time convinces me that I am mistaken, and that during all the time that I thought I was standing at the open hall-door, talking to my beloved, in reality I was lying on my bed in the depths of sleep, with no other company than the scent of the flowers and the light of the moon. At this discovery a great and terrible depression falls on me. I go to my mother to tell her of my vision, and at the end of my narrative I say,

' "Mother, I know well that Bobby is dead, and that I shall never see him any more. I feel assured that he died last night, and that he came himself to tell me of his going. I am sure that there is nothing left for me now but to go too."

'I speak thus far with great calmness, but when I have done I break out into loud and violent weeping. Mother rebukes me gently, telling me that there is nothing more natural than that I should dream of a person who constantly occupies my waking thoughts, nor that, considering the gloomy nature of my appre-hensions about him, my dream should be of a sad and ominous kind; but that, above all dreams and omens, God is good, that He has preserved him hitherto, and that, for her part, no devil-sent apparition shall shake her confidence in His continued clem-ency. I go away a little comforted, though not very much, and still every night I kneel at the open window facing Plymouth and the sea, and pray for my sailor boy. But it seems to me, despite all my self-reasonings, despite all that mother says, that my prayers for him are prayers for the dead.

IV

'Three more weeks pass away; the harvest is garnered, and the pears are growing soft and mellow. Mother's and my outward life goes on in its silent regularity, nor do we talk much to each other of the tumult that rages—of the heartache that burns, within each of us. At the end of the three weeks, as we are sitting as usual, quietly employed, and buried each in our own thoughts, in the parlour, towards evening we hear wheels approaching the hall-door. We both run out as in my dream I had run to the door, and arrive in time to receive my father as he steps out of the carriage that has brought him. Well! at least *one* of our wanderers has come home, but where is the other?

'Almost before he has heartily kissed us both—wife and child—father cries out, "But where is Bobby?"

' "That is just what I was going to ask you," replies mother quickly.

' "Is not he *here* with you?" returns he anxiously.

' "Not he," answers mother, "we have neither seen nor heard anything of him for more than six weeks."

' "Great God!" exclaims he, while his face assumes an expression of the deepest concern, "what *can* have become of him? what *can* have happened to the poor fellow?"

' "Has not he been with you, then?—has not he been in the *Thunderer?*" asks mother, running her words into one another in her eagerness to get them out.

' "I sent him home three weeks ago in a prize, with a letter to you, and told him to stay with you till I came home, and what can have become of him since, God only knows!" he answers with a look of the profoundest sorrow and anxiety.

'There is a moment of forlorn and dreary silence; then I speak. I have been standing dumbly by, listening, and my heart growing colder and colder at every dismal word.

' "It is all my doing!" I cry passionately, flinging myself down in an agony of tears on the straight-backed old settle in the hall. "It is my fault—no one else's! The very last time that I saw him, I told him that he would have to thank me for his death, and he laughed at me, but it has come true. If I had not written *you*, father, that accursed letter, we should have had him here *now* this *minute*, safe and sound, standing in the middle of us—as we never, *never*, shall have him again!'

'I stop, literally suffocated with emotion.

'Father comes over, and lays his kind brown hand on my bent prone head. "My child," he says, "my dear child" (and tears are dimming the clear grey of his own eyes), "you are wrong to make up your mind to what is the worst at once. I do not disguise from you that there is cause for grave anxiety about the dear fellow, but still God is good; He has kept both him and me hitherto; into His hands we must trust our boy."

'I sit up, and shake away my tears.

' "It is no use," I say, "Why should I hope? There is no hope! I know it for a certainty! He is *dead*" (looking round at them both with a sort of calmness); "he died on the night that I had that dream—mother, I told you so at the time. Oh, my Bobby! I knew that you could not leave me for ever without coming to tell me!"

'And so speaking, I fall into strong hysterics and am carried upstairs to bed. And so three or four more lagging days crawl by, and still we hear nothing, and remain in the same state of doubt and uncertainty;

which to me, however, is hardly uncertainty; so convinced am I, in my own mind, that my fair-haired lover is away in the land whence never letter or messenger comes—that he has reached the Great Silence. So I sit at my frame, working my heart's agony into the tapestry, and feebly trying to say to God that He has done well, but I cannot. On the contrary, it seems to me, as my life trails on through the mellow mist of the autumn mornings, through the shortened autumn evenings, that, whoever has done it, it is most evilly done. One night we are sitting round the crackling little wood fire that one does not need for warmth, but that gives a cheerfulness to the room and the furniture, when the butler Stephens enters, and going over to father, whispers to him. I seem to understand in a moment what the purport of his whisper is.

' "Why does he whisper?" I cry, irritably. "Why does not he speak out loud? Why should you try to keep it from me? I know that it is something about Bobby."

'Father has already risen, and is walking towards the door.

' "I will not let you go until you tell me," I cry wildly, flying after him.

' "A sailor has come over from Plymouth," he answers, hurriedly; "he says he has news. My darling, I will not keep you in suspense a moment longer than I can help, and meanwhile pray—both of you pray for him!"

'I sit rigidly still, with my cold hands tightly clasped, during the moments that next elapse. Then father returns. His eyes are full of tears, and there is small need to ask for his message; it is most plainly written on his features—death, and not life.

' "You were right, Phœbe," he says, brokenly, taking hold of my icy hands; "you knew best. He is gone! God has taken him."

'My heart dies. I had thought that I had no hope, but I was wrong. "I knew it!" I say, in a dry stiff voice. "Did not I tell you so? But you would not believe me—go on!—tell me how it was—do not think I cannot bear it—make haste!"

'And so he tells me all that there is now left for me to know—after what manner, and on what day my darling took his leave of this pretty and cruel world. He had had his wish, as I already knew, and had set off blithely home in the last prize they had captured. Father had taken the precaution of having a larger proportion than usual of the French-men ironed, and had also sent a greater number of Englishmen. But to what purpose? They were nearing port, sailing prosperously along on a smooth blue sea, with a fair strong wind, thinking of no evil, when a great and terrible misfortune overtook them. Some of the Frenchmen who were not ironed got the sailors below and drugged their grog; ironed them, and freed their countrymen. Then one of the officers rushed on deck, and holding a pistol to my Bobby's head bade him surrender the vessel or die. Need I tell you which he chose? I think not—well' (with a sigh) 'and so they shot my boy—ah me! how many years ago—and threw him overboard! yes—threw him overboard—it makes me angry and grieved even now to think of it—into the great and greedy sea, and the vessel escaped to France.'

There is a silence between us: I will own to you that I am crying, but the old lady's eyes are dry.

'Well,' she says, after a pause, with a sort of triumph in her tone, 'they never could say again that Bobby Gerard was *afraid!*'

'The tears were running down my father's cheeks, as he told me,' she resumes presently, 'but at the end he wiped them and said, "It is well! He was as pleasant in God's sight as he was in ours, and so He has taken him."'

'And for me, I was glad that he had gone to God—none gladder. But you will not wonder that, for myself, I was past speaking sorry. And so the years went by, and, as you know, I married Mr Hamilton, and lived with him forty years, and was happy in the main, as happiness goes; and when he died I wept much and long, and so I did for each of my sons when in turn they went. But looking back on all my long life, the event that I think stands out most clearly from it is my dream and my boy-lover's death-day. It *was* an odd dream, was not it?'

4

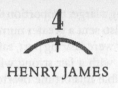

HENRY JAMES

The Ghostly Rental

I was in my twenty-second year, and I had just left college. I was at
liberty to choose my career, and I chose it with much promptness. I
afterwards renounced it, in truth, with equal ardour, but I have never
regretted those two youthful years of perplexed and excited, but also
of agreeable and fruitful experiment. I had a taste for theology, and
during my college term I had been an admiring reader of Dr Channing.
This was theology of a grateful and succulent savour; it seemed to
offer one the rose of faith delightfully stripped of its thorns. And then
(for I rather think this had something to do with it), I had taken a fancy
to the Old Divinity School. I have always had an eye to the back scene
in the human drama, and it seemed to me that I might play my part
with a fair chance of applause (from myself at least), in that detached
and tranquil home of mild casuistry, with its respectable avenue on
one side, and its prospect of green fields and contact with acres of
woodland on the other. Cambridge, for the lovers of woods and fields,
has changed for the worse since those days, and the precinct in
question has forfeited much of its mingled pastoral and scholastic
quietude. It was then a College-hall in the woods—a charming
mixture. What it is now has nothing to do with my story; and I have
no doubt that there are still doctrine-haunted young seniors who, as
they stroll near it in the summer dusk, promise themselves, later, to
taste of its fine leisurely quality. For myself, I was not disappointed. I
established myself in a great square, low-browed room, with deep
window-benches; I hung prints from Overbeck and Ary Scheffer on
the walls; I arranged my books, with great refinement of classifica-
tion, in the alcoves beside the high chimney-shelf, and I began to read

Plotinus and St Augustine. Among my companions were two or three men of ability and of good fellowship, with whom I occasionally brewed a fireside bowl; and with adventurous reading, deep discourse, potations conscientiously shallow, and long country walks, my initiation into the clerical mystery progressed agreeably enough.

With one of my comrades I formed an especial friendship, and we passed a great deal of time together. Unfortunately he had a chronic weakness of one of his knees, which compelled him to lead a very sedentary life, and as I was a methodical pedestrian, this made some difference in our habits. I used often to stretch away for my daily ramble, with no companion but the stick in my hand or the book in my pocket. But in the use of my legs and the sense of unstinted open air, I have always found company enough. I should, perhaps, add that in the enjoyment of a very sharp pair of eyes, I found something of a social pleasure. My eyes and I were on excellent terms; they were indefatigable observers of all wayside incidents, and so long as they were amused I was contented. It is, indeed, owing to their inquisitive habits that I came into possession of this remarkable story. Much of the country about the old College town is pretty now, but it was prettier thirty years ago. That multitudinous eruption of domiciliary pasteboard which now graces the landscape, in the direction of the low, blue Waltham Hills, had not yet taken place; there were no genteel cottages to put the shabby meadows and scrubby orchards to shame—a juxtaposition by which, in later years, neither element of the contrast has gained. Certain crooked crossroads, then, as I remember them, were more deeply and naturally rural, and the solitary dwellings on the long grassy slopes beside them, under the tall, customary elm that curved its foliage in mid-air like the outward dropping ears of a girdled wheatsheaf, sat with their shingled hoods well pulled down on their ears, and no prescience whatever of the fashion of French roofs—weather-wrinkled old peasant women, as you might call them, quietly wearing the native coif, and never dreaming of mounting bonnets, and indecently exposing their venerable brows. That winter was what is called an 'open' one; there was much cold, but little snow; the roads were firm and free, and I was rarely compelled by the weather to forgo my exercise. One grey December afternoon I had sought it in the direction of the adjacent town of

Medford, and I was retracing my steps at an even pace, and watching the pale, cold tints—the transparent amber and faded rose-colour—which curtained, in wintry fashion, the western sky, and reminded me of a sceptical smile on the lips of a beautiful woman. I came, as dusk was falling, to a narrow road which I had never traversed and which I imagined offered me a short cut homeward. I was about three miles away; I was late, and would have been thankful to make them two. I diverged, walked some ten minutes, and then perceived that the road had a very unfrequented air. The wheel-ruts looked old; the stillness seemed peculiarly sensible. And yet down the road stood a house, so that it must in some degree have been a thoroughfare. On one side was a high, natural embankment, on the top of which was perched an apple-orchard, whose tangled boughs made a stretch of coarse black lace-work, hung across the coldly rosy west. In a short time I came to the house, and I immediately found myself interested in it. I stopped in front of it gazing hard, I hardly knew why, but with a vague mixture of curiosity and timidity. It was a house like most of the houses there-abouts, except that it was decidedly a handsome specimen of its class. It stood on a grassy slope, it had its tall, impartially drooping elm beside it, and its old black well-cover at its shoulder. But it was of very large proportions, and it had a striking look of solidity and stoutness of timber. It had lived to a good old age, too, for the woodwork on its doorway and under its eaves, carefully and abundantly carved, referred it to the middle, at the latest, of the last century. All this had once been painted white, but the broad back of time, leaning against the door-posts for a hundred years, had laid bare the grain of the wood. Behind the house stretched an orchard of apple-trees, more gnarled and fantastic than usual, and wearing, in the deepening dusk, a blighted and exhausted aspect. All the windows of the house had rusty shutters, without slats, and these were closely drawn. There was no sign of life about it; it looked blank, bare and vacant, and yet, as I lingered near it, it seemed to have a familiar meaning—an audible eloquence. I have always thought of the impression made upon me at first sight, by that grey colonial dwelling, as a proof that induction may sometimes be near akin to divination; for after all, there was nothing on the face of the matter to warrant the very serious induction that I made. I fell back and crossed the road. The last red light of the sunset disengaged itself, as it was about to vanish, and rested faintly for a moment on the time-silvered front of the old house. It touched, with perfect regularity, the series of small panes in the fan-shaped window above the door, and twinkled there fantastically. Then it died away, and left the place more intensely sombre. At this moment, I said to myself with the accent of profound conviction—'The house is simply haunted!'

Somehow, immediately, I believed it, and so long as I was not shut up inside, the idea gave me pleasure. It was implied in the aspect of the house, and it explained it. Half an hour before, if I had been asked, I would have said, as befitted a young man who was explicitly cultivating cheerful views of the supernatural, that there were no such things as haunted houses. But the dwelling before me gave a vivid meaning to the empty words; it had been spiritually blighted.

The longer I looked at it, the intenser seemed the secret that it held. I walked all round it, I tried to peep here and there, through a crevice in the shutters, and I took a puerile satisfaction in laying my hand on the door-knob and gently turning it. If the door had yielded, would I have gone in?—would I have penetrated the dusky stillness? My audacity, fortunately, was not put to the test. The portal was admirably solid, and I was unable even to shake it. At last I turned away, casting many looks behind me. I pursued my way, and, after a longer walk than I had bargained for, reached the high-road. At a certain distance below the point at which the long lane I have mentioned entered it, stood a comfortable, tidy dwelling, which might have offered itself as the model of the house which is in no sense haunted—which has no sinister secrets, and knows nothing but blooming prosperity. Its clean white paint stared placidly through the dusk, and its vine-covered porch had been dressed in straw for the winter. An old, one-horse chaise, freighted with two departing visitors was leaving the door, and through the undraped windows, I saw the lamp-lit sitting-room, and the table spread with the early 'tea', which had been improvised for the comfort of the guests. The mistress of the house had come to the gate with her friends; she lingered there after the chaise had wheeled creakingly away, half to watch them down the road, and half to give me as I passed in the twilight, a questioning look. She was a comely, quick young woman, with a sharp, dark eye, and I ventured to stop and speak to her.

'That house down that side-road,' I said, 'about a mile from here— the only one—can you tell me whom it belongs to?'

She stared at me a moment, and, I thought, coloured a little. 'Our folks never go down that road,' she said, briefly.

'But it's a short way to Medford,' I answered.

She gave a little toss of her head. 'Perhaps it would turn out a long way. At any rate, we don't use it.'

This was interesting. A thrifty Yankee household must have good reasons for this scorn of time-saving processes. 'But you know the house, at least?' I said.

'Well, I have seen it.'

'And to whom does it belong?'

She gave a little laugh and looked away as if she were aware that, to a stranger, her words might seem to savour of agricultural superstition. 'I guess it belongs to them that are in it.'

'But is there any one in it? It is completely closed.'

'That makes no difference. They never come out, and no one ever goes in.' And she turned away.

But I laid my hand on her arm, respectfully. 'You mean,' I said, 'that the house is haunted?'

She drew herself away, coloured, raised her finger to her lips, and hurried into the house, where, in a moment, the curtains were dropped over the windows.

For several days, I thought repeatedly of this little adventure, but I took some satisfaction in keeping it to myself. If the house was not haunted, it was useless to expose my imaginative whims, and if it was, it was agreeable to drain the cup of horror without assistance. I determined, of course, to pass that way again; and a week later—it was the last day of the year—I retraced my steps. I approached the house from the opposite direction, and found myself before it at about the same hour as before. The light was failing, the sky low and grey; the wind wailed along the hard, bare ground, and made slow eddies of the frost-blackened leaves. The melancholy mansion stood there, seeming to gather the winter twilight around it, and mask itself in it, inscrutably. I hardly knew on what errand I had come, but I had a vague feeling that if this time the door-knob were to turn and the door to open, I should take my heart in my hands, and let them close behind me. Who were the mysterious tenants to whom the good woman at the corner had alluded? What had been seen or heard—what was related? The door was as stubborn as before, and my impertinent fumblings with the latch caused no upper window to be thrown open, nor any strange, pale face to be thrust out. I ventured even to raise the rusty knocker and give it half-a-dozen raps, but they made a flat, dead sound, and aroused no echo. Familiarity breeds contempt; I don't know what I should have done next, if, in the distance, up the road (the same one I had followed), I had not seen a solitary figure advancing. I was unwilling to be observed hanging about this ill-famed dwelling, and I sought refuge among the dense shadows of a grove of pines nearby, where I might peep forth, and yet remain invisible. Presently, the new-comer drew near, and I perceived that he was making straight for the house. He was a little, old man, the most striking feature of whose appearance was a voluminous cloak, of a sort of military cut. He carried a walking-stick, and advanced in a slow, painful, somewhat hobbling fashion, but with an air of extreme resolution. He turned off from the road, and followed the vague wheel-track, and within a few yards of the house he paused. He looked up at it, fixedly and searchingly, as if he were counting the windows, or noting certain familiar marks. Then he took off his hat, and bent over slowly and solemnly, as if he were performing an obeisance. As he stood uncovered, I had a good look at him. He was, as I have said, a diminutive old man, but it would have been hard to decide whether he belonged to this world or to the other. His head reminded me, vaguely, of the portraits of Andrew Jackson. He had a crop of grizzled hair, as stiff as a brush, a lean, pale, smooth-shaven face, and an eye of intense brilliancy, surmounted with thick brows, which had remained perfectly black. His face, as well as his cloak, seemed to belong to an old soldier; he looked like a retired military man of a modest rank; but he struck me as exceeding the classic privilege of even such a personage to be eccentric and grotesque. When he had finished his salute, he advanced to the door, fumbled in the folds of his cloak, which hung down much further in front than behind, and produced a key. This he slowly and carefully inserted into the lock, and then, apparently, he turned it. But the door did not immediately open; first he bent his head, turned his ear, and stood listening, and then he looked up and down the road. Satisfied or reassured, he applied his aged shoulder to one of the deep-set panels, and pressed a moment. The door yielded—opening into perfect darkness. He stopped again on the threshold, and again removed his hat and made his bow. Then he went in, and carefully closed the door behind him.

Who in the world was he, and what was his errand? He might have been a figure out of one of Hoffman's tales. Was he vision or a reality—an inmate of the house, or a familiar, friendly visitor? What had been the meaning, in either case, of his mystic genuflexions, and how did he propose to proceed, in that inner darkness? I emerged from my retirement and observed narrowly, several of the windows. In each of them, at an interval, a ray of light became visible in the chink between the two leaves of the shutters. Evidently, he was lighting up; was he going to give a party—a ghostly revel? My curiosity grew intense, but I was quite at a loss how to satisfy it. For a moment I thought of rapping peremptorily at the door; but I dismissed this idea as unmannerly, and calculated to break the spell, if spell there was. I walked round the house and tried, without violence, to open one of the lower windows. It resisted, but I had better fortune, in a moment, with another. There was a risk, certainly, in the trick I was playing—a risk of being seen from within, or (worse) seeing, myself, something that I should repent of seeing. But curiosity, as I say, had become an inspiration, and the risk was highly agreeable. Through the parting of the shutters I looked into a lighted room—a room lighted by two candles in old brass flambeaux, placed upon the mantel-shelf. It was apparently a sort of back parlour, and it had retained all its furniture. This was of a homely, old-fashioned pattern, and consisted of hair-cloth chairs and sofas, spare mahogany tables, and framed samplers hung upon the walls. But although the room was furnished, it had a strangely uninhabited look; the tables and chairs were in rigid positions, and no small, familiar objects were visible. I could not see everything, and I could only guess at the existence, on my right, of a large folding-door. It was apparently open, and the light of the neighbouring room passed through it. I waited for some time, but the room remained empty. At last I became conscious that a large shadow was projected upon the wall opposite the folding-door—the shadow, evidently, of a figure in the adjoining room. It was tall and grotesque, and seemed to represent a person sitting perfectly motionless, in profile. I thought I recognized the perpendicular bristles and far-arching nose of my little old man. There was a strange fixedness in his posture; he appeared to be seated, and looking intently at something. I watched the shadow a long time, but it never stirred. At last, however, just as my patience began to ebb, it moved slowly, rose to the ceiling, and became indistinct. I don't know what I should have seen next, but by an irresistible impulse, I closed the shutter. Was it delicacy?—was it pusillanimity? I can hardly say. I lingered, nevertheless, near the house, hoping that my friend would reappear. I was not disappointed; for he at last emerged, looking just as when he had gone in, and taking his leave in the same ceremonious fashion. (The lights, I had already observed, had disappeared from the crevice of each of the windows.) He faced about before the door, took off his hat, and made an obsequious bow. As he turned away I had a hundred minds to speak to him, but I let him depart in peace. This, I may say, was pure delicacy;—you will answer, perhaps, that it came too late. It seemed to me that he had a right to resent my observation; though my own right to exercise it (if ghosts were in the question) struck me as equally positive. I continued to watch him as he hobbled softly down the bank, and along the lonely road. Then I musingly retreated in the opposite direction. I was tempted to follow him, at a distance, to see what became of him; but this, too, seemed indelicate; and I confess, moreover, that I felt the inclination to coquet a little, as it were, with my discovery—to pull apart the petals of the flower one by one.

I continued to smell the flower, from time to time, for its oddity of perfume had fascinated me. I passed by the house on the crossroad again, but never encountered the old man in the cloak, or any other wayfarer. It seemed to keep observers at a distance, and I was careful not to gossip about it: one inquirer, I said to myself, may edge his way into the secret, but there is no room for two. At the same time, of course, I would have been thankful for any chance side-light that might fall across the matter—though I could not well see whence it was to come. I hoped to meet the old man in the cloak elsewhere, but as the days passed by without his reappearing, I ceased to expect it. And yet I reflected that he probably lived in that neighbourhood, inasmuch as he had made his pilgrimage to the vacant house on foot. If he had come from a distance, he would have been sure to arrive in some old deep-hooded gig with yellow wheels—a vehicle as venerably grotesque as himself. One day I took a stroll in Mount Auburn cemetery—an institution at that period in its infancy, and full of a sylvan charm which it has now completely forfeited. It contained more maple and birch than willow and cypress, and the sleepers had ample elbow room. It was not a city of the dead, but at the most a village, and a meditative pedestrian might stroll there without too importunate reminder of the grotesque side of our claims to posthumous consideration. I had come out to enjoy the first foretaste of Spring—one of those mild days of late winter, when the torpid earth seems to draw the first long breath that marks the rupture of the spell of sleep. The sun was veiled in haze, and yet warm, and the frost was oozing from its deepest lurking-places. I had been treading for half an hour the winding ways of the cemetery, when suddenly I perceived a familiar figure seated on a bench against a southward-facing evergreen hedge. I call the figure familiar, because I had seen it often in memory and in fancy; in fact, I had beheld it but once. Its back was turned to me, but it wore a voluminous cloak, which there was no mistaking. Here, at last, was my fellow-visitor at the haunted house, and here was my chance, if I wished to approach him! I made a circuit, and came towards him from in front. He saw me, at the end of the alley, and sat motionless, with his hands on the head of his stick, watching me from under his black eyebrows as I drew near. At a distance these black eyebrows looked formidable; they were the only thing I saw in his face. But on a closer view I was reassured, simply because I immediately felt that no man could really be as fantastically fierce as this poor old gentleman looked. His face was a kind of caricature of martial truculence. I stopped in front of him, and respectfully asked leave to sit and rest upon his bench. He granted it with a silent gesture, of much dignity, and I placed myself beside him. In this position I was able, covertly, to observe him. He was quite as much an oddity in the morning sunshine, as he had been in the dubious twilight. The lines in his face were as rigid as if they had been hacked out of a block by a clumsy wood-carver. His eyes were flamboyant, his nose terrific, his mouth implacable. And yet, after awhile, when he slowly turned and looked at me, fixedly, I perceived that in spite of this portentous mask, he was a very mild old man. I was sure he even would have been glad to smile, but, evidently, his facial muscles were too stiff—they had taken a different fold, once for all. I wondered whether he was demented, but I dismissed the idea; the fixed glitter in his eye was not that of insanity. What his face really expressed was deep and simple sadness; his heart perhaps was broken, but his brain was intact. His dress was shabby but neat, and his old blue cloak had known half a century's brushing.

I hastened to make some observation upon the exceptional softness of the day, and he answered me in a gentle, mellow voice, which it was almost startling to hear proceed from such bellicose lips.

'This is a very comfortable place,' he presently added.

'I am fond of walking in graveyards,' I rejoined deliberately; flattering myself that I had struck a vein that might lead to something.

I was encouraged; he turned and fixed me with his duskily glowing eyes. Then very gravely,—'Walking, yes. Take all your exercise now. Some day you will have to settle down in a graveyard in a fixed position.'

'Very true,' said I. 'But you know there are some people who are said to take exercise even after that day.'

He had been looking at me still; at this he looked away.

'You don't understand?' I said, gently.

He continued to gaze straight before him.

'Some people, you know, walk about after death,' I went on.

At last he turned, and looked at me more portentously than ever. 'You don't believe that,' he said simply.

'How do you know I don't'.

'Because you are young and foolish.' This was said without acerbity—even kindly; but in the tone of an old man whose consciousness of his own heavy experience made everything else seem light.

'I am certainly young,' I answered; 'but I don't think that, on the whole, I am foolish. But say I don't believe in ghosts—most people would be on my side.'

'Most people are fools!' said the old man.

I let the question rest, and talked of other things. My companion seemed on his guard, he eyed me defiantly, and made brief answers to my remarks; but I nevertheless gathered an impression that our meeting was an agreeable thing to him, and even a social incident of some importance. He was evidently a lonely creature, and his opportunities for gossip were rare. He had had troubles, and they had detached him from the world, and driven him back upon himself; but the social chord in his antiquated soul was not entirely broken, and I was sure he was gratified to find that it could still feebly resound. At last, he began to ask questions himself; he enquired whether I was a student.

'I am a student of divinity,' I answered.

'Of divinity?'

'Of theology. I am studying for the ministry.'

At this he eyed me with peculiar intensity—after which his gaze wandered away again. 'There are certain things you ought to know, then,' he said at last.

'I have a great desire for knowledge,' I answered. 'What things do you mean?'

He looked at me again awhile, but without heeding my question. 'I like your appearance,' he said. 'You seem to me a sober lad.'

'Oh, I am perfectly sober!' I exclaimed—yet departing for a moment from my soberness.

'I think you are fair-minded,' he went on.

'I don't any longer strike you as foolish then?' I asked.

'I stick to what I said about people who deny the power of departed spirits to return. They *are* fools!' And he rapped fiercely with his staff on the earth.

I hesitated a moment, and then, abruptly, 'You have seen a ghost!' I said.

He appeared not at all startled.

'You are right, sir!' he answered with great dignity. 'With me it's not a matter of cold theory—I have not had to pry into old books to learn what to believe. *I know!* With these eyes I have beheld the departed spirit standing before me as near as you are!' And his eyes, as he spoke, certainly looked as if they had rested upon strange things.

I was irresistibly impressed—I was touched with credulity.

'And was it very terrible?' I asked.

'I am an old soldier—I am not afraid!'

'When was it?—where was it?' I asked.

He looked at me mistrustfully, and I saw that I was going too fast.

'Excuse me from going into particulars,' he said. 'I am not at liberty to speak more fully. I have told you so much, because I cannot bear to hear this subject spoken of lightly. Remember in future, that you have seen a very honest old man who told you—on his honour—that he had seen a ghost!' And he got up, as if he thought he had said enough. Reserve, shyness, pride, the fear of being laughed at, the memory, possibly, of former strokes of sarcasm—all this, on one side, had its weight with him; but I suspected that on the other, his tongue was loosened by the garrulity of old age, the sense of solitude, and the need of sympathy—and perhaps, also, by the friendliness which he had been so good as to express towards myself. Evidently it would be unwise to press him, but I hoped to see him again.

'To give greater weight to my words,' he added, 'let me mention my name—Captain Diamond, sir. I have seen service.'

'I hope I may have the pleasure of meeting you again,' I said.

'The same to you, sir!' And brandishing his stick portentously—though with the friendliest intentions—he marched stiffly away.

I asked two or three persons—selected with discretion—whether they knew anything about Captain Diamond, but they were quite unable to enlighten me. At last, suddenly, I smote my forehead, and, dubbing myself a dolt, remembered that I was neglecting a source of information to which I had never applied in vain. The excellent person at whose table I habitually dined, and who dispensed hospitality to students at so much a week, had a sister as good as herself, and of conversational powers more varied. This sister, who was known as Miss Deborah, was an old maid in all the force of the term. She was deformed, and she never went out of the house; she sat all day at the window, between a birdcage and a flowerpot, stitching small linen articles—mysterious bands and frills. She wielded, I was assured, an exquisite needle, and her work was highly prized. In spite of her deformity and her confinement, she had a little, fresh, round face, and an imperturbable serenity of spirit. She had also a very quick little wit of her own, she was extremely observant, and she had a high relish for a friendly chat. Nothing pleased her so much as to have you—especially, I think, if you were a young divinity student—move your chair near her sunny window, and settle yourself for twenty minutes' 'talk'. 'Well, sir,' she used always to say, 'what is the latest monstrosity in biblical criticism?'—for she used to pretend to be horrified at the rationalistic tendency of the age. But she was an inexorable little philosopher, and I am convinced that she was a keener rationalist than any of us, and that, if she had chosen, she could have propounded questions that would have made the boldest of us wince. Her window commanded the whole town—or rather, the whole country. Knowledge came to her as she sat singing, with her little, cracked voice, in her low rocking-chair. She was the first to learn everything, and the last to forget it. She had the town gossip at her fingers' ends, and she knew everything about people she had never seen. When I asked her how she had acquired her learning, she said simply—'Oh, I observe!' 'Observe closely enough,' she once said, 'and it doesn't matter where you are. You may be in a pitch-dark closet. All you want is something to start with; one thing leads to another, and all things are mixed up. Shut me up in a dark closet and I will observe after a while, that some places in it are darker than others. After that (give me time), and I will tell you what the President of the United States is going to have for dinner.' Once I paid her a compliment. 'Your observation,' I said, 'is as fine as your needle, and your statements are as true as your stitches.'

Of course Miss Deborah had heard of Captain Diamond. He had been much talked about many years before, but he had survived the scandal that attached to his name.

'What was the scandal?' I asked.

'He killed his daughter.'

'Killed her?' I cried; 'how so?'

'Oh, not with a pistol, or a dagger, or a dose of arsenic! With his tongue. Talk of women's tongues! He cursed her—with some horrible oath—and she died!'

'What had she done.'

'She had received a visit from a young man who loved her, and whom he had forbidden the house.'

'The house,' I said—'ah yes! The house is out in the country, two or three miles from here, on a lonely crossroad.'

Miss Deborah looked sharply at me, as she bit her thread.

'Ah, you know about the house?' she said.

'A little,' I answered; 'I have seen it. But I want you to tell me more.'

But here Miss Deborah betrayed an incommunicativeness which was most unusual.

'You wouldn't call me superstitious, would you?' she asked.

'You?—you are the quintessence of pure reason.'

'Well, every thread has its rotten place and every needle its grain of rust. I would rather not talk about that house.'

'You have no idea how you excite my curiosity!' I said.

'I can feel for you. But it would make me very nervous.'

'What harm can come to you?' I asked.

'Some harm came to a friend of mine.' And Miss Deborah gave a very positive nod.

'What had your friend done?'

'She had told me Captain Diamond's secret, which he had told her with a mighty mystery. She had been an old flame of his, and he took her into his confidence. He bade her tell no one, and assured her that if she did, something dreadful would happen to her.'

'And what happened to her?'

'She died.'

'Oh, we are all mortal!' I said. 'Had she given him a promise?'

'She had not taken it seriously, she had not believed him. She repeated the story to me, and three days afterwards, she was taken with inflammation of the lungs. A month afterwards, here where I sit now, I was stitching her grave-clothes. Since then, I have never mentioned what she told me.'

'Was it very strange?'

'It was strange, but it was ridiculous too. It is a thing to make you shudder and to make you laugh, both. But you can't worry it out of me. I am sure that if I were to tell you, I should immediately break a needle in my finger, and die the next week of lock-jaw.'

I retired, and urged Miss Deborah no further; but every two or three days, after dinner, I came and sat down by her rocking-chair. I made no further allusion to Captain Diamond; I sat silent, clipping tape with her scissors. At last, one day, she told me I was looking poorly. I was pale.

'I am dying of curiosity,' I said. 'I have lost my appetite. I have eaten no dinner.'

'Remember Bluebeard's wife!' said Miss Deborah.

'One may as well perish by the sword as by famine!' I answered.

Still she said nothing, and at last I rose with a melodramatic sigh and departed. As I reached the door she called me and pointed to the chair I had vacated. 'I never was hard-hearted,' she said. 'Sit down, and if we are to perish, may we at least perish together.' And then, in very few words, she communicated what she knew of Captain Diamond's secret. 'He was a very high-tempered old man, and though he was very fond of his daughter, his will was law. He had picked out a husband for her, and given her due notice. Her mother was dead, and they lived alone together. The house had been Mrs Diamond's own marriage portion; the Captain, I believe, hadn't a penny. After his marriage they had come to live there, and he had begun to work the farm. The poor girl's lover was a young man with whiskers from Boston. The Captain came in one evening and found them together; he collared the young man, and hurled a terrible curse at the poor girl. The young man cried that she was his wife, and he asked her if it was true. She said, No! Thereupon Captain Diamond, his fury growing fiercer, repeated his imprecation, ordered her out of the house, and disowned her forever. She swooned away, but her father went raging off and left her. Several hours later, he came back and found the house empty. On the table was a note from the young man telling him that he had killed his daughter, repeating the assurance that she was his own wife, and declaring that he himself claimed the sole right to commit her remains to earth. He had carried the body away in a gig! Captain Diamond wrote him a dreadful note in answer, saying that he didn't believe his daughter was dead, but that, whether or no, she was dead to him. A week later, in the middle of the night, he saw her ghost. Then, I suppose, he was convinced. The ghost reappeared several times, and finally began regularly to haunt the house. It made the old man very uncomfortable, for little by little his passion had passed away, and he was given up to grief. He determined at last to leave the place, and tried to sell it or rent it; but meanwhile the story had gone abroad, the ghost had been seen by other persons, the house had a bad name, and it was impossible to dispose of it. With the farm, it was the old man's only property, and his only means of subsistence; if he could neither live in it nor rent it, he was beggared. But the ghost had no mercy, as he had had none. He struggled for six months, and at last he broke down. He put on his old blue cloak and took up his staff, and prepared to wander away and beg his bread. Then the ghost relented, and proposed a compromise. "Leave the house to me!" it said; "I have marked it for my own. Go off and live elsewhere. But to enable you to live, I will be your tenant, since you can find no other. I will hire the house off you and pay you a certain rent." And the ghost named a sum. The old man consented, and he goes every quarter to collect his rent!'

I laughed at this recital, but I confess I shuddered too, for my own observation had exactly confirmed it. Had I not been witness of one of the Captain's quarterly visits, had I not all but seen him sit watching his spectral tenant count out the rent-money, and when he trudged away in the dark, had he not a little bag of strangely gotten coin hidden in the folds of his old blue cloak? I imparted none of these reflections to Miss Deborah, for I was determined that my observations should have a sequel, and I promised myself the pleasure of treating her to my story in its full maturity. 'Captain Diamond,' I asked, 'has no other known means of subsistence?'

'None whatever. He toils not, neither does he spin—his ghost supports him. A haunted house is valuable property!'

'And in what coin does the ghost pay?'

'In good American gold and silver. It has only this peculiarity—that the pieces are all dated before the young girl's death. It's a strange mixture of matter and spirit!'

'And does the ghost do things handsomely; is the rent large?'

'The old man, I believe, lives decently, and has his pipe and his glass. He took a little house down by the river; the door is sidewise to the street, and there is a little garden before it. There he spends his days, and has an old coloured woman to do for him. Some years ago, he used to wander about a good deal, he was a familiar figure in the town, and most people knew his legend. But of late he has drawn back into his shell; he sits over his fire, and curiosity has forgotten him.

I suppose he is falling into his dotage. But I am sure, I trust,' said Miss Deborah in conclusion, 'that he won't outlive his faculties or his powers of locomotion, for, if I remember rightly, it was part of the bargain that he should come in person to collect his rent.'

We neither of us seemed likely to suffer any especial penalty for Miss Deborah's indiscretion; I found her, day after day, singing over her work, neither more nor less active than usual. For myself, I boldly pursued my observations. I went again, more than once, to the great graveyard, but I was disappointed in my hope of finding Captain Diamond there. I had a prospect, however, which afforded me compensation. I shrewdly inferred that the old man's quarterly pilgrimages were made upon the last day of the old quarter. My first sight of him had been on the 31st of December, and it was probable that he would return to his haunted home on the last day of March. This was near at hand; at last it arrived. I betook myself late in the afternoon to the old house on the crossroad, supposing that the hour of twilight was the appointed season. I was not wrong. I had been hovering about for a short time, feeling very much like a restless ghost myself, when he appeared in the same manner as before, and wearing the same costume. I again concealed myself, and saw him enter the house with the ceremonial which he had used on the former occasion. A light appeared successively in the crevice of each pair of shutters, and I opened the window which had yielded to my importunity before. Again I saw the great shadow on the wall, motionless and solemn. But I saw nothing else. The old man reappeared at last, made his fantastic salaam before the house, and crept away into the dusk.

One day, more than a month after this, I met him again at Mount Auburn. The air was full of the voice of Spring; the birds had come back and were twittering over their Winter's travels, and a mild west wind was making a thin murmur in the raw verdure. He was seated on a bench in the sun, still muffled in his enormous mantle, and he recognized me as soon as I approached him. He nodded at me as if he were an old Bashaw giving the signal for my decapitation, but it was apparent that he was pleased to see me.

'I have looked for you here more than once,' I said. 'You don't come often.'

'What did you want of me?' he asked.

'I wanted to enjoy your conversation. I did so greatly when I met you here before.'

'You found me amusing?'

'Interesting!' I said.

'You didn't think me cracked?'

'Cracked?—My dear sir—!' I protested.

'I'm the sanest man in the country. I know that is what insane people always say; but generally they can't prove it. I can!'

'I believe it,' I said. 'But I am curious to know how such a thing can be proved.'

He was silent awhile.

'I will tell you. I once committed, unintentionally, a great crime. Now I pay the penalty. I give up my life to it. I don't shirk it; I face it squarely, knowing perfectly what it is. I haven't tried to bluff it off; I haven't begged off from it; I haven't run away from it. The penalty is terrible, but I have accepted it. I have been a philosopher!'

'If I were a Catholic, I might have turned monk, and spent the rest of my life in fasting and praying. That is no penalty; that is an evasion. I might have blown my brains out—I might have gone mad. I wouldn't do either. I would simply face the music, take the consequences. As I say, they are awful! I take them on certain days, four times a year. So it has been these twenty years; so it will be as long as I last. It's my business; it's my avocation. That's the way I feel about it. I call that reasonable!'

'Admirably so!' I said. 'But you fill me with curiosity and with compassion.'

'Especially with curiosity,' he said, cunningly.

'Why,' I answered, 'if I know exactly what you suffer I can pity you more.'

'I'm much obliged. I don't want your pity; it won't help me. I'll tell you something, but it's not for myself; it's for your own sake.' He paused a long time and looked all round him, as if for chance eavesdroppers. I anxiously awaited his revelation, but he disappointed me. 'Are you still studying theology?' he asked.

'Oh, yes,' I answered, perhaps with a shade of irritation. 'It's a thing one can't learn in six months.'

'I should think not, so long as you have nothing but your books. Do you know the proverb, "A grain of experience is worth a pound of precept?" I'm a great theologian.'

'Ah, you have had experience,' I murmured sympathetically.

'You have read about the immortality of the soul; you have seen Jonathan Edwards and Dr Hopkins chopping logic over it, and deciding, by chapter and verse, that it is true. But I have seen it with these eyes; I have touched it with these hands!' And the old man held up his rugged old fists and shook them portentously. 'That's better!' he went on; 'but I have bought it dearly. You had better take it from the books—evidently you always will. You are a very good young man; you will never have a crime on your conscience.'

I answered with some juvenile fatuity, that I certainly hoped I had my share of human passions, good young man and prospective Doctor of Divinity as I was.

'Ah, but you have a nice, quiet little temper,' he said. 'So have I—now! But once I was very brutal—very brutal. You ought to know that such things are. I killed my own child.'

'Your own child?'

'I struck her down to the earth and left her to die. They could not hang me, for it was not with my hand I struck her. It was with foul and damnable words. That makes a difference; it's a grand law we live under! Well, sir, I can answer for it that *her* soul is immortal. We have an appointment to meet four times a year, and then I catch it!'

'She has never forgiven you?'

'She has forgiven me as the angels forgive! That's what I can't stand—the soft, quiet way she looks at me. I'd rather she twisted a knife about in my heart—O Lord, Lord, Lord!' and Captain Diamond bowed his head over his stick, and leaned his forehead on his crossed hands.

I was impressed and moved, and his attitude seemed for the moment a check to further questions. Before I ventured to ask him anything more, he slowly rose and pulled his old cloak around him. He was unused to talking about his troubles, and his memories overwhelmed him. 'I must go my way,' he said; 'I must be creeping along.'

'I shall perhaps meet you here again,' I said.

'Oh, I'm a stiff-jointed old fellow,' he answered, 'and this is rather far for me to come. I have to reserve myself. I have sat sometimes a month at a time smoking my pipe in my chair. But I should like to see you again.' And he stopped and looked at me, terribly and kindly. 'Some day, perhaps, I shall be glad to be able to lay my hand on a young, unperverted soul. If a man can make a friend, it is always something gained. What is your name?'

I had in my pocket a small volume of Pascal's *Thoughts*, on the flyleaf of which were written my name and address. I took it out and offered it to my old friend. 'Pray keep this little book,' I said. 'It is one I am very fond of, and it will tell you something about me.'

He took it and turned it over slowly, then looking up at me with a scowl of gratitude, 'I'm not much of a reader,' he said; 'but I won't refuse the first present I shall have received since—my troubles; and the last. Thank you, sir!' And with the little book in his hand he took his departure.

I was left to imagine him for some weeks after that sitting solitary in his armchair with his pipe. I had not another glimpse of him. But I was awaiting my chance, and on the last day of June, another quarter having elapsed, I deemed that it had come. The evening dusk in June falls late, and I was impatient for its coming. At last, towards the end of a lovely summer's day, I revisited Captain Diamond's property. Everything now was green around it save the blighted orchard in its rear, but its own immitigable greyness and sadness were as striking as when I had first beheld it beneath a December sky. As I drew near it, I saw that I was late for my purpose, for my purpose had simply been to step forward on Captain Diamond's arrival, and bravely ask him to let me go in with him. He had preceded me, and there were lights already in the windows. I was unwilling, of course, to disturb him during his ghostly interview, and I waited till he came forth. The lights disappeared in the course of time; then the door opened and Captain Diamond stole out. That evening he made no bow to the haunted house, for the first object he beheld was his fair-minded young friend planted, modestly but firmly, near the doorstep. He stopped short, looking at me, and this time his terrible scowl was in keeping with the situation.

'I knew you were here,' I said. 'I came on purpose.'

He seemed dismayed, and looked round at the house uneasily.

'I beg your pardon if I have ventured too far,' I added, 'but you know you have encouraged me.'

'How did you know I was here?'

'I reasoned it out. You told me half your story, and I guessed the other half. I am a great observer, and I had noticed this house in passing. It seemed to me to have a mystery. When you kindly confided to me that you saw spirits, I was sure that it could only be here that you saw them.'

'You are mighty clever,' cried the old man. 'And what brought you here this evening?'

I was obliged to evade this question.

'Oh, I often come; I like to look at the house—it fascinates me.'

He turned and looked up at it himself. 'It's nothing to look at outside.' He was evidently quite unaware of its peculiar outward appearance, and this odd fact, communicated to me thus in the twilight, and under the very brow of the sinister dwelling, seemed to make his vision of the strange things within more real.

'I have been hoping,' I said, 'for a chance to see the inside. I thought I might find you here, and that you would let me go in with you. I should like to see what you see.'

He seemed confounded by my boldness, but not altogether displeased. He laid his hand on my arm. 'Do you know what I see?' he asked.

'How can I know, except as you said the other day, by experience? I want to have the experience. Pray, open the door and take me in.'

Captain Diamond's brilliant eyes expanded beneath their dusky brows, and after holding his breath a moment, he indulged in the first and last apology for a laugh by which I was to see his solemn visage contorted. It was profoundly grotesque, but it was perfectly noiseless. 'Take you in?' he softly growled. 'I wouldn't go in again before my time's up for a thousand times that sum.' And he thrust out his hand from the folds of his cloak and exhibited a small agglomeration of coin, knotted into the corner of an old silk pocket-handkerchief. 'I stick to my bargain no less, but no more!'

'But you told me the first time I had the pleasure of talking with you that it was not so terrible.'

'I don't say it's terrible—now. But it's damned disagreeable!'

This adjective was uttered with a force that made me hesitate and reflect. While I did so, I thought I heard a slight movement of one of the window-shutters above us. I looked up, but everything seemed motionless. Captain Diamond, too, had been thinking; suddenly he turned towards the house. 'If you will go in alone,' he said, 'you are welcome.'

'Will you wait for me here?'

'Yes, you will not stop long.'

'But the house is pitch dark. When you go you have lights.'

He thrust his hand into the depths of his cloak and produced some matches. 'Take these,' he said. 'You will find two candlesticks with candles on the table in the hall. Light them, take one in each hand and go ahead.'

'Where shall I go?'

'Anywhere—everywhere. You can trust the ghost to find you.'

I will not pretend to deny that by this time my heart was beating. And yet I imagine I motioned the old man with a sufficiently dignified gesture to open the door. I had made up my mind that there was in fact a ghost. I had conceded the premise. Only I had assured myself that once the mind was prepared, and the thing was not a surprise, it was possible to keep cool. Captain Diamond turned the lock, flung open the door, and bowed low to me as I passed in. I stood in the darkness, and heard the door close behind me. For some moments, I stirred neither finger nor toe; I stared bravely into the impenetrable dusk. But I saw nothing and heard nothing, and at last I struck a match. On the table were two brass candlesticks rusty from disuse. I lighted the candles and began my tour of exploration.

A wide staircase rose in front of me, guarded by an antique balustrade of that rigidly delicate carving which is found so often in old New England houses. I postponed ascending it, and turned into the room on my right. This was an old-fashioned parlour meagrely furnished, and musty with the absence of human life. I raised my two lights aloft and saw nothing but its empty chairs and its blank walls. Behind it was the room into which I had peeped from without, and which, in fact, communicated with it, as I had supposed, by folding doors. Here, too, I found myself confronted by no menacing spectre.

I crossed the hall again, and visited the rooms on the other side; a dining-room in front, where I might have written my name with my finger in the deep dust of the great square table; a kitchen behind with its pots and pans eternally cold. All this was hard and grim, but it was not formidable. I came back into the hall, and walked to the foot of the staircase, holding up my candles; to ascend required a fresh effort, and I was scanning the gloom above. Suddenly, with an inexpressible sensation, I became aware that this gloom was animated; it seemed to move and gather itself together. Slowly—I say slowly, for to my tense expectancy the instants appeared ages—it took the shape of a large, definite figure, and this figure advanced and stood at the top of the stairs. I frankly confess that by this time I was conscious of a feeling to which I am in duty bound to apply the vulgar name of fear. I may poetize it and call it Dread, with a capital letter; it was at any rate the feeling that makes a man yield ground. I measured it as it grew, and it seemed perfectly irresistible; for it did not appear to come from within but from without, and to be embodied in the dark image at the head of the staircase. After a fashion I reasoned—I remember reasoning. I said to myself, 'I had always thought ghosts were white and transparent; this is a thing of thick shadows, densely opaque.' I reminded myself that the occasion was momentous, and that if fear were to overcome me I should gather all possible impressions while my wits remained. I stepped back, foot behind foot, with my eyes still on the figure and placed my candles on the table. I was perfectly conscious that the proper thing was to ascend the stairs resolutely, face to face with the image, but the soles of my shoes seemed suddenly to have been transformed into leaden weights. I had got what I wanted; I was seeing the ghost. I tried to look at the figure distinctly so that I could remember it, and fairly claim, afterwards, not to have lost my self-possession. I even asked myself how long it was expected I should stand looking, and how soon I could honourably retire. All this, of course, passed through my mind with extreme rapidity, and it was checked by a further movement on the part of the figure. Two white hands appeared in the dark perpendicular mass, and were slowly raised to what seemed to be the level of the head. Here they were pressed together, over the region of the face, and then they were removed, and the face was disclosed. It was dim, white, strange, in every way ghostly. It looked down at me for an instant, after which one of the hands was raised again, slowly, and waved to and fro before it. There was something very singular in this gesture; it seemed to denote resentment and dismissal, and yet it had a sort of trivial, familiar motion. Familiarity on the part of the haunting Presence had not entered into my calculations, and did not strike me pleasantly. I agreed with Captain Diamond that it was 'damned disagreeable.' I was pervaded by an intense desire to make an orderly, and, if possible, a graceful retreat. I wished to do it gallantly, and it seemed to me that it would be gallant to blow out my candles. I turned and did so, punctiliously, and then I made my way to the door, groped a moment and opened it. The outer light, almost extinct as it was, entered for a moment, played over the dusty depths of the house and showed me the solid shadow.

Standing on the grass bent over his stick, under the early glimmering stars, I found Captain Diamond. He looked up at me fixedly for a moment, but asked no questions, and then he went and locked the door. This duty performed, he discharged the other—made his obeisance like the priest before the altar—and then without heeding me further, took his departure.

A few days later, I suspended my studies and went off for the summer's vacation. I was absent for several weeks, during which I had plenty of leisure to analyse my impressions of the supernatural. I took some satisfaction in the reflection that I had not been ignobly terrified; I had not bolted nor swooned—I had proceeded with dignity. Nevertheless, I was certainly more comfortable when I had put thirty miles between me and the scene of my exploit, and I continued for many days to prefer the daylight to the dark. My nerves had been powerfully excited; of this I was particularly conscious when, under the influence of the drowsy air of the seaside, my excitement began slowly to ebb. As it disappeared, I attempted to take a sternly rational view of my experience. Certainly I had seen *something*—that was not fancy; but what had I seen? I regretted extremely now that I had not been bolder, that I had not gone nearer and inspected the apparition more minutely. But it was very well to talk; I had done as much as any man in the circumstances would have dared; it was indeed a physical impossibility that I should have advanced. Was not this paralysis of my powers in itself a supernatural influence? Not necessarily, perhaps, for a sham ghost that one accepted might do as much execution as a real ghost. But why had I so easily accepted the sable phantom that waved its hand? Why had it so impressed itself? Unquestionably, true or false, it was a very clever phantom. I greatly preferred that it should have been true—in the first place because I did not care to have shivered and shaken for nothing, and in the second place because to have seen a well-authenticated goblin is, as things go, a feather in a quiet man's cap. I tried, therefore, to let my vision rest and to stop turning it over. But an impulse stronger than my will recurred at intervals and set a mocking question on my lips. Granted that the apparition was Captain Diamond's daughter; if it was she it certainly was her spirit. But was it not her spirit and something more?

The middle of September saw me again established among the theologic shades, but I made no haste to revisit the haunted house.

The last of the month approached—the term of another quarter with poor Captain Diamond—and found me indisposed to disturb his pilgrimage on this occasion; though I confess that I thought with a good deal of compassion of the feeble old man trudging away, lonely, in the autumn dusk, on his extraordinary errand. On the thirtieth of September, at noonday, I was drowsing over a heavy octavo, when I heard a feeble rap at my door. I replied with an invitation to enter, but as this produced no effect I repaired to the door and opened it. Before me stood an elderly negress with her head bound in a scarlet turban, and a white handkerchief folded across her bosom. She looked at me intently and in silence; she had that air of supreme gravity and decency which aged persons of her race so often wear. I stood interrogative, and at last, drawing her hand from her ample pocket, she held up a little book. It was the copy of Pascal's *Thoughts* that I had given to Captain Diamond.

'Please, sir,' she said, very mildly, 'do you know this book?'

'Perfectly,' said I, 'my name is on the flyleaf.'

'It is your name—no other?'

'I will write my name if you like, and you can compare them,' I answered.

She was silent a moment and then, with dignity—'It would be useless, sir,' she said, 'I can't read. If you will give me your word that is enough. I come,' she went on, 'from the gentleman to whom you gave the book. He told me to carry it as a token—a token—that is what he called it. He is right down sick, and he wants to see you.'

'Captain Diamond—sick?' I cried. 'Is his illness serious?'

'He is very bad—he is all gone.'

I expressed my regret and sympathy, and offered to go to him immediately, if his sable messenger would show me the way. She assented deferentially, and in a few moments I was following her along the sunny streets, feeling very much like a personage in the Arabian Nights, led to a postern gate by an Ethiopian slave. My own conductress directed her steps towards the river and stopped at a decent little yellow house in one of the streets that descend to it. She quickly opened the door and led me in, and I very soon found myself in the presence of my old friend. He was in bed, in a darkened room, and evidently in a very feeble state. He lay back on his pillow staring before him, with his bristling hair more erect than ever, and his intensely dark and bright old eyes touched with the glitter of fever. His apartment was humble and scrupulously neat and I could see that my dusky guide was a faithful servant. Captain Diamond, lying there rigid and pale on his white sheets, resembled some ruggedly carven figure on the lid of a Gothic tomb. He looked at me silently, and my companion withdrew and left us alone.

'Yes, it's you,' he said, at last, 'it's you, that good young man. There is no mistake, is there?'

'I hope not; I believe I'm a good young man. But I am very sorry you are ill. What can I do for you?'

'I am very bad, very bad; my poor old bones ache so!' and, groaning portentously, he tried to turn towards me.

I questioned him about the nature of his malady and the length of time he had been in bed, but he barely heeded me; he seemed impatient to speak of something else. He grasped my sleeve, pulled me towards him and whispered quickly:

'You know my time's up!'

'Oh, I trust not,' I said, mistaking his meaning. 'I shall certainly see you on your legs again.'

'God knows!' he cried. 'But I don't mean I'm dying; not yet a bit. What I mean is, I'm due at the house. This is rent-day.'

'Oh, exactly! But you can't go.'

'I can't go. It's awful. I shall lose my money. If I am dying, I want it all the same. I want to pay the doctor. I want to be buried like a respectable man.'

'It is this evening?' I asked.

'This evening at sunset, sharp.'

He lay staring at me, and, as I looked at him in return, I suddenly understood his motive for sending for me. Morally, as it came into my thought, I winced. But, I suppose I looked unperturbed, for he continued in the same tone. 'I can't lose my money. Some one else must go. I asked Belinda; but she won't hear of it.'

'You believe the money will be paid to another person?'

'We can try, at least. I have never failed before and I don't know. But, if you say I'm as sick as a dog, that my old bones ache, that I'm dying, perhaps she'll trust you. She don't want me to starve!'

'You would like me to go in your place, then?'

'You have been there once; you know what it is. Are you afraid?'

I hesitated.

'Give me three minutes to reflect,' I said, 'and I will tell you.' My glance wandered over the room and rested on the various objects that spoke of the threadbare, decent poverty of its occupant. There seemed to be a mute appeal to my pity and my resolution in their cracked and faded sparseness, Meanwhile Captain Diamond continued, feebly:

'I think she'd trust you, as I have trusted you; she'll like your face; she'll see there is no harm in you. It's a hundred and thirty-three dollars, exactly. Be sure you put them into a safe place.'

'Yes,' I said at last, 'I will go, and, so far as it depends upon me, you shall have the money by nine o'clock tonight.'

He seemed greatly relieved; he took my hand and faintly pressed it, and soon afterwards I withdrew. I tried for the rest of the day not to think of my evening's work, but, of course, I thought of nothing else. I will not deny that I was nervous; I was, in fact, greatly excited, and I spent my time in alternately hoping that the mystery should prove less deep than it appeared, and yet fearing that it might prove too shallow. The hours passed very slowly, but, as the afternoon began to wane, I started on my mission. On the way, I stopped at Captain Diamond's modest dwelling, to ask how he was doing, and to receive such last instructions as he might desire to lay upon me. The old negress, gravely and inscrutably placid, admitted me, and, in answer to my enquiries, said that the Captain was very low; he had sunk since the morning.

'You must be right smart,' she said, 'if you want to get back before he drops off.'

A glance assured me that she knew of my projected expedition, though, in her own opaque black pupil, there was not a gleam of self-betrayal.

'But why should Captain Diamond drop off?' I asked. 'He certainly seems very weak; but I cannot make out that he has any definite disease.'

'His disease is old age,' she said, sententiously.

'But he is not so old as that; sixty-seven or sixty-eight, at most.'

She was silent a moment.

'He's worn out; he's used up; he can't stand it any longer.'

'Can I see him a moment?' I asked; upon which she led me again to his room.

He was lying in the same way as when I had left him, except that his eyes were closed. But he seemed very 'low', as she had said, and he had very little pulse. Nevertheless, I further learned the doctor had been there in the afternoon and professed himself satisfied. 'He don't know what's been going on,' said Belinda, curtly.

The old man stirred a little, opened his eyes, and after some time recognized me.

'I'm going, you know,' I said. 'I'm going for your money. Have you anything more to say?' He raised himself slowly, and with a painful effort, against his pillows; but he seemed hardly to understand me. 'The house, you know,' I said. 'Your daughter.'

He rubbed his forehead, slowly, awhile, and at last, his comprehension awoke. 'Ah, yes,' he murmured, 'I trust you. A hundred and thirty-three dollars. In old pieces—all in old pieces.' Then he added more vigorously, and with a brightening eye: 'Be very respectful—be very polite. If not—if not—' and his voice failed again.

'Oh, I certainly shall be,' I said, with a rather forced smile. 'But, if not?'

'If not, I shall know it!' he said, very gravely. And with this, his eyes closed and he sunk down again.

I took my departure and pursued my journey with a sufficiently resolute step. When I reached the house, I made a propitiatory bow in front of it, in emulation of Captain Diamond. I had timed my walk so as to be able to enter without delay; night had already fallen. I turned the key, opened the door and shut it behind me. Then I struck a light, and found the two candlesticks I had used before, standing on the tables in the entry. I applied a match to both of them, took them up and went into the parlour. It was empty, and though I waited awhile, it remained empty. I passed then into the other rooms on the same floor, and no dark image rose before me to check my steps. At last, I came out into the hall again, and stood weighing the question of going upstairs. The staircase had been the scene of my discomfiture before, and I approached it with profound mistrust. At the foot, I paused, looking up, with my hand on the balustrade. I was acutely expectant, and my expectation was justified. Slowly, in the darkness above, the black figure that I had seen before took shape. It was not an illusion; it was a figure, and the same. I gave it time to define itself, and watched it stand and look down at me with its hidden face. Then, deliberately, I lifted up my voice and spoke.

'I have come in place of Captain Diamond, at his request,' I said. 'He is very ill; he is unable to leave his bed. He earnestly begs that you will pay the money to me; I will immediately carry it to him.' The figure stood motionless, giving no sign. 'Captain Diamond would have come if he were able to move.' I added, in a moment, appealingly; 'but, he is utterly unable.'

At this the figure slowly unveiled its face and showed me a dim, white mask; then it began slowly to descend the stairs. Instinctively I fell back before it, retreating to the door of the front sitting-room. With my eyes still fixed on it, I moved backward across the threshold; then I stopped in the middle of the room and set down my lights. The figure advanced; it seemed to be that of a tall woman, dressed in vaporous black crape. As it drew near, I saw that it had a perfectly human face, though it looked extremely pale and sad. We stood gazing at each other; my agitation had completely vanished; I was only deeply interested.

'Is my father dangerously ill?' said the apparition.

At the sound of its voice—gentle, tremulous, and perfectly human—I started forward; I felt a rebound of excitement. I drew a long breath, I gave a sort of cry, for what I saw before me was not a disembodied spirit, but a beautiful woman, an audacious actress. Instinctively, irresistibly, by the force of reaction against my credulity, I stretched out my hand and seized the long veil that muffled her head. I gave it a violent jerk, dragged it nearly off, and stood staring at a large fair person, of about five-and-thirty. I comprehended her at a glance; her long black dress, her pale, sorrow-worn face, painted to look paler, her very fine eyes—the colour of her father's—and her sense of outrage at my movement.

'My father, I suppose,' she cried, 'did not send you here to insult me!' and she turned away rapidly, took up one of the candles and moved towards the door. Here she paused, looked at me again, hesitated, and then drew a purse from her pocket and flung it down on the floor. 'There is your money!' she said majestically.

I stood there, wavering between amazement and shame, and saw her pass out into the hall. Then I picked up the purse. The next moment, I heard a loud shriek and a crash of something dropping, and she came staggering back into the room without her light.

'My father—my father!' she cried; and with parted lips and dilated eyes, she rushed towards me.

'Your father—where?' I demanded.

'In the hall, at the foot of the stairs.'

I stepped forward to go out, but she seized my arm.

'He is in white,' she cried, 'in his shirt. It's not he!'

'Why, your father is in his house, in his bed, extremely ill,' I answered.

She looked at me fixedly, with searching eyes.

'Dying?'

'I hope not,' I stuttered.

She gave a long moan and covered her face with her hands.

'Oh, heavens, I have seen his ghost!' she cried.

She still held my arm; she seemed too terrified to release it. 'His ghost!' I echoed, wondering.

'It's the punishment of my long folly!' she went on.

'Ah,' said I, 'it's the punishment of my indiscretion—of my violence!'

'Take me away, take me away!' she cried, still clinging to my arm. 'Not there'—as I was turning towards the hall and the front door—'not there, for pity's sake! By this door—the back entrance.' And snatching the other candle from the table, she led me through the neighbouring room into the back part of the house. Here was a door opening from a sort of scullery into the orchard. I turned the rusty lock and we passed out and stood in the cool air, beneath the stars. Here my companion gathered her black drapery about her, and stood for a moment, hesitating. I had been infinitely flurried, but my curiosity touching her was uppermost. Agitated, pale, picturesque, she looked, in the early evening light, very beautiful.

'You have been playing all these years a most extraordinary game,' I said.

She looked at me sombrely, and seemed disinclined to reply. 'I came in perfect good faith,' I went on. 'The last time—three months ago— you remember?—you greatly frightened me.'

'Of course it was an extraordinary game,' she answered at last. 'But it was the only way.'

'Had he not forgiven you?'

'So long as he thought me dead, yes. There have been things in my life he could not forgive.'

I hesitated and then—'And where is your husband?' I asked.

'I have no husband—I have never had a husband.'

She made a gesture which checked further questions, and moved rapidly away. I walked with her round the house to the road, and she kept murmuring—'It was he—it was he!' When we reached the road she stopped, and asked me which way I was going. I pointed to the road by which I had come, and she said—'I take the other. You are going to my father's?' she added.

'Directly,' I said.

'Will you let me know tomorrow what you have found?'

'With pleasure. But how shall I communicate with you?'

She seemed at a loss, and looked about her. 'Write a few words,' she said, 'and put them under that stone.' And she pointed to one of the lava slabs that bordered the old well. I gave her my promise to comply, and she turned away. 'I know my road,' she said. 'Everything is arranged. It's an old story.'

She left me with a rapid step, and as she receded into the darkness, resumed, with the dark flowing lines of her drapery, the phantasmal appearance with which she had at first appeared to me. I watched her till she became invisible, and then I took my own leave of the place. I returned to town at a swinging pace, and marched straight to the little yellow house near the river. I took the liberty of entering without a knock, and, encountering no interruption, made my way to Captain Diamond's room. Outside the door, on a low bench, with folded arms, sat the sable Belinda.

'How is he?' I asked.

'He's gone to glory.'

'Dead?' I cried.

She rose with a sort of tragic chuckle.

'He's as big a ghost as any of them now!'

I passed into the room and found the old man lying there irredeemably rigid and still. I wrote that evening a few lines which I proposed on the morrow to place beneath the stone, near the well; but my promise was not destined to be executed. I slept that night very ill—it was natural—and in my restlessness left my bed to walk about the room. As I did so I caught sight, in passing my window, of a red glow in the north-western sky. A house was on fire in the country, and evidently burning fast. It lay in the same direction as the scene of my evening's adventures, and as I stood watching the crimson horizon I was startled by a sharp memory. I had blown out the candle which lighted me, with my companion, to the door through which we escaped, but I had not accounted for the other light, which she had carried into the hall and dropped—heaven knew where—in her consternation. The next day I walked out with my folded letter and turned into the familiar crossroad. The haunted house was a mass of charred beams and smouldering ashes; the well-cover had been pulled off, in quest of water, by the few neighbours who had had the audacity to contest what they must have regarded as a demon-kindled blaze, the loose stones were completely displaced, and the earth had been trampled into puddles.

5

MARGARET OLIPHANT

The Lady's Walk

I

I was on a visit to some people in Scotland when the events I am about
to relate took place. They were not friends in the sense of long or
habitual intercourse; in short, I had met them only in Switzerland in
the previous year; but we saw a great deal of each other while we were
together, and got into that cosy intimacy which travelling brings
about more readily than anything else. We had seen each other in very
great *déshabillé* both of mind and array in the chilly mornings after a
night's travelling, which perhaps is the severest test that can be applied
in respect to looks; and amid all the annoyances of journeys short and
long, with the usual episodes of lost luggage, indifferent hotels, fusses
of every description, which is an equally severe test for the temper;
and our friendship and liking (I am at liberty to suppose it was mutual,
or they would never have invited me to Ellermore) remained unim-
paired. I have always thought, and still think, that Charlotte Campbell
was one of the most charming young women I ever met with; and her
brothers, if not so entirely delightful, were nice fellows, capital to
travel with, full of fun and spirit. I understood immediately from their
conversation that they were members of a large family. Their allusions to Tom and Jack and little Harry, and the children in the nursery,
might perhaps have been tedious to a harsher critic; but I like to hear
of other people's relations, having scarcely any of my own. I found out
by degrees that Miss Campbell had been taken abroad by her brothers
to recover from a long and severe task of nursing, which had
exhausted her strength. The little ones had all been down with scarlet

fever, and she had not left them night or day. 'She gave up seeing the rest of us and regularly shut herself in,' Charley informed me, who was the younger of the two. 'She would only go out for her walk when all of us were out of the way. That was the worst of it,' the young fellow said, with great simplicity. That his sister should give herself up to the nursing was nothing remarkable; but that she should deny herself their precious company was a heroism that went to her brothers' hearts. Thus, by the way, I learned a great deal about the family. Chatty, as they called her, was the sister-mother, especially of the little ones, who had been left almost in her sole charge since their mother died many years before. She was not a girl, strictly speaking. She was in the perfection of her womanhood and youth—about eight-and-twenty, the age when something of the composure of maturity has lighted upon the sweetness of the earlier years, and being so old enhances all the charm of being so young. It is chiefly among young married women that one sees this gracious and beautiful type, delightful to every sense and every requirement of the mind; but when it is to be met with unmarried it is more celestial still. I cannot but think with reverence that this delicate maternity and maidenhood—the perfect bounty of the one, the undisturbed grace of the other—has been the foundation of that adoring devotion which in the old days brought so many saints to the shrine of the Virgin Mother. But why I should thus enlarge upon Charlotte Campbell at the beginning of this story I can scarcely tell, for she is not in the strict sense of the word the heroine of it, and I am unintentionally deceiving the reader to begin.

They asked me to come and see them at Ellermore when we parted, and, as I have nothing in the way of a home warmer or more genial than chambers in the Temple, I accepted, as may be supposed, with enthusiasm. It was in the first week of June that we parted, and I was invited for the end of August. They had 'plenty of grouse', Charley said, with a liberality of expression which was pleasant to hear. Charlotte added, 'But you must be prepared for a homely life, Mr Temple, and a very quiet one.' I replied, of course, that if I had chosen what I liked best in the world it would have been this combination: at which she smiled with an amused little shake of her head. It did not seem to occur to her that she herself told for much in the matter.

What they all insisted upon was the 'plenty of grouse'; and I do not pretend to say that I was indifferent to that.

Colin, the eldest son, was the one with whom I had been least familiar. He was what people call reserved. He did not talk of everything as the others did. I did not indeed find out till much later that he was constantly in London, coming and going, so that he and I might have seen much of each other. Yet he liked me well enough. He joined warmly in his brother's invitation. When Charley said there was plenty of grouse, he added with the utmost friendliness, 'And ye may get a blaze at a stag.' There was a flavour of the North in the speech of all; not disclosed by mere words, but by an occasional diversity of idiom and change of pronunciation. They were conscious of this and rather proud of it than otherwise. They did not say Scotch, but Scots; and their accent could not be represented by any of the travesties of the theatre, or what we conventionally accept as the national utterance. When I attempted to pronounce after them, my own ear informed me what a travesty it was.

It was to the family represented by these young people that I was going when I started on August 20, a blazing summer day, with dust and heat enough to merit the name of summer if anything ever did. But when I arrived at my journey's end there was just change enough to mark the line between summer and autumn: a little golden haze in the air, a purple bloom of heather on the hills, a touch here and there upon a stray branch, very few, yet enough to swear by. Ellermore lay in the heart of a beautiful district full of mountains and lochs, within the Highland line, and just on the verge of some of the wildest mountain scenery in Scotland. It was situated in the midst of an amphitheatre of hills, not of any very exalted height, but of the most picturesque form, with peaks and couloirs like an Alpine range in little, all glowing with the purple blaze of the heather, with gleams upon them that looked like snow, but were in reality water, white threads of mountain torrents. In front of the house was a small loch embosomed in the hills, from one end of which ran a cheerful little stream, much intercepted by boulders, and much the brighter for the interruptions, which meandered through the glen and fell into another loch of greater grandeur and pretensions. Ellermore itself was a comparatively new house, built upon a fine slope of lawn over the lake, and sheltered by fine trees—great beeches which would not have done discredit to Berkshire, though that is not what we expect to see in Scotland: besides the ashes and firs which we are ready to acknowledge as of northern growth. I was not prepared for the luxuriance of the West Highlands—the mantling green of ferns and herbage everywhere, not to say the wealth of flowers, which formed a centre of still more brilliant colour and cultivation amid all the purple of the hills. Everything was soft and rich and warm about the Highland mansion-house. I had expected stern scenery and a grey atmosphere. I found an almost excessive luxuriance of vegetation and colour everywhere. The father of my friends received me at a door which was constantly open, and where it seemed to me after a while that nobody was ever refused admission. He was a tall old man, dignified but homely, with white hair and moustache and the fresh colour of a rural patriarch, which, however, he was not, but an energetic man of business, as I afterwards found. The Campbells of Ellermore were not great chiefs in that much-extended clan, but they were perfectly well-known people and had held their little estate from remote antiquity. But they had not stood upon their gentility, or refused to avail themselves of the opportunities that came in their way. I have observed that in the great and wealthy region of which Glasgow is the capital the number of the irreconcilables who stand out against trade is few. The gentry have seen all the advantages of combining commerce with tradition. Had it not been for this it is likely that Ellermore would have been a very different place. Now it was overflowing with all those signs of ease and simple luxury which make life so smooth. There was little show, but there was a profusion of comfort. Everything rolled upon velvet. It was perhaps more like the house of a rich merchant than of a family of long descent. Nothing could be more perfect as a pleasure estate than was this little Highland property. They had 'plenty of grouse', and also of trout in a succession of little lochs and mountain streams. They had deer on the hills. They had their own mutton, and everything vegetable that was needed for the large profuse household, from potatoes and cabbage up to grapes and peaches. But with all this primitive wealth there was not much money got out of Ellermore. The 'works' in Glasgow supplied that. What the works were I have never exactly found out, but they afforded occupation for all the family, both father and sons; and that the results were of the most pleasing description as regarded Mr Campbell's banker it was easy to see.

They were all at home with the exception of Colin, the eldest son, for whose absence many apologies, some of which seemed much more elaborate than were at all necessary, were made to me. I was for my own part quite indifferent to the absence of Colin. He was not the one who had interested me most; and though Charley was considerably younger than myself, I had liked him better from the first. Tom and Jack were still younger. They were all occupied at 'the works', and came home only from Saturday to Monday. The little trio in the nursery were delightful children. To see them gathered about Charlotte was enough to melt any heart. Chatty they called her, which is not a very dignified name, but I got to think it the most beautiful in the world as it sounded all over that cheerful, much-populated house. 'Where is Chatty?' was the first question everyone asked as he came in at the door. If she was not immediately found it went volleying through the house, all up the stairs and through the passages— 'Chatty! where are you?'—and was always answered from somewhere or other in a full soft voice, which was audible everywhere though it never was loud. 'Here am I, boys,' she would say, with a pretty inversion which pleased me. Indeed, everything pleased me in Chatty—too much, more than reason. I found myself thinking what would become of them all if, for example, she were to marry, and entered into a hot argument with myself on one occasion by way of proving that it would be the most selfish thing in the world were this family to work upon Chatty's feelings and prevent her from marrying, as most probably, I could not help feeling, they would. At the same time I perceived with a little shudder how entirely the whole thing would collapse if by any chance Chatty should be decoyed away.

I enjoyed my stay beyond description. In the morning we were out on the hills or about the country. In the evening it very often happened that we all strolled out after dinner, and that I was left by Chatty's side, 'the boys' having a thousand objects of interest, while Mr Campbell usually sat in his library and read the newspapers, which arrived at that time either by the coach from Oban or by the boat. In this way I went over the whole 'policy', as the grounds surrounding a country house are called in Scotland, with Chatty, who would not be out of reach at this hour, lest her father should want her, or the children. She would bid me not to stay with her when no doubt it would be more amusing for me to go with the boys; and when I assured her my pleasure was far greater as it was, she gave me a gracious, frank smile, with a little shake of her head. She laughed at me softly, bidding me not to be too polite or think she would mind if I left her; but I think, on the whole, she liked to have me with her in her evening walk.

'There is one thing you have not told me of,' I said, 'and that you must possess. I cannot believe that your family has been settled here so long without having a ghost.'

She had turned round to look at me, to know what it was that had been omitted in her descriptions. When she heard what it was she smiled a little, but not with the pleasant mockery I had expected. On the contrary, it was a sort of gentle smile of recognition that something had been left out.

'We don't call it a ghost,' she said. 'I have wondered if you had never noticed. I am fond of it for my part; but then I have been used to it all my life. And here we are, then,' she added as we reached the top of a little ascent and came out upon a raised avenue, which I had known by its name of the Lady's Walk without as yet getting any explanation what that meant. It must have been, I supposed, the avenue to the old house, and now encircled one portion of the grounds without any distinct meaning. On the side nearest the gardens and house it was but slightly raised above the shrubberies, but on the other side was the summit of a high bank sloping steeply to the river, which, after it escaped from the loch, made a wide bend round that portion of the grounds. A row of really grand beeches rose on each side of the path, and through the openings in the trees the house, the bright gardens, the silvery gleam of the loch were visible. The evening sun was slanting into our eyes as we walked along; a little soft yet brisk air was pattering among the leaves, and here and there a yellow cluster in the middle of a branch showing the first touch of a cheerful decay. 'Here we are, then.' It was a curious phrase; but there are some odd idioms in the Scotch—I mean Scots'—form of our common language, and I had become accustomed now to accept them without remark.

'I suppose,' I said, 'there must be some back way to the village or to the farmhouse under this bank, though there seems no room for a path?'

'Why do you ask?' she said, looking at me with a smile.

'Because I always hear some one passing along—I imagine down there. The steps are very distinct. Don't you hear them now? It has puzzled me a good deal, for I cannot make out where the path can be.'

She smiled again, with a meaning in her smile, and looked at me steadily, listening, as I was. And then, after a pause, she said, 'That is what you were asking for. If we did not hear it, it would make us unhappy. Did you not know why this was called the Lady's Walk?'

When she said these words I was conscious of an odd enough change in my sensations—nay, I should say in my very sense of hearing, which was the one appealed to. I had heard the sound often, and, after looking back at first to see who it was and seeing no one, had made up my mind that the steps were on some unseen byway and heard them accordingly, feeling quite sure that the sound came from below. Now my hearing changed, and I could not understand how I had ever thought anything else: the steps were on a level with us, by our side—as if some third person were accompanying us along the avenue. I am no believer in ghosts, nor the least superstitious, so far as I had ever been aware (more than everybody is), but I felt myself get out of the way with some celerity and a certain thrill of curious sensation. The idea of rubbing shoulders with something unseen startled me in spite of myself.

'Ah!' said Charlotte, 'it gives you an—unpleasant feeling. I forgot you are not used to it like me.'

'I am tolerably well used to it, for I have heard it often,' I said, somewhat ashamed of my involuntary movement. Then I laughed, which I felt to be altogether out of place and fictitious, and said, 'No doubt there is some very easy explanation of it—some vibration or echo. The science of acoustics clears up many mysteries.'

'There is no explanation,' Chatty said, almost angrily. 'She has walked here far longer than anyone can remember. It is an ill sign for us Campbells when she goes away. She was the eldest daughter, like me; and I think she has got to be our guardian angel. There is no harm going to happen as long as she is here. Listen to her,' she cried, standing still with her hand raised. The low sun shone full on her, catching her brown hair, the lucid clearness of her brown eyes, her cheeks so clear and soft, in colour a little summer-brown, too. I stood and listened with a something of excited feeling which I could not control: the sound of this third person, whose steps were not to be mistaken though she was unseen, made my heart beat: if, indeed, it was not merely the presence of my companion, who was sweet enough to account for any man's emotion.

'You are startled,' she said with a smile.

'Well! I should not be acting my part, should I, as I ought, if I did not feel the proper thrill? It must be disrespectful to a ghost not to be afraid.'

'Don't say a ghost,' said Chatty; 'I think *that* is disrespectful. It is the Lady of Ellermore; everybody knows about her. And do you know,' she added, 'when my mother died—the greatest grief I have ever known—the steps ceased? Oh! it is true! You need not look me in the face as if there was anything to laugh at. It is ten years ago, and I was only a silly sort of girl, not much good to anyone. They sent me out to get the air when she was lying in a doze; and I came here. I was crying, as you may suppose, and at first I did not pay any attention. Then it struck me all at once—the Lady was away. They told me afterwards that was the worst sign. It is always death that is coming when she goes away.'

The pathos of this incident confused all my attempts to touch it with levity, and we went on for a little without speaking, during which time it is almost unnecessary to say that I was listening with all my might to those strange footsteps, which finally I persuaded myself were no more than echoes of our own.

'It is very curious,' I said politely. 'Of course you were greatly agitated and too much absorbed in real grief to have any time to think of the other: and there might be something in the state of the atmosphere——'

She gave me an indignant look. We were nearly at the end of the walk; and at that moment I could have sworn that the footsteps, which had got a little in advance, here turned and met us going back. I am aware that nothing could sound more foolish, and that it must have been some vibration or atmospheric phenomenon. But yet this was how it seemed—not an optical but an aural delusion. So long as the steps were going with us it was less impossible to account for it; but when they turned and audibly came back to meet us! Not all my scepticism could prevent me from stepping aside to let them pass. This time they came directly between us, and the naturalness of my withdrawal out of the way was more significant than the faltering laugh with which I excused myself. 'It is a very curious sound indeed,' I said with a tremor which slightly affected my voice.

Chatty gave me a reassuring smile. She did not laugh at me, which was consolatory. She stood for a moment as if looking after the visionary passenger. 'We are not afraid,' she said, 'even the youngest; we all know she is our friend.'

When we had got back to the side of the loch, where, I confess, I was pleased to find myself, in the free open air without any perplexing shadow of trees, I felt less objection to the subject. 'I wish you would tell me the story; for of course there is a story,' I said.

'No, there is no story—at least nothing tragical or even romantic. They say she was the eldest daughter. I sometimes wonder,' Chatty said with a smile and a faint increase of colour, 'whether she might not be a little like me. She lived here all her life, and had several generations to take care of. Oh no, there was no murder or wrong about our Lady; she just loved Ellermore above everything; but my idea is that she has been allowed the care of us ever since.'

'That is very sweet, to have the care of you,' I said, scarcely venturing to put any emphasis on the pronoun; 'but, after all, it must be slow work, don't you think, walking up and down there for ever? I call that a poor sort of reward for a good woman. If she had been a bad one it might have answered very well for a punishment.'

'Mr Temple!' Chatty said, now reddening with indignation, 'do you think it is a poor thing to have the care of your own people, to watch over them, whatever may happen—to be all for them and their service? I don't think so; I should like to have such a fate.'

Perhaps I had spoken thus on purpose to bring about the discussion. 'There is such a thing as being too devoted to your family. Are they ever grateful? They go away and marry and leave you in the lurch.'

She looked up at me with a little astonishment. 'The members may vary, but the family never goes away,' she said; 'besides, that can apply to us in our present situation only. *She* must have seen so many come and go; but that need not vex her, you know, because they go where she is.'

'My dear Miss Campbell, wait a bit, think a little,' I said: 'where she is! That is in the Lady's Walk, according to your story. Let us hope that all your ancestors and relations are not there.'

'I suppose you want to make me angry,' said Chatty. 'She is in heaven—have you any doubt of that?—but every day when the sun is setting she comes back home.'

'Oh, come!' I said, 'if it is only at the sunset that is not so bad.'

Miss Campbell looked at me doubtfully, as if not knowing whether to be angry. 'You want to make fun of it,' she said, 'to laugh at it; and yet,' she added with a little spirit, 'you were rather nervous half an hour ago.'

'I acknowledge to being nervous. I am very impressionable. I believe that is the word. It is a luxury to be nervous at the fit moment. Frightened you might say, if you prefer plain speaking. And I am very glad it is at sunset, not in the dark. This completes the round of my Highland experiences,' I said; 'everything now is perfect. I have shot grouse on the hill and caught trout on the loch, and been soaked to the skin and then dried in the wind; I wanted nothing but the family ghost. And now I have seen her, or at least heard her——'

'If you are resolved to make a joke of it I cannot help it,' said Chatty, 'but I warn you that it is not agreeable to me, Mr Temple. Let us talk of something else. In the Highlands,' she said with dignity, 'we take different views of many things.'

'There are some things,' I said, 'of which but one view is possible—that I should have the audacity and impertinence to laugh at anything for which you have a veneration! I believe it is only because I was so frightened——'

She smiled again in her lovely motherly way, a smile of indulgence and forgiveness and bounty. 'You are too humble now,' she said, 'and I think I hear someone calling me. It is time to go in.'

And to be sure there was someone calling her: there always was, I think, at all hours of the night and day.

II

To say that I got rid of the recollection of the Lady of Ellermore when I went upstairs after a cheerful evening through a long and slippery gallery to my room in the wing would be untrue. The curious experience I had just had dwelt in my mind with a feeling of not unpleasant perplexity. Of course, I said to myself, there must be something to account for those footsteps—some hidden way in which the sounds could come. Perhaps my first idea would turn out to be correct—that there was a by-road to the farm, or to the stables, which in some states of the atmosphere—or perhaps it might even be always—echoed back the sounds of passing feet in some subterranean vibration. One has heard of such things; one has heard, indeed, of every kind of natural wonder, some of them no more easy to explain than the other kind of prodigy; but so long as you have science with you, whether you understand it or not, you are all right. I could not help wondering, however, whether, if by chance I heard those steps in the long gallery outside my door, I should refer the matter comfortably to the science of acoustics. I was tormented, until I fell asleep, by a vague expectation of hearing them. I could not get them out of my mind or out of my ears, so distinct were they—the light step, soft but with energy in it, evidently a woman's step. I could not help recollecting, with a tingling sensation through all my veins, the distinctness of the turn it gave—the coming back, the steps going in a line opposite to ours. It seemed to me that from moment to moment I must hear it again in the gallery, and then how could it be explained?

Next day—for I slept very well after I had succeeded in getting to sleep, and what I had heard did not by any means haunt my dreams—next day I managed to elude all the pleasant occupations of the house, and, as soon as I could get free from observation, I took my way to the Lady's Walk. I had said that I had letters to write—a well-worn phrase, which of course means exactly what one pleases. I walked up and down the Lady's Walk, and could neither hear nor see anything. On this side of the shrubbery there was no possibility of any concealed path; on the other side the bank went sloping to the water's edge. The avenue ran along from the corner of the loch half-way round the green plateau on which the house was planted, and at the upper end came out upon the elevated ground behind the house; but no road crossed it, nor was there the slightest appearance of any mode by which a steady sound not its own could be communicated here. I examined it all with the utmost care, looking behind the bole of every tree as if the secret might be there, and my heart gave a leap when I perceived what seemed to me one narrow track worn along the ground. Fancy plays us curious pranks even when she is most on her guard. It was a strange idea that I, who had come here with the purpose of finding a way of explaining the curious phenomenon upon which so long and lasting a superstition had been built, should be so quickly infected by it. I saw the little track, quite narrow but very distinct, and though of course I did not believe in the Lady of Ellermore, yet within myself I jumped at the certainty that this was her track. It gave me a curious sensation. The certainty lay underneath the scepticism as if they were two things which had no connection with each other. Had anyone seen me it must have been supposed that I was looking for something among the bushes, so closely did I scrutinize every foot of the soil and every tree.

It exercised a fascination upon me which I could not resist. The Psychical Society did not exist in those days, so far as I know, but there are many minds outside that inquisitive body to whom the authentication of a ghost story, or, to speak more practically, the clearing up of a superstition, is very attractive. I managed to elude the family arrangements once more at the same hour at which Miss Campbell and I had visited the Lady's Walk on the previous evening. It was a lovely evening, soft and warm, the western sky all ablaze with colour, the great branches of the beeches thrown out in dark maturity of greenness upon the flush of orange and crimson melting into celestial rosy red as it rose higher, and flinging itself in airy masses rose-tinted across the serene blue above. The same wonderful colours glowed in reflection out of the loch. The air was of magical clearness, and earth and sky seemed stilled with an almost awe of their own loveliness, happiness, and peace.

> The holy time was quiet as a nun,
> Breathless with adoration.

For my part, however, I noticed this only in passing, being intent on other thoughts. From the loch there came a soft tumult of voices.

It was Saturday evening, and all the boys were at home. They were getting out the boats for an evening row, and the white sail of the toy yacht rose upon the gleaming water like a little white cloud among the rosy clouds of that resplendent sky. I stood between two of the beeches that formed a sort of arch, and looked out upon them, distracted for an instant by the pleasant distant sound which came softly through the summer air. Next moment I turned sharply round with a start, in spite of myself—turned quickly to see who it was coming after me. There was, I need not say, not a soul within sight. The beech leaves fluttered softly in the warm air; the long shadows of their great boles lay unbroken along the path; nothing else was visible, not even a bird on a bough. I stood breathless between the two trees, with my back turned to the loch, gazing at nothing, while the soft footsteps came quietly on, and crossed me—passed me! with a slight waft of air, I thought, such as a slight figure might have made; but that was imagination perhaps. Imagination! was it not all imagination? or what was it? No shadows or darkness to conceal a passing form by; full light of day radiant with colour; the most living delightful air, all sweet with pleasure. I stood there speechless and without power to move. They went along softly, without changing the gentle regularity of the tread, to the end of the walk, growing fainter as they went further and further from me. I never listened so intently in my life. I said to myself, 'If they go out of hearing I shall know it is merely an excited imagination.' And on they went, almost out of hearing, only the faintest touch upon the ground; then there was a momentary pause, and my heart stood still, but leaped again to my throat and sent wild waves of throbbing to my ears next moment: they had turned and were coming back.

I cannot describe the extraordinary effect. If it had been dark it would have been altogether different. The brightness, the life around, the absence of all that one associates with the supernatural, produced a thrill of emotion to which I can give no name. It was not fear; yet my heart beat as it had never in any dangerous emergency (and I have passed through some that were exciting enough) beat before. It was simple excitement, I suppose; and in the commotion of my mind I instinctively changed the pronoun which I had hitherto used, and asked myself, would *she* come back? She did, passing me once more, with the same movement of the air (or so I thought). But by that time my pulses were all clanging in my ears, and perhaps the sense itself became confused with listening. I turned and walked precipitately away, descending the little slope and losing myself in the shrubberies which were beneath the range of the low sun, now almost set, and felt dank and cold in the contrast. It was something like plunging into a bath of cold air after the warmth and glory above.

It was in this way that my first experience ended. Miss Campbell looked at me a little curiously with a half-smile when I joined the party at the lochside. She divined where I had been, and perhaps something of the agitation I felt, but she took no further notice; and as I was in time to find a place in the boat, where she had established herself with the children, I lost nothing by my meeting with the mysterious passenger in the Lady's Walk.

I did not go near the place for some days afterwards, but I cannot say that it was ever long out of my thoughts. I had long arguments with myself on the subject, representing to myself that I had heard the sound before hearing the superstition, and then had found no difficulty in believing that it was the sound of some passenger on an adjacent path, perhaps invisible from the Walk. I had not been able to find that path, but still it might exist at some angle which, according to the natural law of the transmission of sounds—Bah! what jargon this was! Had I not heard *her* turn, felt her pass me, watched her coming back? And then I paused with a loud burst of laughter at myself. 'Ass! you never had any of these sensations before you heard the story,' I said. And that was true; but I heard the steps before I heard the story; and, now I think of it, was much startled by them, and set my mind to work to account for them, as you know. 'And what evidence have you t' it the first interpretation was not the right one?' myself asked me with scorn; upon which question I turned my back with a hopeless contempt of the pertinacity of that other person who has always so many objections to make. Interpretation! could any interpretation ever do away with the effect upon my actual senses of that invisible passer-by? But the most disagreeable effect was this, that I could not shut out from my mind the expectation of hearing those same steps in the gallery outside my door at night. It was a long gallery running the full length of the wing, highly polished and somewhat slippery, a place in which any sound was important. I never went along to my room without a feeling that at any moment I might hear those steps behind me, or after I had closed my door might be conscious of them passing. I never did so, but neither have I ever got free of the thought.

A few days after, however, another incident occurred that drove the Lady's Walk and its invisible visitor out of my mind. We were all returning home in the long northern twilight from a mountain expedition. How it was that I was the last to return I do not exactly recollect. I think Miss Campbell had forgotten to give some directions to the coachman's wife at the lodge, which I volunteered to carry for her. My nearest way back would have been through the Lady's Walk, had not some sort of doubtful feeling restrained me from taking it. Though I have said and felt that the effect of these mysterious footsteps was enhanced by the full daylight, still I had a sort of natural reluctance to put myself in the way of encountering them when the darkness began to fall. I preferred the shrubberies, though they were darker and less attractive. As I came out of their shade, however, some one whom I had never seen before—a lady—met me, coming apparently from the house. It was almost dark, and what little light there was was behind her, so that I could not distinguish her features. She was tall and slight, and wrapped apparently in a long cloak, a dress usual enough in those rainy regions. I think, too, that her veil was over her face. The way in which she approached made it apparent that she was going to speak to me, which surprised me a little, though there was nothing extraordinary in it, for of course by this time all the neighbourhood knew who I was and that I was a visitor at Ellermore. There was a little air of timidity and hesitation about her as she came forward, from which I supposed that my sudden appearance startled her a little, and yet was welcome as an unexpected way of getting something done that she wanted. *Tant de choses en un mot*, you will say—nay, without a word—and yet it was quite true. She came up to me quickly as soon as she had made up her mind. Her voice was very soft, but very peculiar, with a sort of far-away sound as if the veil or evening air interposed a visionary distance between her and me. 'If you are a friend to the Campbells,' she said, 'will you tell them——' then paused a little and seemed to look at me with eyes that shone dimly through the shadows like stars in a misty sky.

'I am a warm friend to the Campbells; I am living there,' I said.

'Will you tell them—the father and Charlotte—that Colin is in great trouble and temptation, and that if they would save him they should lose no time?'

'Colin!' I said, startled; then, after a moment, 'Pardon me, this is an uncomfortable message to entrust to a stranger. Is he ill? I am very sorry, but don't let me make them anxious without reason. What is the matter? He was all right when they last heard——'

'It is not without reason,' she said; 'I must not say more. Tell them just this—in great trouble and temptation. They may perhaps save him yet if they lose no time.'

'But stop,' I said, for she seemed about to pass on. 'If I am to say this there must be something more. May I ask who it is that sends the message? They will ask me, of course. And what is wrong?'

She seemed to wring her hands under her cloak, and looked at me with an attitude and gesture of supplication. 'In great trouble,' she said, 'in great trouble! and tempted beyond his strength. And not such as I can help. Tell them, if you wish well to the Campbells. I must not say more.'

And, notwithstanding all that I could say, she left me so, with a wave of her hand, disappearing among the dark bushes. It may be supposed that this was no agreeable charge to give to a guest, one who owed nothing but pleasure and kindness to the Campbells, but had no acquaintance beyond the surface with their concerns. They were, it is true, very free in speech, and seemed to have as little *dessous des cartes* in their life and affairs as could be imagined. But Colin was the one who was spoken of less freely than any other in the family. He had been expected several times since I came, but had never appeared. It seemed that he had a way of postponing his arrival, and 'of course', it was said in the family, never came when he was expected. I had wondered more than once at the testy tone in which the old gentleman spoke of him sometimes, and the line of covert defence always adopted by Charlotte. To be sure he was the eldest, and might naturally assume a more entire independence of action than the other young men, who were yet scarcely beyond the time of pupilage and in their father's house.

But from this as well as from the still more natural and apparent reason that to bring them bad news of any kind was most disagreeable and inappropriate on my part, the commission I had so strangely received hung very heavily upon me. I turned it over in my mind as I dressed for dinner (we had been out all day, and dinner was much later than usual in consequence) with great perplexity and distress. Was I bound to give a message forced upon me in such a way? If the lady had news of any importance to give, why did she turn away from the house, where she could have communicated it at once, and confide it to a stranger? On the other hand, should I be justified in keeping back anything that might be of so much importance to them? It might perhaps be something for which she did not wish to give her authority. Sometimes people in such circumstances will even condescend to write an anonymous letter to give the warning they think necessary, without betraying to the victims of misfortune that anyone whom they know is acquainted with it. Here was a justification for the strange step she had taken. It might be done in the utmost kindness to them, if not to me; and what if there might be some real danger afloat and Colin be in peril, as she said? I thought over these things anxiously before I went downstairs, but even to the moment of entering that bright and genial drawing-room, so full of animated faces and cheerful talk, I had not made up my mind what I should do. When we returned to it after dinner I was still uncertain. It was late, and the children had been sent to bed. The boys went round to the stables to see that the horses were not the worse for their day's work. Mr Campbell retired to his library. For a little while I was left alone, a thing that very rarely happened. Presently Miss Campbell came downstairs from the children's rooms, with that air about her of rest and sweetness, like a reflection of the little prayers she has been hearing and the infant repose which she has left, which hangs about a young mother when she has disposed her babies to sleep. Charlotte, by her right of being no mother, but only a voluntary mother by deputy, had a still more tender light about her in the sweetness of this duty which God and her goodwill, not simple nature, had put upon her. She came softly into the room with her shining countenance. 'Are you alone, Mr Temple?' she said with a little surprise. 'How rude of those boys to leave you,' and came and drew her chair towards the table where I was, in the kindness of her heart.

'I am very glad they have left me if I may have a little talk with you,' I said; and then before I knew I had told her. She was the kind of woman to whom it is a relief to tell whatever may be on your heart. The fact that my commission was to her, had really less force with me in telling it, than the ease to myself. She, however, was very much surprised and disturbed. 'Colin in trouble? Oh, that might very well be,' she said, then stopped herself. 'You are his friend,' she said; 'you will not misunderstand me, Mr Temple. He is very independent, and not so open as the rest of us. That is nothing against him. We are all rather given to talking; we keep nothing to ourselves—except Colin. And then he is more away than the rest.' The first necessity in her mind seemed to be this, of defending the absent. Then came the question, From whom could the warning be? Charley came in at this moment, and she called him to her eagerly. 'Here is a very strange thing happened. Somebody came up to Mr Temple in the shrubbery and told him to tell us that Colin was in trouble.'

'Colin!' I could see that Charley was, as Charlotte had been, more distressed than surprised. 'When did you hear from him last?' he said.

'On Monday; but the strange thing is, who could it be that sent such a message? You said a lady, Mr Temple?'

'What like was she?' said Charley.

Then I described as well as I could. 'She was tall and very slight; wrapped up in a cloak, so that I could not make out much, and her veil down. And it was almost dark.'

'It is clear she did not want to be recognized,' Charley said.

'There was something peculiar about her voice, but I really cannot describe it, a strange tone unlike anything——'

'Marion Gray has a peculiar voice; she is tall and slight. But what could she know about Colin?'

'I will tell you who is more likely,' cried Charley, 'and that is Susie Cameron. Her brother is in London now; they may have heard from him.'

'Oh! Heaven forbid! oh! Heaven forbid! the Camerons of all people!' Charlotte cried, wringing her hands. The action struck me as so like that of the veiled stranger that it gave me a curious shock. I had not time to follow out the vague, strange suggestion that it seemed to breathe into my mind, but the sensation was as if I had suddenly, groping, came upon some one in the dark.

'Whoever it was,' I said, 'she was not indifferent, but full of concern and interest——'

'Susie would be that,' Charley said, looking significantly at his sister, who rose from her chair in great distress.

'I would telegraph to him at once,' she said, 'but it is too late tonight.'

'And what good would it do to telegraph? If he is in trouble it would be no help to him.'

'But what can I do? what else can I do?' she cried. I had plunged them into sudden misery, and could only look on now as an anxious but helpless spectator, feeling at the same time as if I had intruded myself upon a family affliction: for it was evident that they were not at all unprepared for 'trouble' to Colin. I felt my position very embarrassing, and rose to go away.

'I feel miserably guilty,' I said, 'as if I had been the bearer of bad news; but I am sure you will believe that I would not for anything in the world intrude upon——'

Charlotte paused to give me a pale sort of smile, and pointed to the chair I had left. 'No, no,' she said, 'don't go away, Mr Temple. We do not conceal from you that we are anxious—that we were anxious even before—but don't go away. I don't think I will tell my father, Charley. It would break his rest. Let him have his night's rest whatever happens; and there is nothing to be done tonight——'

'We will see what the post brings tomorrow,' Charley said.

And then the consultation ended abruptly by the sudden entrance of the boys, bringing a gust of fresh night air with them. The horses were not a preen the worse though they had been out all day; even old grumbling Geordie, the coachman, had not a word to say. 'You may have them again tomorrow, Chatty, if you like,' said Tom. She had sat down to her work, and met their eyes with an unruffled countenance. 'I hope I am not so unreasonable,' she said with her tranquil looks; only I could see a little tremor in her hand as she stooped over the socks she was knitting. She laid down her work after a while, and went to the piano and played accompaniments, while first Jack and then Tom sang. She did it without any appearance of effort, yielding to all the wishes of the youngsters, while I looked on wondering, How can women do this sort of thing? It is more than one can divine.

Next morning Mr Campbell asked 'by the bye', but with a pucker in his forehead, which, being now enlightened on the subject, I could understand, if there was any letter from Colin? 'No,' Charlotte said (who for her part had turned over all her letters with a swift, anxious scrutiny). 'But that is nothing,' she said, 'for we heard on Monday.' The old gentleman uttered an 'Umph!' of displeasure. 'Tell him I think it a great want in manners that he is not here to receive Mr Temple.' 'Oh, father, Mr Temple understands,' cried Charlotte; and she turned upon me those mild eyes, in which there was now a look that went to my heart, an appeal at once to my sympathy and my forbearance, bidding me not to ask, not to speak, yet to feel with her all the same. If she could have known the rush of answering feeling with which my heart replied! but I had to be careful not even to *look* too much knowledge, too much sympathy.

After this two days passed without any incident. What letters were sent, or other communications, to Colin I could not tell. They were great people for the telegraph and flashed messages about continually. There was a telegraph station in the little village, which had been very surprising to me at first, but I no longer wondered, seeing their perpetual use of it. People who have to do with business, with great 'works' to manage, get into the way more easily than we others. But either no answer or nothing of a satisfactory character was obtained, for I was told no more. The second evening was Sunday, and I was returning alone from a ramble down the glen. It was Mr Campbell's custom to read a sermon on Sunday evenings to his household, and as I had, in conformity to the custom of the family, already heard two, I had deserted on this occasion, and chosen the freedom and quiet of a rural walk instead. It was a cloudy evening, and there had been rain. The clouds hung low on the hills, and half the surrounding peaks had retired altogether into the mist. I had scarcely set foot within the gates when I met once more the lady whose message had brought so much pain. The trees arched over the approach at this spot, and even in full daylight it was in deep shade. Now in the evening dimness it was dark as night. I could see little more than the slim straight figure, the sudden perception of which gave me—I could scarcely tell why—a curious thrill of something like fear. She came hurriedly towards me, an outline, nothing more, until the same peculiar voice, sweet but shrill, broke the silence. 'Did you tell them?' she said.

It cost me an effort to reply calmly. My heart had begun to beat with an excitement over which I had no control, like a horse that takes fright at something which its rider cannot see. I said, 'Yes, I told them,' straining my eyes, yet feeling as if my faculties were restive like that same horse and would not obey me, would not look or examine her appearance as I desired. But indeed it would have been in vain, for it was too dark to see.

'But nothing has been done,' she said. 'Did they think I would come for nothing?' And there was again that movement, the same as I had seen in Charlotte, of wringing her hands.

'Pardon me,' I said, 'but if you will tell me who you are? I am a stranger here; no doubt if you would see Miss Campbell herself, or if she knew who it was——'

I felt the words somehow arrested in my throat, I could not tell why; and she drew back from me with a sudden movement. It is hard to characterize a gesture in the dark, but there seemed to be a motion of impatience and despair in it. 'Tell them again Colin wants them. He is in sore trouble, trouble that is nigh death.'

'I will carry your message; but for God's sake if it is so important tell me who sends it,' I said.

She shook her head and went rapidly past me, notwithstanding the anxious appeals that I tried to make. She seemed to put out a hand to wave me back as I stood gazing after her. Just then the lodge door opened. I suppose the woman within had been disturbed by the sound of the voices, and a gleam of firelight burst out upon the road. Across this gleam I saw the slight figure pass quickly, and then a capacious form with a white apron came out and stood in the door. The sight of the coachman's wife in her large and comfortable proportions gave me a certain ease, I cannot tell why. I hurried up to her. 'Who was that that passed just now?' I asked.

'That passed just now? There was naebody passed. I thought I heard a voice, and that it was maybe Geordie; but nobody has passed here that I could see.'

'Nonsense! you must have seen her,' I cried hastily; 'she cannot be out of sight yet. No doubt you would know who she was—a lady tall and slight—in a cloak——'

'Eh, sir, ye maun be joking,' cried the woman. 'What lady, if it werna Miss Charlotte, would be walking here at this time of the night? Lady! it might be, maybe, the schoolmaster's daughter. She has one of those ulsters like her betters. But nobody has passed here this hour back; o' that I'm confident,' she said.

'Why did you come out, then, just at this moment?' I cried. The woman contemplated me in the gleam from the fire from top to toe. 'You're the English gentleman that's biding up at the house?' she said. ''Deed, I just heard a step, that was nae doubt your step, and I thought it might be my man; but there has naebody, far less a lady, whatever she had on, passed my door coming or going. Is that you, Geordie?' she cried suddenly as a step became audible approaching the gate from the outer side.

'Ay, it's just me,' responded her husband out of the gloom.

'Have ye met a lady as ye came along? The gentleman here will have it that there's been a lady passing the gate, and there's been no lady. I would have seen her through the window even if I hadna opened the door.'

'I've seen no lady,' said Geordie, letting himself in with consider-able noise at the foot entrance, which I now remembered to have closed behind me when I passed through it a few minutes before. 'I've met no person; it's no an hour for ladies to be about the roads on Sabbath day at e'en.'

It was not till this moment that a strange fancy, which I will explain hereafter, darted into my mind. How it came I cannot tell. I was not the sort of man, I said to myself, for any such folly. My imagination had been a little touched, to be sure, by that curious affair of the footsteps; but this, which seemed to make my heart stand still and sent a shiver through me, was very different, and it was a folly not to be entertained for a moment. I stamped my foot upon it instantly, crushing it on the threshold of the mind. 'Apparently either you or I must be mistaken,' I said with a laugh at the high tone of Geordie, who himself had evidently been employed in a jovial way—quite con-sistent, according to all I had heard, with very fine principles in respect to the Sabbath. I had a laugh over this as I went away, insisting upon the joke to myself as I hurried up the avenue. It was extremely funny, I said to myself; it would be a capital story among my other Scotch experiences. But somehow my laugh died away in a very feeble sort of quaver. The night had grown dark even when I emerged from under the trees, by reason of a great cloud, full of rain, which had rolled up over the sky, quenching it out. I was very glad to see the lights of the house gleaming steadily before me. The blind had not been drawn over the end window of the drawing-room, and from the darkness without I looked in upon a scene which was full of warmth and household calm. Though it was August there was a little glimmer of fire. The reading of the sermon was over. Old Mr Campbell still sat at a little table with the book before him, but it was closed. Charlotte in the foreground, with little Harry and Mary on either side of her, was 'hearing their Paraphrase'.[1] The boys were putting a clever dog through his tricks in a sort of clandestine way behind backs, at whom Charlotte would shake a finger now and then with an admonitory smiling look. Charley was reading or writing at the end of the room. The soft little chime of the children's voices, the suppressed laughter and whispering of the boys, the father's leisurely remark now and then, made up a soft murmur of sound which was like the very breath of quietude and peace. How did I dare, their favoured guest, indebted so deeply as I was to their kindness, to go in among them with that mysterious message and disturb their tranquillity once more?

When I went into the drawing-room, which was not till an hour later, Charlotte looked up at me smiling with some playful remark as to my flight from the evening reading. But as she caught my eye her countenance changed. She put down her book, and after a little consideration walked to that end window through which I had looked, and which was in a deep recess, making me a little sign to follow her. 'How dark the night is,' she said with a little pretence of looking out; and then in a hurried under-tone, 'Mr Temple, you have heard something more?'

'Not anything more, but certainly the same thing repeated. I have seen the lady again.'

'And who is she? Tell me frankly, Mr Temple. Just the same thing— that Colin is in trouble? no details? I cannot imagine who can take so much interest. But you asked her for her name?'

[1] The Paraphrases are a selection of hymns always printed along with the metrical version of the Psalms in use in Scotland, and more easy, being more modern in diction, to be learnt by heart.

'I asked her, but she gave me no reply. She waved her hand and went on. I begged her to see you, and not to give me such a commission; but it was of no use. I don't know if I ought to trouble you with a vague warning that only seems intended to give pain.'

'Oh yes,' she cried, 'oh yes, it was right to tell me. If I only knew who it was! Perhaps you can describe her better, since you have seen her a second time. But Colin has friends—whom we don't know. Oh, Mr Temple, it is making a great claim upon your kindness, but could not you have followed her and found out who she was?'

'I might have done that,' I said. 'To tell the truth, it was so instant-aneous and I was—startled.'

She looked up at me quickly with a questioning air, and grew a little pale, gazing at me; but whether she comprehended the strange wild fancy which I could not even permit myself to realize I cannot tell; for Charley seeing us standing together, and being in a state of nervous anxiety also, here came and joined us, and we stood talking together in an undertone till Mr Campbell called to know if anything was the matter. 'You are laying your heads together like a set of con-spirators,' said the old gentleman with a half-laugh. His manner to me was always benign and gracious; but now that I knew something of the family troubles I could perceive a vein of suppressed irritation, a certain watchfulness which made him alarming to the other mem-bers of the household. Charlotte gave us both a warning look. 'I will tell him tomorrow—I will delay no longer—but not tonight,' she said. 'Mr Temple was telling us about his ramble, father. He has just come in in time to avoid the rain.'

'Well,' said the old man, 'he cannot expect to be free from rain up here in the Highlands. It is wonderful the weather we have had.' And with this the conversation fell into an easy domestic channel. Miss Campbell this time could not put away the look of excitement and agi-tation in her eyes. But she escaped with the children to see them put to bed, and we sat and talked of politics and other mundane subjects. The boys were all going to leave Ellermore next day—Tom and Jack for the 'works', Charley upon some other business. Mr Campbell made me formal apologies for them. 'I had hoped Colin would have been at home by this time to do the honours of the Highlands: but we expect him daily,' he said. He kept his eye fixed upon me as if to give emphasis to his words and defy any doubt that might arise in my mind.

Next morning I was summoned by Charley before I came down-stairs to 'come quickly and speak to my father'. I found him in the library, which opened from the dining-room. He was walking about the room in great agitation. He began to address me almost before I was in sight. 'Who is this, sir, that you have been having meetings with about Colin? some insidious gossip or other that has taken ye in. I need not tell you, Mr Temple, a lawyer and an Englishman, that an anonymous statement——' For once the old gentleman had forgot-ten himself, his respect for his guest, his fine manners. He was irri-tated, obstinate, wounded in pride and feeling. Charlotte touched him on the arm with a murmured appeal, and turned her eyes to me in anxious deprecation. But there was no thought further from my mind than that of taking offence.

'I fully feel it,' I said; 'nor was it my part to bring any disagreeable suggestion into this house—if it had not been that my own mind was so burdened with it and Miss Campbell so clear-sighted.'

He cast a look at her, half affectionate, half displeased, and then he said to me testily, 'But who was the woman? That is the question; that is what I want to know.'

My eyes met Charlotte's as I looked up. She had grown very pale, and was gazing at me eagerly, as if she had divined somehow the wild fancy which once more shot across my mind against all reason and without any volition of mine.

III

Mr Campbell was not to be moved. He was very anxious, angry, and ill at ease; but he refused to be influenced in any way by this strange communication. It would be some intrusive woman, he said; some busybody—there were many about—who, thinking she might escape being found out in that way, had thought it a grand opportun-ity of making mischief. He made me a great many apologies for his first hasty words. It was very ill-bred, he said; he was ashamed to think that he had let himself be so carried away; but he would hear nothing of the message itself. The household, however, was in so agitated a state that, after the brothers departed to their business on Monday, I made a pretext of a letter calling me to town, and arranged my departure for the same evening. Both Charlotte and her father evidently divined my motive, but neither attempted to detain me: indeed she, I thought, though it hurt my self-love to see it, looked forward with a little eagerness to my going. This however, explained itself in a way less humiliating when she seized the opportunity of our last walk together to beg me to 'do something for her'.

'Anything,' I cried; 'anything—whatever man can.'

'I knew you would say so; that is why I have scarcely said I am sorry. I have not tried to stop you. Mr Temple, I am not shutting my eyes to it, like my father. I am sure that, whoever it was that spoke to you, the warning was true. I want you to go to Colin,' she said abruptly, after a momentary pause, 'and let me know the truth.'

'To Colin?' I cried. 'But you know how little acquainted we are. It was not he who invited me but—Charley——'

'And I——. You don't leave me out, I hope,' she said, with a faint smile; 'but what could make a better excuse than that you have been here? Mr Temple, you will go when I ask you? Oh, I do more—I entreat you! Go, and let me know the truth.'

'Of course I shall go—from the moment you bid me, Miss Campbell,' I said. But the commission was not a pleasant one, save in so far that it was for her service.

We were walking up and down by the side of the water, which every moment grew more and more into a blazing mirror, a burnished shield decked with every imaginable colour, though our minds had no room for its beauty, and it only touched my eyesight in coming and going. And then she told me much about Colin which I had not known or guessed—about his inclinations and tastes, which were not like any of the others, and how his friends and his ways were unknown to them. 'But we have always hoped this would pass away,' she said, 'for his heart is good; oh, his heart is good! You remember how kind he was to me when we met you first. He is always kind.' Thus we walked and talked until I had seen a new side at once of her character and life. The home had seemed to me so happy and free from care; but the dark shadow was there as everywhere, and her heart often wrung with suspense and anguish. We then returned slowly towards the house, still absorbed in this conversation, for it was time that I should go in and eat my last meal at Ellermore.

We had come within sight of the door, which stood open as always, when we suddenly caught sight of Mr Campbell posting towards us with a wild haste, so unlike his usual circumspect walk, that I was startled. His feet seemed to twist as they sped along, in such haste was he. His hat was pushed back on his head, his coat-tails flying behind him—precipitate like a man pursued, or in one of those panics which take away breath and sense, or, still more, perhaps as if a strong wind were behind him, blowing him on. When he came within speech of us, he called out hurriedly, 'Come here! come here, both of you!' and turning, hastened back with the same breathless hurry, beckoning with his hand. 'He must have heard something more,' Charlotte said, and rushed after him. I followed a few steps behind. Mr Campbell said nothing to his daughter when she made up to him. He almost pushed her off when she put her hand through his arm. He had no leisure even for sympathy. He hurried along with feet that stumbled in sheer haste till he came to the Lady's Walk, which lay in the level sunshine, a path of gold between the great boles of the trees. It was a slight ascent, which tried him still more. He went a few yards along the path, then stopped and looked round upon her and me, with his hand raised to call our attention. His face was perfectly colourless. Alarm and dismay were written on every line of it. Large drops of perspiration stood upon his forehead. He seemed to desire to speak, but could not; then held up his finger to command our attention. For the first moment or two my attention was so concentrated upon the man and the singularity of his look and gesture, that I thought of nothing else. What did he want us to do? We stood all three in the red light, which seemed to send a flaming sword through us. There was a faint stir of wind among the branches overhead, and a twitter of birds; and in the great stillness the faint lap of the water upon the shore was audible, though the loch was at some distance. Great stillness—that was the word; there was nothing moving but these soft stirrings of nature. Ah! this was what it was! Charlotte grew perfectly pale, too, like her father, as she stood and listened. I seem to see them now: the old man with his white head, his ghastly face, the scared and awful look in his eyes, and she gazing at him, all her faculties involved in the act of listening, her very attitude and drapery listening too, her lips dropping apart, the life ebbing out of her, as if something was draining the blood from her heart.

Mr Campbell's hand dropped. 'She's away,' he said. 'She's away'—in tones of despair; then, with a voice that was shaken by emotion—'I thought it was, maybe, my fault. By times you say I am getting stupid.' There was the most heartrending tone in this I ever heard—the pained humility of old age, confessing a defect, lit up with a gleam of feverish hope that in this case the defect might be a welcome explanation.

'Father, dear,' cried Charlotte, putting her hand on his arm—she had looked like fainting a moment before, but recovered herself—'It may be only a warning. It may not be desperate even now.'

All that the old man answered to this was a mere repetition, pathetic in its simplicity. 'She's away, she's away!' Then, after a full minute's pause, 'You mind when that happened last?' he said.

'Oh, father! oh, father!' cried Charlotte. I withdrew a step or two from this scene. What had I, a stranger, to do with it? They had forgotten my presence, and at the sound of my step they both looked up with a wild eager look in their faces, followed by blank disappointment. Then he sighed, and said, with a return of composure, 'You will throw a few things into a bag, and we'll go at once, Chatty. There is no time to lose.'

They went up with me to town that night. The journey has never seemed to me so long or so fatiguing, and Mr Campbell's state, which for once Charlotte in her own suspense and anxiety did not specially remark, was distressing to see. It became clear afterwards that his illness must have been coming on for some time, and that he was not then at all in a condition to travel. He was so feeble and confused when we reached London that it was impossible for me to leave them, and I was thus, without any voluntary intrusion of mine, a witness of all the melancholy events that followed. I was present even at the awful scene which the reader probably will remember as having formed the subject of many a newspaper article at the time. Colin had 'gone wrong' in every way that a young man could do. He had compromised the very existence of the firm in business; he had summed up all his private errors by marrying a woman unfit to bear any respectable name. And when his father and sister suddenly appeared before him, the unfortunate young man seized a pistol which lay suspiciously ready to his hand, and in their very presence put an end to his life. All the horror and squalor and dismal tragedy of the scene is before me as I write. The wretched woman, whom (I felt sure) he could not endure the sight of in Charlotte's presence, the heap of letters on his table announcing ruin from every quarter, the consciousness so suddenly brought upon him that he had betrayed and destroyed all who were most dear to him, overthrew his reason or his self-command. And the effect of so dreadful an occurrence on the unhappy spectators needs no description of mine. The father, already wavering under the touch of paralysis, fell by the same blow, and I had myself to bring Charlotte from her brother dead to her father dying, or worse than dying, struck dumb and prostrate in that awful prison of all the faculties. Until Charley arrived I had everything to do for both dead and living, and there was no attempt to keep any secret from me, even had it been possible. It seemed at first that there must be a total collapse of the family altogether; but afterwards some points of consolation appeared. I was present at all their consultations. The question at last came to be whether the 'Works', the origin of their wealth, should be given up, and the young men disperse to seek their fortune as they might, or whether a desperate attempt should be made to keep up the business by retrenching every expense and selling Ellermore. Charley, it was clear to me, was afraid to suggest this dreadful alternative to his sister; but she was no weakling to shrink from any necessity. She made up her mind to the sacrifice without a moment's hesitation. 'There are so many of us—still,' she said; 'there are the boys to think of, and the children.' When I saw her standing thus, with all those hands clutching at her, holding to her, I had in my own mind a sensation of despair. But what was that to the purpose? Charlotte was conscious of no divided duty. She was ready to serve her own with every faculty, and shrank from no sacrifice for their sake.

It was some time before Mr Campbell could be taken home. He got better indeed after a while, but was very weak. And happily for him he brought no consciousness of what had happened out of the temporary suspension of all his faculties. His hand and one side were almost without power, and his mind had fallen into a state which it would be cruel to call imbecility. It was more like the mind of a child recovering from an illness, pleased with, and exacting constant attention. Now and then he would ask the most heartrending questions: what had become of Colin, if he was ill, if he had gone home? 'The best place for him, the best place for him, Chatty,' he would repeat; 'and if you got him persuaded to marry, that would be fine.' All this Charlotte had to bear with a placid face, with quiet assent to the suggestion. He was in this condition when I took leave of him in the invalid carriage they had secured for the journey. He told me that he was glad to go home; that he would have left London some time before but for Chatty, who 'wanted to see a little of the place'. 'I am going to join my son Colin, who has gone home before us—isn't that so, Chatty?' 'Yes, father,' she said. 'Yes, yes, I have grown rather doited, and very very silly,'[1] the old man said, in a tone of extraordinary pathos. 'I am sometimes not sure of what I am saying; but Chatty keeps me right. Colin has gone on before; he has a grand head for business; he will soon set everything right—connected,' he added, with a curious sense which seemed to have outlived his other powers, that somehow explanation of Colin's actions was necessary—'connected with my retirement. I am past business; but we'll still hope to see you at Ellermore.'

I ought perhaps to say, though at the risk of ridicule, that up to the moment of their leaving London, I constantly met, or seemed to meet—for I became confused after a while, and felt incapable of distinguishing between feeling and fact—the same veiled lady who had spoken to me at Ellermore. Wherever there was a group of two or three people together, it appeared to me that she was one of them. I saw her in advance of me in the streets. I saw her behind me. She seemed to disappear in the distance wherever I moved. I suppose it was imagination—at least that is the most easy thing to say: but I was so convinced at the moment that it was not imagination, that I have hurried along many a street in pursuit of the phantom who always, I need not say, eluded me. I saw her at Colin's grave: but what need to linger longer on this hallucination, if it was one? From the day the Campbells left London, I saw her no more.

[1] Used in Scotland in the sense of weakness of body—invalidism.

IV

Then there ensued a period of total stillness in my life. It seemed to me as if all interest had gone out of it. I resumed my old occupations, such as they were, and they were not very engrossing. I had enough, which is perhaps of all conditions of life, if the most comfortable, the least interesting. If it was a disciple of Solomon who desired that state, it must have been when he was like his master, blasé, and had discovered that both ambition and pleasure were vanity. There was little place or necessity for me in the world. I pleased myself, as people say. When I was tired of my solitary chambers, I went and paid visits. When I was tired of England, I went abroad. Nothing could be more agreeable, or more unutterably tedious, especially to one who had even accidentally come across and touched upon the real events and excitements of life. Needless to say that I thought of the household at Ellermore almost without intermission. Charlotte wrote to me now and then, and it sometimes seemed to me that I was the most callous wretch on earth, sitting there watching all they were doing, tracing every step and vicissitude of their trouble in my own assured well-being. It was monstrous, yet what could I do? But if, as I have said, such impatient desire to help were to come now and then to those who have the power to do so, is political economy so infallible that the world would not be the better for it? There was not a word of complaint in Charlotte's letters, but they made me rage over my impotence. She told me that all the arrangements were being completed for the sale of Ellermore, but that her father's condition was still such that they did not know how to communicate to him the impending change. 'He is still ignorant of all that has passed,' Charlotte wrote, 'and asks me the most heartrending questions; and I hope God will forgive me all that I am obliged to say to him. We are afraid to let him see anyone lest he should discover the truth; for indeed falsehood, even with a good meaning, is always its own punishment. Dr Maxwell, who does not mind what he says when he thinks it is for his patient's good, is going to make believe to send him away for change of air; and this is the artifice we shall have to keep up all the rest of his life to account for not going back to Ellermore.' She wrote another time that there was every hope of being able to dispose of it by private bargain, and that in the meantime friends had been very kind, and the 'Works' were going on. There was not a word in the letter by which it would have been divined that to leave Ellermore was to the writer anything beyond a matter of necessity. She said not a word about her birthplace, the home of all her associations, the spot which I knew was so dear. There had been no hesitation, and there was no repining. Provided only that the poor old man, the stricken father, deprived at once of his home and firstborn, without knowing either, might be kept in that delusion—this was all the exemption Charlotte sought.

And I do not think they asked me to go to them before they left the place. It was my own doing. I could not keep away any longer. I said to Charlotte, and perhaps also to myself, by way of excuse, that I might help to take care of Mr Campbell during the removal. The fact was that I could not stay away from her any longer. I could have risked any intrusion, thrust myself in anyhow, for the mere sake of being near her and helping her in the most insignificant way.

It was, however, nearly Christmas before I yielded to my impatience. They were to leave Ellermore in a week or two. Mr Campbell had been persuaded that one of the soft and sheltered spots where Scotch invalids are sent in Scotland would be better for him. Charlotte had written to me, with a half despair, of the difficulties of their removal. 'My heart almost fails me,' she said; and that was a great deal for her to say. After this I could hesitate no longer. She was afraid even of the revival of life that might take place when her father was brought out of his seclusion, of some injudicious old friend who could not be staved off, and who might talk to him about Colin. 'My heart almost fails me.' I went up to Scotland by the mail train that night, and next day, while it was still not much more than noon, found myself at Ellermore.

What a change! The heather had all died away from the hills; the sunbright loch was steely blue; the white threads of water down every crevice in the mountains were swollen to torrents. Here and there on the higher peaks there was a sprinkling of snow. The fir-trees were the only substantial things in the nearer landscape. The beeches stood about all bare and feathery, with every twig distinct against the blue. The sun was shining almost as brightly as in summer, and scattered a shimmer of reflections everywhere over the wet grass, and across the rivulets that were running in every little hollow. The house stood out amid all this light, amid the bare tracery of the trees, with its Scotch-French *tourelles*, and the sweep of emerald lawn, more green than ever, at its feet, and all the naked flower-beds; the blue smoke rising peacefully into the air, the door open as always. There was little stir or movement, however, in this wintry scene. The outdoor life was checked. There was no son at home to leave traces of his presence. The lodge was shut up, and vacant. I concluded that the carriage had been given up, and all luxuries, and the coachman and his family were gone. But this was all the visible difference. I was received by one of the maids, with whose face I was familiar. There had never been any wealth of male attendants at Ellermore. She took me into the drawing-room, which was deserted, and bore a more formal look than of old. 'Miss Charlotte is mostly with her papa,' the woman said. 'He is very frail; but just wonderful contented, like a bairn. She's always up the stair with the old gentleman. It's no good for her. You'll find her white, white, sir, and no like hersel'.' In a few minutes Charlotte came in. There was a gleam of pleasure (I hoped) on her face, but she was white, white, as the woman said, worn and pale. After the first greeting, which had brightened her, she broke down a little, and shed a few hasty tears, for which she excused herself, faltering that everything came back, but that she was glad, glad to see me! And then she added quickly, that I might not be wounded, 'It has come to that, that I can scarcely ever leave my father; and to keep up the deception is terrible.'

'You must not say deception.'

'Oh, it is nothing else; and that always punishes itself. It is just the terror of my life that some accident will happen; that he will find out everything at once.' Then she looked at me steadily, with a smile that was piteous to see, 'Mr Temple, Ellermore is sold.'

'Is it so—is it so?' I said, with a sort of groan. I had still thought that perhaps at the last moment something might occur to prevent the sacrifice.

She shook her head, not answering my words, but the expression of my face. 'There was nothing else to be desired,' she said; and, after a pause, 'We are to take him to the Bridge of Allan. He is almost pleased to go; he thinks of nothing further—oh, poor old man, poor old man!

If only I had him there safe; but I am more terrified for the journey than I ever was for anything in my life.'

We talked of this for some time, and of all the arrangements she had made. Charley was to come to assist in removing his father; but I think that my presence somehow seemed to her an additional safeguard, of which she was glad. She did not stay more than half an hour with me. 'It will be dull, dull for you, Mr Temple,' she said, with more of the lingering cadence of her national accent than I had perceived before— or perhaps it struck me more after these months of absence. 'There is nobody at home but the little ones, and they have grown far too wise for their age, because of the many things that they know must never be told to papa; but you know the place, and you will want to rest a little.' She put out her hand to me again—'And I am glad, glad to see you!' Nothing in my life ever made my heart swell like those simple words. That she should be 'glad, glad' was payment enough for anything I could do. But in the meantime there was nothing that I could do. I wandered about the silent place till I was tired, recalling a hundred pleasant recollections; even to me, a stranger, who a year ago had never seen Ellermore, it was hard to give it up; and as for those who had been born there, and their fathers before them, it seemed too much for the cruellest fate to ask. But Nature was as indifferent to the passing away of the human inhabitants, whose little spell of a few hundred years was as nothing in her long history, as she would have been to the falling of a rock on the hillside, or the wrenching up of a tree in the woods. For that matter, of so small account are men, the rock and tree would both have been older dwellers than the Campbells; and why for that should the sun moderate his shining, or the clear skies veil themselves?

My mind was so taken up by these thoughts that it was almost inadvertence that took me, in the course of my solitary rambles about, to the Lady's Walk. I had nearly got within the line of the beech-trees, however, when I was brought hurriedly back to the strange circumstances which had formed an accompaniment to this family history. To hear once more the footsteps of the guardian of Ellermore had a startling effect upon me. She had come back then! After that first thrill of instinctive emotion this gave me a singular pleasure. I stood between the trees and heard the soft step coming and going with absolute satisfaction. It seemed to me that they were not altogether abandoned so long as she was here. My heart rose in spite of myself. I began to speculate on the possibility even yet of saving the old house. I asked myself how it could be finally disposed of without Mr Campbell's consent and signature; and tried to believe that at the last moment some way might open, some wonderful windfall come. But when I turned back to the house, this fantastic confidence naturally failed me. I began to contemplate the other side of the question—the new people who would come in. Perhaps 'some Englishman', as Charley had said with a certain scorn; some rich man, who would buy the moors and lochs at many times their actual value, and bring down, perhaps, a horde of Cockney sportsmen to banish all quiet and poetry from Ellermore. I thought with a mingled pity and anger of what the Lady would do in such hands. Would she still haunt her favourite walk when all whom she loved were gone? Would she stay there in forlorn faithfulness to the soil, or would she go with her banished race? or would she depart altogether, and cut the tie that had bound her to earth? I thought—for fancy once set out goes far without any conscious control from the mind—that these were circumstances in which the intruders into the home of the Campbells might be frightened by noises and apparitions, and all those vulgarer powers of the unseen of which we hear sometimes. If the Lady of Ellermore would condescend to use such instruments, no doubt she might find lower and less elevated spirits in the unseen to whom this kind of play would be congenial. I caught myself up sharply in this wandering of thought, as if I were forming ideas derogatory to a dear friend, and felt myself redden with shame. She connect her lovely being with tricks of this kind! I was angry with myself, as if I had allowed it to be suggested that Charlotte would do so. My heart grew full as I pursued these thoughts. Was it possible that some mysterious bond of a kind beyond our knowledge connected her with this beloved soil? I was overawed by the thought of what she might suffer, going upon her solitary watch, to see the house filled with an alien family—yet, perhaps, by-and-by, taking them into amity, watching over them as she had done over her own, in that sweetness of self-restraint and tender love of humankind which is the atmosphere of the blessed. All through this spiritual being was to me a beatified shadow of Charlotte. You will say all this was very fantastic, and I do not deny that the sentence is just.

Next day passed in something the same way. Charlotte was very anxious. She had wished the removal to take place that afternoon, but when the moment came she postponed it. She said 'Tomorrow,' with a shiver. 'I don't know what I am afraid of,' she said, 'but my heart fails me—my heart fails me.' I had to telegraph to Charley that it was deferred: and another long day went by. It rained, and that was an obstacle. 'I cannot take him away in bad weather,' she said. She came downstairs to me a dozen times a day, wringing her hands. 'I have no resolution,' she cried. 'I cannot—I cannot make up my mind to it. I feel that something dreadful is going to happen.' I could only take her trembling hand and try to comfort her. I made her come out with me to get a little air in the afternoon. 'You are killing yourself,' I said. 'It is this that makes you so nervous and unlike yourself.' She consented, though it was against her will. A woman who had been all her life in their service, who was to go with them, whom Charlotte treated, as she said, 'like one of ourselves', had charge of Mr Campbell in the meantime. And I think Charlotte got a little pleasure from this unusual freedom. She was very tremulous, as if she had almost forgotten how to walk, and leant upon my arm in a way which was very sweet to me. No word of love had ever passed between us; and she did not love me, save as she loved Charley and Harry, and the rest. I think I had a place among them, at the end of the brothers. But yet she had an instinctive knowledge of my heart; and she knew that to lean upon me, to show that she needed me, was the way to please me most. We wandered about there for a time in a sort of forlorn happiness; then, with a mutual impulse, took our way to the Lady's Walk. We stood there together, listening to the steps. 'Do you hear them?' said Charlotte, her face lighting up with a smile. 'Dear lady! that has always been here since ever I mind!' She spoke as the children spoke in the utter abandonment of her being, as if returning for refreshment to the full simplicity of accent and idiom, the soft native speech to which she was born. 'Will she stay after us, do ye think?' Charlotte said; and then, with a little start, clinging to my arm, 'Was that a sound—was that a cry?'

Not a cry, but a sigh. It seemed to wander over all the woods and thrill among the trees. You will say it was only the wind. I cannot tell. To me it was a sigh, personal, heart-rending. And you may suppose what it was to her. The tears dropped from her full eyes. She said, speaking to the air, 'We are parting, you and me. Oh, go you back to Heaven, and let us trouble you no more. Oh, go back to your home, my bonnie lady, and let us trouble you no more!'

'Charlotte!' I cried, drawing her arm more closely through mine. She cast me a glance, a smile, like one who could not even in the midst of the highest thoughts neglect or be unkind, but drew her hand away and clasped it in the other. 'We are of one stock,' she said, the tears always falling; 'and the same heart. We are too anxious, but God is above us all. Go back to your pleasant place, and say to my mother that I will never leave them. Go away, my bonnie lady, go away! You and me, we must learn to trust them to God.'

We waited, and I think she almost expected some reply. But there was none. I took her arm within mine again, and led her away trembling. The moment, the excitement had been too much for me also. I said, 'You tell her to go, that she is too anxious, that she must trust you to God—and in the same breath you pledge yourself never to leave them. Do you think if God does not want her, He wants you to stand between Him and them?' I grasped her arm so closely and held it so to my side in my passion that I think I almost hurt her. She gave me a startled look, and put up her hand to dry her wet eyes.

'It is very different,' she said; 'I am living and can work for them. It has come to me all in a moment to see that She is just like me after all. Perhaps to die does not make a woman wise any more than life does. And it may be that nobody has had the thought to tell her. She will have imagined that she could stop any harm that was coming, being here; but if it was not God's pleasure to stop it, how could she? You know she tried,' said Charlotte, looking at me wistfully; 'she tried—God bless her for that! Oh, you know how anxious she was; but neither she nor I could do it—neither she nor I!'

At this moment we were interrupted by some one flying towards us from the house, calling, 'Miss Charlotte, Miss Charlotte! you are wanted,' in a wild and agitated tone. It was the woman who had been left in charge of Mr Campbell, and Charlotte started at the sight of her. She drew her hand from my arm, and flew along the path. 'Oh, Marg'ret, why did you leave him?' she said.

'It was no blame of mine,' said the woman, turning, following her mistress. I hurried on, too, after them, and the explanation was addressed to both of us. 'He would come down to the library: nothing would stop him. I tried all I could; but what could I do? And there is nothing to be frighted for, Miss Charlotte. Ah! I've nae breath to tell it. \He is just real like himself!'

Charlotte flew along the path like a creature flying for life. She paused an instant at the door of the house to beckon me to follow her. The library, the room where her father had gone, was one of those which had been partially dismantled. The pictures had been taken down from the walls, a number of books which she meant to take with her collected on the tables. Mr Campbell had displaced some of the books in order to seat himself in his favourite seat. He looked at her curiously, almost with severity, as she came in anxious and breathless. He was greatly changed. He had been robust and hale, like a tower, when I first entered Ellermore, not yet six months since. Now he had shrunken away into half his size. The coat which he had not worn for months hung loosely upon him; his white hair was long, and he wore a beard which changed his appearance greatly. All this change had come since the time I parted with him in London, when he told me he was going to join his son Colin; but there was another change more remarkable, which I with awe, and Charlotte with terror, recognized at a glance—the prostration of his mind was gone. He looked his daughter in the face with intelligent, almost sternly intelligent eyes.

'Oh, father, you have wanted me!' Charlotte cried. 'I went out for a mouthful of air—I went out—for a few minutes——'

'Why should you not have gone out, Chatty?' he said. 'And why was Marg'ret left in charge of me? I have been ill, I make no doubt; but why should I be watched and spied about my own house?'

She gave me a glance of dismay, and then she faltered, 'Oh, not that, father—not that!'

'But I tell you it was that. She would have hindered my coming downstairs, that woman'—he gave a little laugh, which was terrible to us in the state of our feelings—'and here are you rushing in out of breath, as if there was some cause of fear. Who is that behind ye? Is it one of your brothers—or——'

'It is Mr Temple, father,' she said, with a new alarm.

'Mr Temple,' he said, with a shade of displeasure passing over his face. Then he recovered himself, and his old-world politeness. 'I am glad to see ye,' he said. 'So far as I can remember, the house was much disorganized when you were here before, Mr Temple. You will think we are always out of order; but I've been ill, and everything has fallen out of gear. This is not a place,' he added, turning to Charlotte, 'to receive a stranger in. What is all this for?' he added, in a sharp tone, waving his hand towards the books, of which some were heaped at his feet on the floor.

Once more she made a pause of dismay. 'They are some books to take with us,' she said; 'you remember, father, we are going away.'

'Going away!' he cried, irritably. 'Where are my letters? Where are your brothers? What are you doing with a gentleman visitor (I beg ye a thousand pardons, Mr Temple!) and the place in such a state? It is my opinion that there is something wrong. Where are my letters? It is not in reason that there should be no letters. After being laid aside from business for a time, to have your letters kept back from you, you will allow, Mr Temple,' he said, turning to me with an explanatory air, 'is irritating. It is perhaps done with a mistaken notion that I am not equal to them; but if you think I will allow myself to be treated as a child——'

He stammered a little now and then, in his anger, but made a great effort to control himself. And then he looked up at us, once more a little severely, and brought confusion to all our hopes with one simple question. 'Where is Colin?' he said.

What could be more natural? Charlotte gave me one look, and stood, white as death, motionless, her fingers twisting together. How truly she had said that falsehood was its own punishment, even such falsehood as this! She had answered him with ambiguous words when he was in the state of feebleness from which he had thus awoke, and he had been easily satisfied and diverted from too close enquiry. But now she was confounded by the sudden question. She could not confront with a subterfuge her father's serious eyes; her head drooped, her hands caught at each other with a pitiful clasp, while he sat looking at her with an authoritative, but as yet unalarmed, look. All this time the door had been left ajar, and Marg'ret stood waiting outside, listening to all that went on, too much interested and anxious to feel herself out of place. But when she heard this demand the woman was struck with horror. She made a step within the door. 'Oh, Ellermore!'

124

she cried. 'Oh! my auld maister, dinna break her heart and mine! To hear ye asking for Colin! and Colin in his grave this four long months, poor lad, poor lad!' She threw her apron over her head as she spoke, and burst forth into loud sobs and tears. Charlotte had put out a hand to stop the revelation, but dropped it again, and stood by speechless, her head bent, and wringing her hands, a silent image of grief and guilt, as if it had been her from whom the blow came.

The old man sat and listened with a countenance growing ashy pale, and with intent eyes, that seemed to flicker as if beyond his control. He tried to speak, but in the trembling of his lips could articulate nothing. Then he slowly raised himself up and stood pallid and dizzy, like a man on the edge of a precipice.

'My son is dead, and I knew it not,' he said slowly, pausing between the words. He stood with his trembling lips falling apart, his countenance all moving and twitching, transfixed, it seemed, by a sort of woeful amaze, wondering at himself. Then he turned upon Charlotte, with a piteous appeal. 'Was I told, and have I forgotten?' he asked. The humiliation of that thought overpowered his re-awakened soul.

She came to him quickly and put her arm round him. 'Father, dear, you were so ill, they would not let us tell you. Oh, I have known, I have known it would be so much the worse when it came!'

He put her away from him, and sat down again feebly in his chair. In that dreadful moment he wanted no one. The horror of the individual humiliation, the idea that he could have heard and forgotten, was more terrible even than the dreadful news which thus burst upon him. 'I'm glad,' he said, 'I'm glad,' babbling with his loose lips. I shrank away, feeling it a profanation to be here, a spectator of the last mystery of nature; but Charlotte made a faint motion that kept me from withdrawing altogether. For the first time she was afraid; her heart had failed her.

For some minutes her father continued silent in his chair. The sunset had faded away, the misty twilight was falling. Marg'ret, guilty and miserable, but still unable altogether to subdue her sobs, throwing her white apron from her head, and looking round with a deprecating, apologetic glance, had withdrawn to the other side of the room. All was silence after that broken interchange of words. He lay back, clasping and unclasping his hands, his lips and features all moving, whether with a wish to speak or with the mere workings of emotions unspeakable, I cannot tell. When suddenly, all at once, with the voice of a strong man loud and full, he broke out into the cry which has sounded through all the world—the utterance of every father's anguish. 'Oh, Absalom, my son, my son! Would God that I had died for thee, my son, my son——'

We both rushed towards him simultaneously. He did not remark me, fortunately; but again he put Charlotte away. 'What are you afraid for?' he said, almost sternly; 'that I will fall back and be ill again? That is not possible. Ye think sorrow kills; but no, it stings ye back to life: it stings ye back to life,' he repeated, raising himself in his chair. Then he looked round him solemnly. 'Marg'ret, my woman, come here, and give me your hand. We're partners in trouble, you and me, and never shall we part. As long as this is my house there is a place in it for you. Afterwards, when it goes to—— ah! when it goes to Charley,' he cried, with a sudden burst of unforeseen sobs.

Charlotte looked at me again. Her face was white with despair. How was this last news to be broken to him?

'Father,' she said, standing behind him, 'you are sorely tried. Will you not come back to your room and rest till tomorrow, and then you will hear all? Then we will tell you—about all that has happened——'

Her voice shook like a leaf in the wind, but she managed to show no other sign of her terror and despair. There was a long pause after this, and we stood waiting, not knowing how the moment would terminate. I believe it was the sight of me that decided it after all. A quick movement of irritation passed over his face.

'I think you are right, Chatty,' he said; 'I think you are right. I am not fit, in my shattered state, and with the information I have just received, to pay the attention I would like to pay——' He paused, and looked at me fixedly. 'It is a great trouble to me that we have never been able to show you proper attention, Mr Temple. You see, my son was detained; and now he is dead—and I've never known it till this moment. You will excuse a reception which is not the kind of reception I would like to give you.' He waved his hand. 'You were my Colin's friend. You will know how to make allowances. Yes, my dear,

I am best in my own chamber. I will just go, with Mr Temple's per-
mission—go—to my bed.'

A faint groan burst from him as he said these words; a kind of
dreary smile flickered on his lips. 'To my bed,' he repeated; 'that is all
we can do, we old folk, when we are stricken by God's hand. Lie
down, and turn our faces to the wall—our faces to the wall.' He rose
up, and took his daughter's arm, and made a few steps towards the
door, which I was holding open for him. Then he turned and looked
round with the air of one who has a favour to bestow. 'You may come
too, Marg'ret,' he said. 'You can come and help me to my bed.'

This strange interruption of all plans, which it was evident filled
Charlotte with despair, gave me much to think of, as I stayed behind in
the slowly darkening room. It was evident that now nothing could be
concealed from him; and who was there so bold as to tell the bereaved
father, in his first grief for his firstborn, what horrors had accompanied Colin's death, and what a penalty the family had to pay? It
seemed to me that the premonition of some fresh calamity was in the
air; and when Charlotte came down about half an hour later, like a
ghost through the dim-coming shadows, I almost expected to hear
that it had already occurred. But even in these depths of distress it was
a happiness to me to feel that she came to me for relief. She told me
that he had gone to bed without asking any further questions, and
that Margaret, who had been Colin's nurse, seemed almost more
agreeable to him than herself. He had turned his face to the wall as he
had said, and nothing but a long-drawn, occasional sigh told that he
was awake. 'I think he is not worse—in body,' she said. 'He has borne
it far better than we could have thought possible. But how am I to tell
him the way it happened, and how am I to tell him about Ellermore?'
She wept with a prostration and self-abandonment which alarmed
me; but she stopped my remonstrances and entreaties with a motion
of her hand. 'Oh, let me cry! It is the only ease I have,' she said.

When she had gone away from me, restless, anxious, afraid to be
out of hearing, I went out, myself, as restless, as incapable of banish-
ing all these anxieties from my mind as she. The night was almost
dark, soft and mild. It was one of those nights when the moon, without being visible, softens and ameliorates the gloom, and makes of
night a sort of twilight. While I went pacing softly about, to occupy

myself, a soft small rain began to fall; but this did not affect me in any way. It was rather soothing than disagreeable. I went down to the side of the loch, where the pale light on the water was touched by innumerable dimplings of the rain, then up again, round and round the house, not caring where I went. At this hour I had always avoided the Lady's Walk, I can scarcely tell why. Tonight, in my strange familiarity with everything, and carelessness of all but one subject, I suddenly turned into it with a caprice I could not account for, perhaps with an unexpressed wish for company, for somebody who might understand my thoughts. The mystic footsteps gave me a sort of pleasure. Whether it was habit or some new sense of human fellowship which Charlotte's impassioned words had caused, I can scarcely tell; but the excitement with which I had always hitherto regarded the mysterious watcher here was altogether gone out of my mind. I felt a profound and tender pity for her rising in me instead. Was it possible that a spirit could be 'over-anxious', as Charlotte said, endeavouring vainly, and yet not undutifully, to take God's supreme guardianship out of His hands? The thought was new to me. To think that a good and blessed creature could so err, could mistake so humanly and persevere so patiently, though never able to remedy the evils, seemed somehow more possible than that a guardian from Heaven could watch and watch for generations with so little result. This gave me a great compassion for the lonely watcher thus rebelling in a heavenly way of love against the law of nature that separated her from visible life. My old idea, that it might be Charlotte herself in an unconscious shadow-shape, whose protecting motherly love made these efforts unawares, glided gratefully into the feeling that it was an earlier Charlotte, her very kin and prototype, who could not even now let God manage her race without her aid. While I was thus thinking, I was startled once more by the same sigh which I had heard with Charlotte. Yes, yes, it might be the wind. I had no time to bandy explanations with myself. It was a soft long sigh, such as draws the very breath out of an over-laden bosom. I turned half round, it was so near to me; and there, by my side, so close that I could have touched her, stood the Lady whom I had seen so often—the same figure which I had met in the London streets and in the woods of Ellermore. I suppose I stepped back, with a little thrill of the old sensations, for she seemed to put out a hand in the pale gloom, and began to speak softly, quickly, as if there was scarcely time enough for what she had to say.

'I am going away like the rest,' she said. 'None of them have ever bid me go before; but it is true—it is true what she says. I have never done any good—just frightened them, or pleased them. It is in better hands—it is in better hands.'

With this there came the familiar movement, the wringing of the hands, which was like Charlotte, and she seemed to weep; but before I could say anything (and what could I have said?) she cried with eagerness, 'I came to you because you loved her, but you were too late—and now again, again! you may help if you will. It will be set before you to help, if you will.'

'How can I help?' I cried. 'Tell me, Lady, whoever you are; I will do it, I will do it!—but how can I do it? Tell me——'

I put out my hand to touch her dress, but it melted out of my hold. She withdrew with a swift, shy movement. 'It will be set before you,' she said, with a breathless faintness as if of haste; and already her voice was further off breathing away. 'It will be set before you—I must not say more. One can never say more.'

'What can I do?' I cried; so much had I forgot the old terror that I put myself in her path, stopping the way. 'Tell me how, how! Tell me, for God's sake, and because of Charlotte!'

The shadowy figure retreated before me. It seemed to fade, then reappeared, then dissolved altogether into the white dimness, while the voice floated away, still saying, as in a sigh, 'You may help, you may help, you may save——' I could hear no more. I went after this sighing voice to the end of the Walk; it seemed to me that I was pursuing, determined to hear her message, and that she softly fled, the hurrying footsteps becoming almost inaudible as they flew before me. I went on hotly, not knowing what I did, determined only to know what it was; to get an explanation, by what means I did not care. Suddenly, before I knew, I found my steps stumbling down the slope at the further end, and the pale water alive with all the dimplings of the rain appearing at my very feet. The steps sank upon the loch-side, and ceased with a thrill like the acutest sound. A silence more absolute than any I have heard in nature ensued. I stood gasping, with my foot touching the edge of the water; it was all I could do to arrest myself there.

I hurried back to the house in a state of agitation, which I cannot describe. It was partly nervous dread. I do not disguise this; but partly it was a bewildered anxiety and eagerness to know what the chance was which was to be set before me. That I had the most absolute faith in it I need hardly say. 'You may help them if you will! You may help them if you will! I said it over and over to myself a thousand times with a feverish hurry and eagerness. Indeed, I did nothing but repeat it. When Charlotte came down late to tell me her father was asleep, that the doctor who had been sent for had pronounced his recovery real, I was walking up and down the half-lighted drawing-room, saying these words over and over to myself.

'He says it is wonderful, but it may be complete recovery,' Charlotte said; 'only to tell him nothing we can help, to keep all the circumstances from him; especially, if it is possible, about Ellermore. But how is it possible? how can I do it? "Help if you will?" Mr Temple, what are you saying?'

'It is nothing,' I said; 'some old rhyme that has got possession of me.'

She looked very anxiously into my face. 'Something else has happened? You have seen or heard——' Her mind was so alive to every tone and glance that it was scarcely possible to conceal a thought from her.

'I have been in the Walk,' I said, 'and being excited and restless, it was more than my nerves could bear.'

She looked at me again wistfully. 'You would not deceive me, Mr Temple,' she said; then returned to her original subject. The doctor was anxious, above all things, that Mr Campbell should leave Ellermore tomorrow, that he should go early, and above all that he should not suspect the reason why. She had the same dread of the removal as ever, but there was no alternative, and not even a day's delay was to be thought of, for every day, every hour, made the chances of discovery more.

'But you cannot keep up the delusion for ever,' I said, 'and when it is found out?'

Again she wrung her hands. 'It is against my judgement; but what can I do?' She paused a moment, and then said, with a melancholy dignity, 'It can but kill him, soon or syne. I would not myself have my life saved by a lie; but I am weak where my father is concerned, and God understands all. Oh, I am beginning to feel that so, Mr Temple! We search and search, and think what is best, and we make a hundred mistakes, but God sees the why and the wherefore. Whoever misunderstands, He never misunderstands.'

She went away from me in the calm of this thought, the secret of all calm. It seemed to me that I, in my blind anxiety guessing at the enigma that had been given to me, and my poor Lady vagrant from the skies, still trying to be the providence of this house, were left alike behind.

Next morning Charlotte came down to breakfast with me, which she had not done before. She told me that her father had passed a good night, that he had shed tears on awaking, and began to talk tenderly and calmly of Colin, and that everything seemed to promise that the softening and mournful preoccupation of grief, distracting his mind from other matters, would be an advantage to him. He was pleased to be left with Margaret, who had adored her nursling, and who had been fully warned of the necessity of keeping silence as to the circumstances of Colin's death. The post-bag came in while we were talking. It lay on the table for a few minutes untouched, for neither of us were anxious for our correspondence. We were alone at table, and Charlotte had rested, though I had not, and was almost cheerful now that the moment had arrived for the final severance. The necessity of doing inspired her; and perhaps, though I scarcely dared to think so, this tranquil table at which we sat alone, which might have been our table, in our home, in a new life full of peace and sober happiness, soothed her. The suggestion it conveyed made the blood dance in my veins. For the moment it seemed as if the hope I dared not even entertain, for one calm hour of blessedness and repose, had come true.

At last she gave me the key, and asked me to open the bag. 'I have been loth to disturb this peaceful moment,' she said, with a smile which was full of sweetness and confidence, 'and nothing outside seems of much consequence just now; but the boys may have something to tell, and there will be your letters—will you open it, Mr Temple?' I, too, was loth, more loth than she, to disturb the calm, and the outside world was nothing to me, while I sat here with her, and could fancy her my own. But I did what she told me. Letters are like fate, they must be encountered with all that is good and evil in them. I gave her hers, and laid out some, probably as important to them, though they seemed to me so trifling and unnecessary, that were for the servants. Then I turned to my own share. I had two letters, one with a broad black border, which had been forwarded from one place to another in search of me, and was nearly ten days old; for, like most people, I examined the outside first; the other a large, substantial blue letter, which meant business. I can remember now the indifference with which I opened them, the mourning envelope first. There were so many postmarks on it, that that of its origin, which would have enlightened me at once, never struck me at all.

Heaven above! what was this that met my eyes? An announcement, full of the periphrasis of formal regret, of the death of my old cousin Jocelyn ten days before. I gave a sort of fierce cry—I can hear it now— and tore open the second, the official letter. Of course I knew what it was; of course I was aware that nothing could interfere; and yet the opportuneness of the announcement was such, that human nature, accustomed to be balked, would not allow me to believe in the possibility. Then I sprang from my seat. 'I must go,' I cried; 'there is not a moment to lose. Stop all proceedings—do nothing about the going, for God's sake, till I come back.'

'Mr Temple, what has happened? Charley——,' cried Charlotte, blanched with terror. She thought some other catastrophe had happened, some still more fatal news that I would not tell her. But I was too much absorbed in my own excitement to think of this.

'Do nothing,' I said; 'I will meet Charley on the way, and tell him. All will be right, all will be right, only wait till I come back.' I rushed to the door in my haste, then came back again, not knowing what I did, and had caught her in my arms before I was aware—not in my arms, but with my hands on her shoulders, holding her for one wild moment. I could hardly see her for the water in my eyes. 'Wait,' I said, 'wait till I come back! Now I can do what she said! Now my time is come; do nothing till I come back.' I let my hands drop down to hers, and caught them and kissed them in a wild tremor, beyond explanation. Then I rushed away. It was a mile or more to the little quay where the morning boat carried communications back to the world. I seemed to be there as on wings, and scarcely came to myself till

I descended into the noise, the haze, the roar of the damp streets, the crowds and traffic of Glasgow. Next moment (for time flew and I with it, so that I took no note of its progress or my own) I was in the clamour of the 'Works', making my way through the grime and mud of a great courtyard, with machinery clanging round me on every side, from the big skeleton houses with their open windows—into the office, where Charley, in close converse with a stranger, jumped up with terror at the sight of me. 'What has happened?' he cried; 'my father?' I had scarcely breath enough to say what I had to say. 'Your father,' I cried, 'has come to himself. You can make no sale without him—every arrangement must be stopped at once.' All that I was capable of knowing was with a certainty, beyond all proof, that the man with whom Charley was talking, a sportsman in every line of his countenance and clothes, was the intending purchaser of Ellermore.

I remember little of the conversation that followed. It was stormy and excited, for neither would Charley be convinced nor would the other consent to be off his bargain. But I made my point clear. Mr Campbell having recovered his faculties, it was clear that no treaty could be concluded without his consent. (It could not have been legal in any case, but I suppose they had in some way got over this.) I remember Charley turning upon me with a passionate remonstrance, when, almost by violence and pertinacity, I had driven his Cockney sportsman away. 'I cannot conceive what is your object, Temple,' he said. 'Are you mad? my father must give his consent; there is no possibility of a question about it. Ellermore must be sold—and as well to him as to another,' he said, with a sigh. I took out my blue letter, which I had huddled into my pocket, and laid it before him. 'It is to me that Ellermore must be sold,' I said.

My inheritance had come—there was nothing wonderful about it—it was my right; but never did inheritance come at a more suitable moment. Charley went back with me that afternoon, after a hurried conference with his young brothers, who came round me, shaking my arms nearly off, and calling to each other in their soft young basses, like rolls of mild thunder, that, whatever happened, I was a good fellow, a true friend. If they had not been so bashful they would have embraced me, less I verily believe from the sense of escape from a great misery which they had scarcely realized, than from generous pleasure in what they thought a sort of noble generosity: that was their view of it. Charley perhaps was more enlightened. He was very silent during the journey, but at one point of it burst out suddenly upon me. 'You are doing this for Chatty, Temple. If you take her away, it will be as bad as losing Ellermore.' I shook my head. Then, if never before, I felt the hopelessness of the position. 'There is but one thing you can do for me: say not a word of that to her,' I said.

And I believe he kept counsel. It was of her own accord that Charlotte came up to me after the hurried interview in which Charley laid my proposal before her. She was very grave, though the sweetness of her look drew the heart out of my breast. She held out her hands to me, but her eyes took all warm significance out of this gesture. 'Mr Temple,' she said, 'you may think me bold to say it, but we are friends that can say anything to one another. If in your great generosity there may yet be a thought—a thought that a woman might recompense what was done for her and hers——' Her beautiful countenance, beautiful in its love and tenderness and noble dignity, but so pale, was suddenly suffused with colour. She took her hands out of mine, and folded them together—'That is out of my power—that is out of my power!' she said.

'I like it better so,' I cried. God help me! it was a lie, and so she knew. 'I want no recompense. It will be recompense enough to know you are here.'

And so it has remained ever since, and may, perhaps, for ever—I cannot tell. We are dear friends. When anything happens in the family I am sent for, and all is told to me. And so do I with her. We know all each other's secrets—those secrets which are not of fortune or incident, but of the soul. Is there anything better in marriage than this? And yet there is a longing which is human for something more.

That evening I went back to the Lady's Walk, with a sort of fanciful desire to tell her, the other, that I had done her bidding, that she had been a true guardian of her race to the last. I paced up and down through the dim hour when the sun ought to have been setting, and later, long into the twilight. The rain fell softly, pattering upon the dark glistening leaves of the evergreens, falling straight through the bare branches. But no soft step of a living soul was on the well-worn track. I called to her, but there was no answer, not even the answer of

a sigh. Had she gone back heartsick to her home in Heaven, acknow-
ledging at last that it was not hers to guard her race? It made my heart
ache for her to think so; but yet it must have been a sweet grief and easily healed to know that those she loved were most safe in God's only
care when hers failed—as everything else must fail.

6

SIR HERBERT STEPHEN

No. 11 Welham Square

I

We were sitting in the drawing-room of our house at Bayswater one evening after dinner, in high good-humour. I had that day been appointed to a certain post at the British Museum which would afford me ample opportunity for the studies in which I was most interested, and put me in possession of what I expected to find an ample competence. We had been talking over my prospects, and the only cloud I could discern upon the horizon was that I should have to be at my post at an earlier hour in the morning than was comfortably compatible with the three-mile walk from our house to the Museum.

'What a pity,' said my youngest sister Patricia, 'that we don't still live in the dear old house in Welham Square! You could have got to the Museum from there in five minutes.'

I was born after we left Welham Square, but Patricia was six years my senior, and could remember her nursery days there.

'Not at all,' said my father, very abruptly; 'the walk will do you all the good in the world.'

As the old gentleman had been, to all appearance, fast asleep for at least ten minutes, I was rather surprised at the energy with which he spoke. Looking up, I saw my mother making anxious signals to Patricia, which she followed up by instantly changing the subject.

A few days afterwards, as I descended reluctantly into the bowels of the earth at the Edgware Road Metropolitan Station, on the way to my new work for the first time, this episode recurred to my mind, and I began to speculate upon what might be the reasons that made the mention of Welham Square distasteful to my parents. I determined to consult my eldest sister Ellen on the subject, and from her, and some other sources, I gradually accumulated the facts which I will present here in the form of a continuous narrative.

No. 11 Welham Square has always been the freehold property of my family. It was built, together with several adjoining houses, about the beginning of the eighteenth century by the owner of a plot of land in which the houses stand, a retired attorney, who had two nephews. These were Andrew Masey, my great-great-great-grandfather, and his cousin, Ronald Masey. Ronald, who was generally thought to be his uncle's favourite, and probable heir, was an exceedingly tall and powerful young man, with a forbidding and melancholy expression of countenance. As a boy he was singularly backward, and his incapacity for mental exertion seemed to develop, as he grew up, into something not far removed from downright idiocy. His weakness of mind caused him to be remarkably subject to the influence of those with whom he lived, and in particular his cousin Andrew, my ancestor, was supposed to exercise over him an influence almost amounting to fascination, and to be able to mould him to all the purposes of an exceptionably vigorous will. Shortly after the building of the houses in what is now Welham Square, the uncle of these young men died, and Andrew took possession of all his property under the provisions, as he asserted, of a will, the existence of which no one except Ronald had any interest in disputing, and which no one except Andrew, the sole executor and devisee, ever saw. Shortly before his uncle's death, Ronald had become engaged to a young lady named Lettice White, to whom he was passionately attached, and it was generally supposed among the neighbours that upon his accession to the avuncular wealth the marriage would take place. But when a barely decent interval had occurred since the old gentleman's obsequies, the fair Lettice was led to the altar, not by the impecunious Ronald, but by his more fortunate cousin Andrew. The newly married pair took up their residence in No. 11, and Ronald came to live with them.

When it was represented to Andrew by some of his few intimate acquaintances that this arrangement was so singular as almost to be thought improper, he curtly gave them to understand that Ronald's mental condition was not such as to permit of his only living relation allowing him to live alone, and that he was compelled by the merest considerations of family affection to take the unfortunate young man into his own household. So the three lived on in the stately and somewhat gaunt mansion, Andrew collecting his rents with methodical regularity, and otherwise giving his neighbours but little concern. As for Ronald, there soon came to be little doubt in anyone's mind of his confirmed imbecility. He appeared seldom, and when he did, was for the most part silent, regarding his cousin and former betrothed with an expression of the profoundest submission, which at times merged into a look of wild and hardly human apprehension, 'like a terrified brute-beast', as it was put by an old lady who was one of the few friends occasionally privileged to partake of the gloomy hospitality of this uncomfortable establishment. Nothing more was ever known of the condition in which my ancestor, his wife, and his cousin lived, and no one was specially interested when, about six years after the marriage, Ronald, who had not been seen for many months, died, and was buried in a frugal manner.

Before he had been dead a year, Andrew and Lettice suddenly left their house and took up their abode elsewhere, and after a while a tenant was found for No. 11. Thirty years later, the lease of the house having expired, Andrew's son, who had succeeded to his father's property, came to reside there, but not for long. He left the house suddenly after a few years, and a rumour went abroad that it was haunted, probably by the ghost of the unfortunate Ronald. From this time No. 11 descended from father to son, the adjoining property being sold piecemeal as the family necessities dictated. Occasionally the successive freeholders made attempts to live there, but they never stayed more than a few months, and on each occasion of their removal the rumours of ghostly possession were renewed. These, however, would die away, and tenants would after a time be found, who never suffered from any inconvenience. The last occupation by the owner was that of my father, who moved into the house when my sister Patricia was a little girl. After living there a year he left precipitately, but Ellen could give me no particulars of his reasons for doing so, and knew only that he disliked any reference to the house, and never mentioned it himself. The house was now let to a stockbroker with a family.

II

Five years had elapsed since the conversation I related at the beginning of the previous chapter. My parents had both died, and Patricia was married and living with her husband in a provincial town. My career at the Museum had been a prosperous one, and I was now entrusted with a more responsible and better paid office. The tenant of No. 11 Welham Square had just given me notice of his intention to depart from it, and it occurred to me that it would be interesting to follow what seemed to be the family destiny, and try living in the house myself, to say nothing of the fact that it was admirably suited to my requirements. I felt fully capable of confronting any number of ghosts, and my wife was neither timid nor superstitious. Accordingly at the beginning of the new year we established ourselves, with our two babies, and my sister Ellen, who lived with us, in Welham Square, greatly delighted with the proximity of my work, with the solid masonry, spacious apartments, and roomy passages of our new abode, and with the remnant of eighteenth-century fashion and grandeur which seemed to pervade the neighbourhood. And in Welham Square we lived prosperously, without any kind of disturbance, for upwards of six months.

In the course of July my wife and the children left home to spend a couple of months at the seaside. I intended to join them when the time came to take my holiday, and in the meantime I stayed in London, going daily to my work. Ellen stayed on with me to keep house in the absence of her sister-in-law.

One evening, four or five days after my wife's departure, I was sitting in my study, a large room with a door leading into the drawing-room, and a heavy curtain hung over my side of the door. It was past eleven; my sister had retired half an hour before, and the two maids who were left in the house were presumably in bed and asleep. I was therefore surprised to hear heavy and somewhat slow footsteps, apparently those of a large man, ascending the stairs from the ground-floor. The front door I knew was locked and chained, nor had I heard anyone ring. The steps paused for a moment on the landing outside my door, and then I heard the intruder proceed to go up the next flight of stairs leading to the bedrooms on the second floor. I sprang up, seized a candle, and opened the door. As I stood on the threshold of my room I seemed to hear footsteps, as of a man heavily mounting the stairs at the top of the flight leading up from my door. But, though I held the light above my head, I could see no one. Everything wore its usual aspect. I walked quickly up the stairs, but nobody was visible. I searched all the empty rooms, but with no result. I called up Ellen and the maids, but none of them had seen or heard anything. I am ashamed to say that I made a specially rigorous investigation of a large room at the back of the house, which we used for a night nursery, and which tradition declared to have been the abode of my ill-fated kinsman Ronald Masey. I then went downstairs and completed my search of the entire premises. Everything was in order, and at the end of an hour I went back to my study and my book, rather annoyed with myself for having spent so much time in so fruitless an exploration, and determined to think nothing more about the matter.

It was the next night after this that I suddenly started up very wide awake with a conviction that somebody was in my bedroom. I seemed to hear still ringing in my ears the sound of a long-drawn human sigh. I sat up, trembling with excitement, and looked about in the dim twilight of dawn in late July. I could see no one, but I did not feel alone. The feeling of suspense became unbearable. I jumped out of bed, and walked with nervous determination to the window, where I turned round and faced the room, such light as there was being behind me. I saw no one. Again I walked across the room, and as I did so I felt unmistakably that wave of air that meets one walking in the streets when someone on foot passes close to him in the opposite direction. I seemed to feel the light graze of a passing substance against my nightgown. I was dimly conscious of a faint, indescribable odour, calling up recollections of a time of life long but indefinitely past. And while I stood fixed to the spot with surprise and horror, my heart beating violently, I heard distinctly four long heavy steps passing from me towards the window. The floor creaked under their weight. The next instant I felt that I was alone. But it was not until long after the morning was as light as noon that I fell asleep again.

I awoke much troubled in mind, and doubting whether I should not, like my fathers, be compelled to leave this uncanny dwelling; but when in some measure restored by breakfast, I determined to say nothing to my sister at present, but to wait and see whether the situation would in any way develop itself. My resolution was fated to be put to the test sooner than I expected.

I did not get home that evening till close upon dinner-time. When I entered the drawing-room Ellen greeted me with, 'Oh, Edward! what do you think has happened? Sikes is dead!'

Now Sikes was a grey parrot belonging to my wife. He was so called because when he first came to us it was affirmed of him, perhaps rather libellously, that, like the hero of Mr Calverley's poem, he 'habitually swore'. He certainly did from time to time blaspheme somewhat unreservedly.

I was secretly not altogether sorry to hear of his demise. So I answered with much composure, 'Did the cat eat him?'

'No,' said Ellen, 'he died in the most horrible convulsions.'

I went up to get ready for dinner, thinking more of how to prevent my wife from replacing Sikes by another clamorous bird than of the manner of the lost one's death, but in the course of our meal it occurred to me that his fate was an odd one.

'How did Sikes come to have convulsions?' I asked.

'Why, it was most curious,' answered Ellen. 'I was going to tell you about it. I was in the drawing-room writing letters, and suddenly I heard a tremendous screaming and flapping, and I looked up, and there was Sikes turning over and over in the air, and pecking, and clawing, and flapping his wings, and screaming, and before I could get to him he suddenly twisted his head right round two or three times, and tumbled down dead on the floor.'

'But do you mean,' I said, 'that he was carrying on these gymnastics up in the air?'

'Yes; when I saw him he was quite up above his cage, which was on the little table, and in his struggles he must have wrung his own neck.'

'That seems rather remarkable.'

'Yes; and another remarkable thing was that he must have opened the door of his cage and got out all by himself, which I never heard of his doing before, because I had been feeding him with cake after lunch, and I know the door was fastened then. I found it open when he was dead.'

'Had he been out long?'

'No. He must have been seized almost directly he got out, because it so happened that about five minutes before he began to scream, I fancied I heard the door open, and looked up to see if anyone was coming in, and no one was there, but I happened to see the parrot, and he was in his cage just as usual.'

'Well,' I said, 'I suppose he's dead, and there's an end of it; but it is a very singular catastrophe. I hope Marion won't be inconsolable.'

During the rest of dinner I was conscious of being rather poor company. Following close upon the mysterious occurrences I have described, Sikes's unhappy fate troubled me. My suspicions were, however, so undefined, and seemed even to me, when I tried to contemplate them from an impartial point of view, so ridiculous, that I could not bring myself to communicate them to Ellen, and incur the contempt which would be the deserved portion of a grown-up man who confessed to being seriously disturbed by an odd sound in an empty house, and by a commonplace nightmare. I have no hesitation in revealing these sentiments now that subsequent events have justified them. But that evening I again determined to wait. I did not have to wait long.

It was a cold evening, and, after bidding goodnight to my sister, I lighted a fire in my study and sat down to enjoy a new novel I had long been wishing to read. I was about halfway through my volume when I suddenly felt a sensation of cold. I looked up. The fire was burning brightly, but I did not feel its warmth. It was as though some opaque body, or a large glass screen, had been interposed between me and it. A moment afterwards I felt the heat fall on my face again. Had I heard the muffled sound of a footstep on the hearth-rug close to me? I put out my hand and felt nothing but the warmth of the fire. As I gazed about the room in surprise my eye fell on an armchair standing on the other side of the fire. It was a nearly new chair, which I had bought shortly after coming to Welham Square. It had a leather seat, smooth and unworn, with particularly good and yielding springs. Hung upon its back was an antimacassar, worked aesthetically in crewels. As I looked at this chair it struck me that the seat was considerably depressed, as though some one had recently sat down upon it, and the seat had failed to resume its ordinary level. This surprised me, for I had sat in the chair that morning and felt sure the springs had then been in good order. I looked at the antimacassar. Towards the top it was pushed up in wrinkles. As I looked, it occurred to me that it was impossible for it to hang in such a manner by itself. It looked for all the world as if an invisible but substantial human frame was then actually sitting in the chair. When this notion occurred to me, I sat dazed with an indescribable horror, staring stupidly at the chair, which did not move. In an access of frenzied terror, I hurled the book I was reading at the chair. Did it strike the seat, or did it glance away a few inches from the edge and fall on the hearth-rug? The next instant the seat of the chair rose up audibly to its normal level, and the antimacassar fell out into its usual folds, still preserving, however, the traces of its previous wrinkles. I started up, and rushing to the chair, began to prod it. I could discover nothing unusual in its condition. As I was doing so I felt a hand, beyond all doubt, laid steadily on my shoulder. I faced round and saw nothing. 'Who are you?' I shouted. 'What do you want?' But no answer came. I was alone.

I sat cogitating till one o'clock, and then I went to bed. Just as I was getting into bed it occurred to me that perhaps I might be annoyed in the dark, and though I had not yet seen anything, the prospect seemed rather awful, and with a slightly trembling hand I lighted a night-light. When I had done so, and got into bed, I was rather disposed to be ashamed of myself, and thought I would put it out, but, partly no doubt from a disinclination to get out of bed, I determined that in any case it would do no harm, and that I would leave it as it was. It occurred to me what an odd thing it is that one feels safer in bed than anywhere else, whereas in fact one is never in a more defenceless situation. Then I went to sleep.

I do not know what time I woke. It seemed to me that the air was blowing in upon my chest where the bedclothes should have covered me up. And—yes, certainly there was an odd depression in my pillow, close in front of my face, as if some heavy weight were pressing it down. I put up my hand to investigate. I touched something on the pillow. I caught hold of it, and turned cold with terror. For I held tightly in my hand, another hand, neither cold nor warm, but large and solid. My light was still burning, and there was no one to be seen. The hand was suddenly jerked away from me. I sprang out of bed, and rushed to the fireplace with a despairing feeling that someone followed close behind me. I seized the poker, turned round, and struck wildly at the air. Whether I hit anything or not I do not know. I remember only that as I was recovering myself from a frantic lunge at nothing, I received a sharp and stunning blow on the back of my head. When I came to myself it was six in the morning, and I was lying on the floor where I had fallen. The night-light was out, and the morning sunlight was streaming in at my window. There was a very large and painful bruise where I had been struck.

III

I felt that this was getting beyond a joke. It was all very well to frighten me, but when my ghostly enemy took to knocking me down like a ninepin, I was not going to keep it to myself any longer. I had no intention of surrendering, for the blood of the Maseys was up, and the fact that each of my ancestors since the house was built had sooner or later evacuated the premises made me all the more determined not to be driven away without making some further resistance. So I unbosomed to my sister Ellen the whole of my experience in the matter. She was decidedly sceptical about the ghost, if ghost it could be called, and suggested that I was not well. I vowed that I was as well as any man with a great hole in the back of his head could be, and she consented to the arrangement that I proposed—that she should sit up for a night or two in the drawing-room, while I was in my study, with the door open between us, and that if any remarkable incident occurred, I should call her in. In order not to be wholly without male assistance in case I should be attacked, I invited a college friend of mine named Prescott, a strong, sensible, and energetic young doctor who lived near us, to keep my sister company in the drawing-room. He, when he heard my story, was, as befitted a scientific young professional man, exceedingly facetious at my expense, but he willingly consented to share our watch, and to sleep in the house. That evening I sat up as usual in my study, while Prescott and Ellen beguiled the hours in the drawing-room with light literature, until about half-past two, when, nothing having occurred, we settled to go to bed, and separated; Prescott divided between high spirits at the temporary triumph of incredulity, and a tinge of disappointment at the non-occurrence of anything in the shape of a row, and Ellen rather indignant with me for having kept her up so long to no purpose. After the stormy experiences of the two preceding nights I thoroughly enjoyed an unbroken sleep.

I prevailed upon my sister and my friend to give the ghost one more chance, and the next evening saw us again comfortably established in the two rooms, separated only by the curtain which hung over the door of communication.

It may have been eleven o'clock when I heard a board creak just behind my chair. Uttering a shout, I sprang up, and dashed at the spot from which the noise had come. I came into heavy contact with what felt like a gigantic human figure. Prescott and Ellen hurried into the room and beheld me wildly grappling, apparently with nothing at all. 'By Jove!' said Prescott, 'he has got them.' 'Them' I believe meant some kind of hallucinations upon which Prescott professed to be an authority, but I was struggling furiously with my unseen antagonist, and had no breath for explanations.

'Seize him! seize him!' I cried.

At that moment my prey burst from me, hurling me with prodigious violence across the room.

Prescott rushed forward, and as he did so was tripped up by what he afterwards described as a heavy kick from an unseen foot, and sent sprawling on the floor. Fortunately I was prostrate at the other end of the room, and could not be suspected of having had a hand, or a foot, in this outrage.

As we struggled to our feet, while Ellen stared wildly about, we all heard two or three hurried steps, as of a man running; there was a tremendous crash, and all was still. But the curtains had swung violently back into the window, and the window itself, plate-glass, frame, and all, was burst clean away outwards.

Prescott was as white as a sheet, and the sensible and strong-minded Ellen was actually crying, which impressed me more than anything else in the scene.

'Let us leave this horrible house,' she said; 'something worse will happen if we stay.'

But I was filled with an unreasonable kind of courage at having, as it seemed, put our inexplicable visitor to flight; and I was besides conscious of a certain degree of pride in the assurance that Prescott had been converted, and would hardly talk again about my having 'got them'.

'We can't go tonight,' I said, 'and as our gentleman seems to have taken himself off for the present, we had better consider what's to be done next. I am sure Prescott wants to stay and investigate the phenomenon.'

We shut the shutters over the wreck of the window, and sat talking over the event until late at night. By degrees I contrived to infuse into my companions some of my courage, and at last, no further disturbance having taken place, we all went to bed in pretty good spirits. I placed a loaded double-barrelled pistol on the table by my bedside, thinking that if a ghost could be struggled with, he ought to be able to be shot, and Prescott placed within reach a large bowie-knife, which he had brought back from America, and had long been wishing for an opportunity to make use of.

When I woke I thought my last hour had come. My throat was tightly grasped by two extremely strong hands. A crushing weight was on my chest. I tried to shout, but could not. I was rapidly being strangled. And as I lay writhing, my eyes, forced half out of their sockets, glared through the light of the night-light at the opposite wall, which looked precisely as usual, except that, as the squeezing of my throat grew more and more intolerable, my view of the room slowly darkened. But of the horrible and only too palpable form that was killing me I could see no trace. In unavailing despair I clutched at the iron wrists that held me down. In another moment I believe I should have become unconscious. Then, a last gleam of hope, the thought of my pistol, flashed through my mind. I stretched out my hand, and as I lay I could just reach the end of the barrel. I drew it towards me, and with an expiring effort pushed the muzzle of it close against what I took to be the invisible body of my tormentor, and fired. We never found the bullet, or any trace of it afterwards. Instantly the hands relaxed their grip on my throat a little, and with a violent effort I wrenched my neck away; then a heavy body fell sideways from my bed to the ground, and I fell too, grappling with it. At that moment Ellen and Prescott, who had been aroused by the sound of the shot, burst into the room. There they saw me struggling, partly on the floor, and partly kneeling apparently on space. They rushed to my assistance. Both of them felt the thing, both of them grappled with it. The struggles of our enemy became fainter.

Managing to get one hand free I repossessed myself of the pistol, which had fallen on the floor, and emptied the second barrel into what I judged to be the breast of the spectre. I fired straight downwards, apparently at the floor, but of that bullet we saw no more than of the other. Meanwhile Prescott stabbed furiously with the bowie-knife, and each time he dashed the blade down its progress was arrested before it reached the carpet. Then the struggles ceased, and nothing was heard except our rapid panting. We were all kneeling on and holding down what looked like space, and felt like the form of a tall and athletic man.

'We've done for it, whatever it is,' said I hoarsely.

Prescott burst into a foolish giggle. 'By Jove!' he said, 'we'll make a cast of it and see what it's like.'

As he spoke the form of our victim was agitated by a desperate convulsion, which shook us all off. Before we could seize it again a deep groan burst from the place where we had held it, and the word 'Lettice!' rang through the room in a tone of sepulchral melancholy. Then there was silence.

I threw myself on the floor—not, as I had intended, on the prostrate figure. We searched the room, and then the house, but we could find absolutely nothing. Nor from that day to this has anyone, to the best of my knowledge, seen, heard, or felt anything whatever of this ghastly being.

After much consideration we determined to keep the adventure to ourselves, for a time at any rate. Indeed, it was only last summer, when we had lived in the house for a good number of years without any kind of ghostly interruption, that I described the circumstances herein narrated to my wife. She doesn't believe them, and I am sorry I told her.

Was it the ghost of Ronald Masey? Did it voluntarily depart and leave us alone because it considered that the annoyances it had inflicted upon my ancestors and me were sufficient, and that the tale of its vengeance upon our house, for the wrongs, whatever they were, inflicted upon Ronald in his lifetime by Andrew and Lettice, was complete? Or did we actually kill it? Perhaps we did. He was a poor weak creature when he was alive.

EDWARD MASEY

11 WELHAM SQUARE, 1885

7

B. M. CROKER

The Khitmatgar

'Whence and what art thou, execrable shape?'—MILTON.

Perhaps you have seen them more than once on railway platforms in the North-West Provinces. A shabby, squalid, weary-looking group, sitting on their battered baggage, or scrambling in and out of inter-mediate compartments; I mean Jackson, the photographer, and his belongings. Jackson is not his real name, but it answers the purpose. There are people who will tell you that Jackson is a man of good fam-ily, that he once held a commission in a crack cavalry regiment, and that his brother is Lord-Lieutenant of his county, and his nieces are seen at Court balls. Then how comes their kinsman to have fallen to such low estate—if kinsman he be—this seedy-looking, unshorn reprobate, with a collarless flannel shirt, greasy deerstalker, and broken tennis shoes? If you look into his face, who runs may read the answer—Jackson drinks; or his swollen features, inflamed nose, and watery and uncertain eye greatly belie him.

Jackson was a *mauvais sujet* from his youth upwards, if the truth must be confessed. At school he was always in trouble and in debt. At Oxford his scrapes were so prominent that he had more than one nar-row escape of being sent down. Who would believe, to look at him *now*, that he had once been a very pretty boy, the youngest and best-looking of a handsome family, and naturally his mother's darling? Poor woman! whilst she lived she shielded him from duns and dons, and from his father's wrath; she pawned her diamonds and handed over her pin-money to pay his bills; she gave him advice—and he gave her kisses. By the time he had joined his regiment, this reckless youth had lost his best friend, but his bad luck—as *he* termed it—still clung to him and overwhelmed him. His father had a serious interview with his colonel, paid up like a liberal parent, and agreed to his son's exchange into a corps in India. 'India may steady him,' thought this sanguine old gentleman; but, alas! it had anything but the desired effect. In India the prodigal became more imprudent than ever. Cards, racing, simpkin, soon swallowed up his moderate allowance, and he fell headlong into the hands of the soucars—a truly fatal fall! Twenty per cent per month makes horrible ravages in the income of a subaltern, and soon he was hopelessly entangled in debt, and had acquired the disagreeable reputation of being 'a man who never paid for anything, and always let others in, when it was a question of rupees'. Then his name was whispered in connection with some very shady racing transaction, and finally he was obliged to leave the service, bankrupt alike in honour and credit. His father was dead, his brothers unanimously disowned him, and for twenty years he fell from one grade to another, as he roamed over India from Peshawar to Madras, and Rangoon to Bombay. He had been in turn planter, then planter's clerk, house agent, tonga agent; he had tried touting for a tailoring firm and manufacturing hill jams; and here he was at fifty years of age, with a half-caste wife, a couple of dusky children, and scarcely an anna in his pocket. Undoubtedly he had put the coping-stone on his misfortunes when he took for his bride the pretty, slatternly daughter of a piano-tuner, a girl without education, without energy, and without a penny.

Ten years ago Fernanda Braganza had been a charming creature (with the fleeting beauty of her kind), a sylph in form, with superb dark eyes, fairy-like feet, and a pronounced taste for pink ribbons, patchouli, and pearl-powder. This vision of beauty, who had gushed to Jackson with her soul in her exquisite eyes, and who was not insensible to the honour of marrying a gentleman, was she the selfsame individual as this great fat woman, in carpet slippers, and a bulging tweed ulster, who stood with a sallow, hungry-looking child in either hand? Alas! she was.

The Jacksons had come to try their fortunes at Panipore—a small up-country station, where there were two European regiments and half a battery of Artillery—for is not Tommy Atkins ever a generous patron to an inexpensive photographer? The finances of the family were at a very low ebb that February afternoon, as they stood on the platform collecting their belongings, a camera and chemicals, a roll of frowsy bedding, a few cooking things, a couple of boxes, also a couple of grimy servants—in India the poorest have a following, and third-class tickets are cheap. Jackson had a 'three-finger' peg at the bar, although there was but little in his pocket, besides a few cards and paper posters, and thus invigorated proceeded to take steps respecting the removal of his family.

Poverty forbade their transit in a couple of ticca gharries, and pride shrank from an ekka; therefore Jackson left his wife in the waiting-room whilst he tramped away in the blinding sun and powdery white dust to see if there was accommodation at the Dâk Bungalow. It proved to be crammed, and he had not yet come down to the Serai, or native halting-place. He was (when sober) a man of some resource. He made his way up to the barracks and asked questions, and heard that the station was in the same condition as the Dâk Bungalow, quite full. Even Fever Hall and Cholera Villa were occupied, and the only shelter he could put his head into was the big two-storied bungalow in the Paiwene road. It had been empty for years; it was to be had at a nominal rent—say two rupees a week—and there was no fear of any one disturbing him *there!* It was large and close to the barracks, but greatly out of repair. With this useful intelligence, Mr Jackson rejoined his impatient circle, and, with their goods in a hand-cart, they started off for this house of refuge without delay.

Past the native bazaar, past the officers' mess, past the church, then along a straight wide road, where the crisp dead leaves crackled underfoot, a road lined with dusty half-bare trees, whose branches stood out in strong relief against a hard blue sky, whilst a vast tract of grain country, covered with green barley and ripe sugar-cane, stretched away on the right. On the left were a pair of great gaunt gate piers, leading by a grass-grown approach, to the two-storeyed bunga-low—an imposing-looking house, that was situated well back from the highway amid a wilderness of trees, and rank and rotting vegeta-tion. Distance in this case certainly had lent enchantment to the view! When the little party arrived under the wide, dilapidated portico, they found all the doors closed, the lower windows stuffed with boards, matting, and even paper in default of glass; weeds and creepers abounded, and there was a dangerous fissure in the front wall. After knocking and calling for about ten minutes, an ancient chowkidar appeared, looking half asleep. At first he thought it was merely a party from the station, wishing, as was their eccentric custom, 'to go over' the haunted house, the Bhootia Bungalow; but he soon learnt his mistake from the voluble, shrill-tongued memsahib.

This family of shabby Europeans, who had arrived on foot, with all their belongings in a '*tailer*' from the station, had actually come to stay, to sleep, to *live* on the premises! Grumbling to himself, he conducted them up an exceedingly rickety, not to say dangerous, staircase—for the lower rooms were dark and damp—to three or four large and cheerful apartments, opening on a fine verandah. Mrs Jackson was accustomed to pitching her tent in queer places, and in a very short time she had procured from the bazaar a table, a few chairs, and a couple of charpoys, and furnished two rooms—she had but little to unpack—whilst Kadir Bux, the family slave, vibrated between cooking and chemicals. Meanwhile Mr Jackson, having washed, shaved, and invested himself in his one linen collar and black alpaca coat, set forth on a tour of inspection, to stick up posters and distribute cards. His wife also made her rounds; the upper rooms were habitable, and the verandah commanded a fine view; it overlooked the park-like but neglected compound, intersected with short-cut paths, and which, despite its two grand entrance gates, was now without hedge or paling, and quite open to the road, a road down which not a few ladies and gentlemen in bamboo carts or on ponies were trotting past for their evening airing. Below the suite Mr Jackson had chosen, were the dismal vault-like rooms, the chowkidar with his charpoy and hukka, and beyond, at the back of the bungalow, the servants' quarters and stables, both roofless. Behind these ruins, stretched an immense overgrown garden (with ancient, dried-up fruit trees, faint traces of walks and water-channels, and a broken fountain and sundial) now abandoned to cattle. On the whole, Mrs Jackson was pleased with her survey. She had never as yet inhabited such a lordly looking mansion, and felt more contented than she had done for a long time, especially as Jackson was on his best behaviour—he had no friends in the place, and scarcely any funds.

In a short time Mr Jackson had acquired both. His good address, his gentlemanly voice, and the whisper of his having once been an officer who had come to grief—who had been unfortunate—went far in a military station. With extraordinary discretion he kept his belongings entirely out of sight; he also kept sober, and consequently received a number of orders for photographs of groups, of bungalows, and of polo ponies. He had the eye of an artist and really knew his business, and although some were startled at the strength of the pegs which he accepted, he had a large and lucrative connection in less than no time, and rupees came flowing in fast. As he and the invaluable Kadir worked together, he talked glibly to portly field-officers and smooth-faced sub-alterns, of men whom *he* had known, men whose names at least were familiar to them—distinguished veterans, smart soldiers, and even cele-brated personages. He attended church, and sang lustily out of a little old Prayer-book, and looked such a picture of devout, decayed gentility, that the tender-hearted ladies pitied him and thought him quite romantic, and hastened to order photographs of all their children, or, children being lacking, dogs. Little did they know that Mr Jackson's shabby Prayer-book would have been sold for drink years previously, only that he found it an absolutely unmarketable article!

Meanwhile Mrs Jackson was convinced that she was positively about to be 'a lady at last'. She purchased frocks for her sallow girls, a dress and boots for herself; she set up a rocking-chair and a cook, and occasionally drove to the bazaar in a 'ticca' gharry, where she looked down with splendid dignity on the busy bargaining wives of Tommy Atkins. The chaplain's lady had called upon her, also the barrack-sergeant's wife, who lived in a small bungalow or quarters beyond the garden. She had haughtily snubbed this good woman at first, but sub-sequently had thawed toward her, for several reasons. Jackson, having been uproariously drunk, and unpleasantly familiar to an officer, had now fallen back on the sergeants' mess for his society, and on private soldiers for his patrons. He was still doing a roaring trade, especially in cartes-de-visite at six rupees a dozen. He bragged and talked, and even wept, to his listeners in the barrack-rooms, and in the canteen: listen-ers who thought him an uncommonly fine fellow, liberal as a lord, flinging his coin right and left. They little guessed the usual sequel, or of how the Jackson family were wont to steal out of a station by rail in the grey dawn of an Indian morning, leaving many poor natives, who had supplied their wants in the shape of bread and meat, coffee, and even clothes, to bewail their too abrupt departure. Jackson was 'on the drink', as his wife frankly expressed it, never home before twelve o'clock at night, and then had to be helped upstairs, and Mrs Jackson found these evenings extremely wearisome. She rarely read, but she did a little crochet and not a little scolding; she slept a good deal; and, as long as her coffee and her curry were well and punctually served, she was fairly content, for she was naturally lethargic and indolent. But still she liked to *talk*, and here she had no one with whom to exchange a word. She pined for the sound of another female tongue, and accordingly one afternoon she arrayed herself in her new hat with scarlet cock's feathers, also her yellow silk gloves, and with the cook as a body-servant and to carry her umbrella, she sallied forth to return the visit of the barrack-sergeant's wife. She had not far to go—only through the garden and across the road. The barrack-sergeant's wife was knitting outside in her verandah, for the weather was 'warming up', when Mrs Jackson, all-gorgeous in her best garments, loomed upon her vision. Now, Mrs Clark 'had no notion of the wives of drunken photographers giving themselves hairs! And don't go for to tell *her* as ever that Jackson was a gentleman! A fellow that went reeling home from the canteen every night!' But she dissembled her feelings and stood up rather stiffly, and invited her visitor into her drawing-room, a small apartment, the walls coloured grey, furnished with cheap straw chairs, covered in gaudy cretonne, further embellished by billowy white curtains, tottering little tables, and a quantity of photographs in cotton velvet frames—a room of some pretensions, and Mrs Clark's pride. Its unexpected grandeur was a blow to Mrs Jackson, as was also the appearance of two cups of tea on a tray, accompanied by a plate of four water-biscuits. It seemed to her that Mrs Clark also set up for being quite the lady, although *her* husband was not a gentleman. The two matrons talked volubly, as they sipped their tea, of bazaar prices, cheating hawkers, and the enormities of their servants. 'My cook,' was continually in Mrs Jackson's mouth. They played a fine game of brag, in which Mrs Jackson, despite her husband who had been an officer, of her cook, and of her large house, came off second best!

'I can't think,' she said, looking round contemptuously, 'how you can bear to live in these stuffy quarters. I am sure *I* couldn't; it would kill me in a week. You should see the splendid rooms we have; they do say it was once a palace, and built by a nabob.'

'May be so,' coolly rejoined her hostess. 'I know it was a mess-house, and after that an officers' chummery, fifteen or twenty years ago; but no one would live there now, unless they had *no other* roof to cover them, and came to a place like a parcel of beggars!'

'Why, what's up with it?' enquired Mrs Jackson, suddenly becoming of a dusky puce, even through her pearl-powder.

'Don't you know—and *you* there this two months and more?'

'Indeed I don't; what is there to know?'

'And haven't you seen him?' demanded Mrs Clarke, in a key of intense surprise—'I mean the Khitmatgar?'

'I declare I don't know what you are talking about,' cried the other, peevishly. 'What Khitmatgar?'

'What Khitmatgar? Hark at her! Why, a short, square-shouldered man, in a smart blue coat, with a regimental badge in his turban. He has very sticking-out, curling black whiskers, and a pair of wicked eyes that look as if they could stab you, though he salaams to the ground whenever you meet him.'

'I believe I *have* seen him, now you mention it,' rejoined Mrs Jackson; 'rather a tidy-looking servant, with, as you say, a bad expression. But bless you! *we* have such crowds of officers' messengers coming with chits to my husband, I never know who they are! I've seen him now and then, of an evening, I'm sure, though I don't know what brought him, or whose servant he is.'

'Servant!' echoed the other. 'Why, he is a ghost—the ghost what haunts the bungalow!'

'Ah, now, Mrs Clark,' said her visitor, patronizingly, 'you don't tell me you believe such rubbish?'

'Rubbish!' indignantly, 'is it? Oh, just you wait and see. Ask old Mr Soames, the pensioner, as has been here this thirty year—ask any-one—and they will all tell you the same story.'

'Story, indeed!' cried Mrs Jackson, with a loud, rude laugh.

'Well, it's a true story, ma'am—but you need not hear it unless you like it.'

'Oh, but I should like to hear it very much,' her naturally robust curiosity coming to the front. 'Please do tell it to me.'

'Well, twenty years ago, more or less, some young officers lived in that bungalow, and one of them in a passion killed his Khitmatgar. They say he never meant to do it, but the fellow was awfully cheeky, and he threw a bottle at his head and stretched him dead. It was all hushed up, but that young officer came to a bad end, and the house began to get a bad name—people died there so often; two officers of *delirium tremens;* one cut his throat, another fell over the verandah and broke his neck—and so it stands empty! No one stays a week.'

'And why?' demanded the other, boldly. 'Lots of people die in houses; they must die somewhere.'

'But *not* as they do there!' shrilly interrupted Mrs Clark. 'The Khitmatgar comes round at dusk, or at night, just like an ordinary servant, with pegs or lemonade and so on. Whoever takes anything from his hand seems to get a sort of madness on them, and goes and destroys themselves.'

'It's a fine tale, and you tell it very well,' said Mrs Jackson, rising and nodding her red cock's feathers, and her placid, dark, fat face. 'There does be such in every station; people must talk, but they won't frighten *me.*'

And having issued this manifesto, she gave her hostess a limp shake of the hand and waddled off.

'She's jealous of the grand big house, and fine compound, fit for gentry,' said Mrs Jackson to herself, 'and she thinks to get me out of it. Not that *she* could get in! for she has to live in quarters; and she is just a dog in the manger, and, anyways, it's a made-up story from first to last!'

As she reached her abode, and called '*Qui hai! buttie lao!*' a figure came out from the passage, salaamed respectfully, and, by the light of a two-anna lamp on the staircase, she descried the strange Khitmatgar, whose appearance was perfectly familiar to her—a short, square, surly looking person. No doubt he was one of Kadir's many friends; the lower rooms were generally overrun with his visitors.

'Send Kadir!' she said imperiously, and went upstairs, and as she spoke the man salaamed again and vanished.

The wife of his bosom had a fine tale to tell Mr Jackson the next morning, as, with a very shaky hand, he was touching up some plates in his own room.

'A Khitmatgar that offers free pegs!' he exclaimed, with a shout of laughter. 'Too good to be true. Why, I'd take a whisky and soda from the devil himself—and glad to get it. My mouth is like a lime-kiln at this moment—*Qui hai! whisky-pani do!*'

Many days, warm and sweltering days, rolled on; the hot winds blew the crackling leaves before them, blew great clouds of red dust along the roads, blew ladies up to the hills, and dispersed many of Jackson's patrons. But he did not care; he had made a good many rupees; he had more than one boon-companion, and he drank harder than ever. 'Why not?' he demanded; 'he had earned the money, and had the best right to spend it.' He was earning none now. When customers came, Kadir always informed them the sahib was *sota* (asleep). Yes, sleeping off the effects of the preceding night. Mrs Jackson was accustomed to this state of affairs, and what she called his 'attacks'. She rocked herself, fanned herself and dozed, and did a little crochet, whilst the two children played quietly in a back room, with old photographs and bits of cardboard. When her husband did awake, and enjoy a few hours' lucid interval, it was only to recall bills and duns, and flashes of his old life: the cool green park at home, the hunting-field, reviews at Aldershot, his pretty cousin Ethel. Then the chill reality forced itself upon his half-crazy brain. The park was this great, barren, scorched compound, with the hot winds roaring across it; the figure in the verandah was not Ethel in her riding-habit, but Fernanda in carpet slippers and a greasy old dressing-gown. Was this life worth living?

Mrs Jackson had seen the Khitmatgar several times; once she noticed him looking down at her as she ascended the stairs, once he had appeared in answer to her call, carrying a tray and glasses, but she had boldly waved him away, and said, 'Send Kadir; why does he allow strangers to do his work?' There was something far too human about the appearance of the man for her to give a moment's credence to the ghost-story.

One still hot night, a night as bright as day, Mrs Jackson found the air so oppressive that she could not sleep. She lay tossing from side to side on her charpoy, looking out on the moon-flooded verandah, and listening to the indefatigable brain-fever bird, when suddenly she heard her husband's familiar call, '*Qui hai, peg lao!*' He had been drinking as usual, and had fallen into a sodden sleep in his own room.

After an unusually short interval, steps came up the stairs, shoes were audibly slipped off, and there were sounds of the jingling of a glass and bottle.

The door of Mrs Jackson's apartment opened into the verandah and stood wide, on account of the intense breathless heat of that Indian night. In a few moments someone came and paused on the threshold, tray in hand, some one who surveyed her with a grin of Satanic satisfaction. It was the strange Khitmatgar! There was a triumphant expression in his eyes that made her blood run cold, and whilst she gazed, transfixed with horror, he salaamed and was gone. In a second she had jumped out of bed; she ran into the verandah. Yes, the long verandah was empty—he had disappeared. She called excitedly to her husband; no answer. She rushed into his room, to unfold her experience. Jackson was sitting at the table, or rather half lying across it, his hands clenched, his features convulsed, his eyes fixed—quite dead.

He had swallowed one of his chemicals, a fatal poison. Of course, there was the usual ephemeral excitement occasioned by a tragedy in the station, the usual inquest and verdict of temporary insanity, and then a new nameless grave in the corner of the cantonment cemetery.

8

MARY LOUISA MOLESWORTH

Old Gervais

... and now, as to your questions about that long-ago story. What put it into your head, I wonder? You have been talking 'ghosts' like everybody else nowadays, no doubt, and you want to have something to tell that you had at 'first hand'. Ah well, I will try to recall my small experience of the kind as accurately as my old brain is capable of doing at so long a distance. Though, after all, that is scarcely a correct way of putting it. For, like all elderly people, I find it true, strikingly true, that the longer ago the better, as far as memory is concerned. I can recollect events, places—nay, words and looks and tones, material impressions of the most trivial, such as scents and tastes, of forty or fifty years ago, far more vividly, more minutely, than things of a year or even a month past. It is strange, but I like it. There is something consolatory and suggestive about it. It seems to show that we are still all there, or all here, rather; that there is a something—an innermost 'I'—which goes on, faithful and permanent, however rusty and dull the machinery may grow with the wear and tear of time and age.

But you won't thank me for reflections of this kind. You want my little personal experience of the 'more things', and you shall have it.

You know, of course, that by birth—by descent, that is to say—I am a little, a quarter or half a quarter, French. And by affection I have always felt myself much more than that. It is often so; there is a sort of loyalty in us to the weaker side of things. Just because there is really so much less French than English in me, because I have spent nearly all my threescore and —! years in Great Britain, I feel bound to stand up for the Gallic part of me, and to feel quite huffed and offended if France or 'Frenchness' is decried. It is silly, I dare say; but somehow

I cannot help it. We don't know, we can't say in what proportions our ancestors are developed in us. It is possible that I am really, paradoxical as it may sound, more French than English, after all.

You know all about me, but if you want to tell my bit of a ghost-story to others, you will understand that I am not actuated by egotism in explaining things. It was through my being a little French that I came to pay long visits to old friends of my mother's in Normandy. *They* were not relations, but connections by marriage, and bound by the closest ties of association and long affection to our cousins. And the wife of the head of the family, dear Madame de Viremont, was my own godmother. She had visited us in England and Scotland—she loved both, and she was cosmopolitan enough to think it only natural that even as a young girl I should be allowed to cross the Channel to stay with her for weeks, nay, months at a time, in her old château of Viremont-les-bocages. Not that I travelled over there *alone*—ah no, indeed! Girls, even of the unmistakably upper classes, *do* travel alone now, I am assured, still I can't say that it has ever come within my own knowledge that a young lady should journey by herself to Normandy, though I believe such things are done. But it was very different in my young days. My father himself took me to Paris—I am speaking just now of the first time I went, with which indeed only, I am at present concerned—and after a few days of sightseeing there, Madame de Viremont's own maid came to escort me to my destination—the château.

We travelled by diligence, of course—the journey that five or six hours would now see accomplished took us the best part of two days. At Caen, my godmother met us, and I spent a night in her 'hotel' there—the town residence of the family—dear old house that it was! Many a happy day have I spent there since. And then, at Caen, I was introduced for the first time to my godmother's granddaughters, her son's children, Albertine and Virginie. Albertine was older than I, Virginie two years younger. We were dreadfully shy of each other, though Albertine was too well bred to show it, and talked formalities in a way that I am sure made her grandmother smile. Virginie, dear soul, did not speak at all, which you must remember is *not* bad manners in a French girl before she is out, and I, as far as I recollect, spoke nonsense in very bad French, and blushed at the thought of it afterwards. It was stupid of me, for I really could speak the language very decently.

But that all came right. I think we took to each other in spite of our shyness and awkwardness, at once. It must have been so, for we have remained friends ever since, staunch friends, though Albertine's life has been spent among the great ones of the earth (she is a great-grandmother now) and I only see my Virginie once a year, or once in two or three years, for a few hours, at the convent of which she has long, long been the head; and I am an old-fashioned, narrow-minded perhaps, Scotch maiden lady of a very certain age, who finds it not always easy to manage the journey to France even to see her dear old friends.

How delightful, how unspeakably exciting and interesting and fascinating that first real glimpse into the home life of another nation was! The queernesses, the extraordinary differences, the indescribable mingling of primitiveness with ultra refinement, of stateliness and dignity of bearing and customs with odd unsophisticatedness such as I had imagined medieval at least—all added to the charm.

How well I remember my first morning's waking in my bedroom at the château! There was no carpet on the floor; no looking-glass, except a very black and unflattering one which might have belonged to Noah's wife, over the chimney-piece; no attempt at a dressing-table; a ewer and basin in the tiny cabinet-de-toilette which would have delighted my little sister for her dolls. Yet the cup in which old Désirée brought me my morning chocolate was of almost priceless china, and the chocolate itself such as I do not *think* I ever have tasted elsewhere, so rich and fragrant and steaming hot—the roll which accompanied it, though sour, lying on a little fringed doyley marked with the Viremont crest in embroidery which must have cost somebody's eyes something.

It seemed to me like awaking in a fairy-tale in a white cat's château. And the charm lasted till I had come to feel so entirely at home with my dear, courteous, kindly hosts, that I forgot to ask myself if I were enjoying myself or no. Nay, longer than till then, did it last—indeed, I have never lost the *feeling* of it—at any moment I can hear the tapping of my godmother's stoutly shod feet as she trotted about early in the morning, superintending her men and maidens, and giving orders for the day; I can scent the perfume of Monsieur's pet roses; I can hear the sudden wind, for we were not far from the sea, howling and crying through the trees as I lay in my alcove bed at night.

It was not a great house, though called a château. It was one of the still numerous moderate-sized old country houses which escaped the destruction of that terrible time now nearly a century past. The de Viremonts were of excellent descent, but they had never been extremely wealthy, nor very prominent. They were pious, home-loving, cultivated folk—better read than most of their class in the provinces, partly perhaps thanks to their English connections which had widened their ideas, partly because they came of a scholarly and thoughtful race. The house was little changed from what it must have been for a century or more. The grounds, so Madame de Viremont told me, were less well tended than in her husband's childhood, for it was increasingly difficult to get good gardeners, and she herself had no special gift in that line, such as her mother-in-law had been famed for. And though Monsieur loved his roses, his interest in horticulture began and ended with them. I don't think he minded how untidy and wilderness-like the grounds were, provided the little bit near the house was pretty decent. For there, round the 'lawn' which he and Madame fondly imagined was worthy of the name, bloomed his beloved flowers.

If it had been my own home, the wildness of the unkempt grounds would have worried me sadly. I have always been old-maidish about neatness and tidiness, I think. But as it was not my home, and I there-fore felt no uncomfortable responsibility, I think I rather liked it. It was wonderfully picturesque—here and there almost mysterious. One terrace I know, up and down which Virginie and I were specially fond of pacing, always reminded me of the garden in George Sand's *Château de Pictordu*, if only there had been a broken statue at one end!

The time passed quickly, even during the first two or three weeks, when my only companions were 'Marraine', as Madame made me call her, and her husband. I was not at all dull or bored, though my kind friends would scarcely believe it, and constantly tried to cheer my supposed loneliness by telling me how pleasant it would be when *les petites*—Albertine and Virginie—joined us, as they were to do before long. I didn't feel very eager about their coming. I could not forget my shyness; though, of course, I did not like to say so. I only repeated to my godmother that I *could* not feel dull when she and Monsieur de Viremont were doing so much to amuse me. And for another reason I was glad to be alone with my old friends at first. I was very anxious to improve my French, and I worked hard at it under Monsieur's directions. He used to read aloud to us in the evenings; he read splendidly, and besides the exercises and dictations he gave me, he used to make me read aloud too. I hated it at first, but gradually I improved very much, and then I liked it.

So passed three or four weeks; then at last one morning came a letter announcing the granddaughters' arrival on the following day. I could not but try to be pleased, for it was pretty to see how delighted every one at the château was, to hear the news.

'They must be nice girls,' I thought, 'otherwise all the servants and people about would not like them so much,' and I made myself take an interest in going round with my godmother superintending the little preparations she was making for the girls.

They were to have separate rooms. Albertine's was beside mine, Virginie's on the floor above. There was a good deal of excitement about Virginie's room, for a special reason. Her grandmother was arranging a surprise for her, in the shape of a little oratory. It was a tiny closet—a dark closet it had been, used originally for hanging up dresses, in one corner of her room, and here on her last visit, the girl had placed her *prie-Dieu*, and hung up her crucifix. Madame de Viremont had noticed this, and just lately she had had the door taken away, and the little recess freshly painted, and a small window knocked out, and all made as pretty as possible for the sacred purpose.

I felt quite interested in it. It was a queer little recess—almost like a turret—and Madame showed me that it ran up the whole height of the house from the cellars where it began, as an out-jut, with an arched window to give light to one end of the large 'cave' at that side, which would otherwise have been quite dark.

'The great cellar used to be a perfect rat-warren,' she told me, 'till light and air were thus thrown into it. What that odd out-jut was originally, no one knows. There goes a story that a secret winding-staircase, very, very narrow, of course, once ran up it to the roof. There were some doubts, I know, as to the solidity of the masonry—it has sunk a little at one side, you can see it in the cellar. But I expect it has all 'settled', as they call it, long ago. Old Gervais, whom we employed to knock out the new window in Virginie's little oratory, had no doubt about it, and he is a clever mason.'

'Old Gervais,' I repeated; 'who is he, Marraine? I don't think I have seen him, have I?'

For she had spoken of him as if I must have known whom she meant.

'Have you not?' she said. 'He is a dear old man—one of our great resources. He is so honest and intelligent. But no—I dare say you have not seen him. He does not live in our village, but at Plaudry, a mere hamlet about three miles off. And he goes about a good deal; the neighbouring families know his value, and he is always in request for some repairs or other work. He is devout, too,' my godmother added; 'a simple, sincere, and yet intelligent Christian. And that is very rare nowadays: the moment one finds a thoughtful or intelligent mind among our poor, it seems to become the prey of all the sad and hopeless teaching so much in the air.'

And Madame de Viremont sighed. But in a moment or two she spoke again in her usual cheerful tone.

'It was quite a pleasure to see Gervais' interest in this little place,' she said—we were standing in the oratory at the time. 'He has the greatest admiration for our Virginie, too,' she added, 'as indeed everyone has who knows the child.'

'She does look *very* sweet,' I said, and truly. But as I had scarcely heard Virginie open her lips, I could not personally express admiration of anything *but* her looks! In those days too, the reputation of unusual 'goodness'—as applied to Virginie de Viremont, I see now that the word 'sanctity' would scarcely be too strong to use—in one so young, younger than myself, rather alarmed than attracted me.

But her grandmother seemed quite pleased.

'You will find the looks a true index,' she said.

I was examining the oratory—and wondering if there was any little thing I could do to help to complete it. Suddenly I exclaimed to my godmother—

'Marraine, the floor does sink decidedly at one side—just move across slowly, and you will feel it.'

'I know,' she replied composedly, 'that is the side of the settling

I told you of. It is the same in the two intermediate storeys—one of them is my own cabinet-de-toilette. If Virginie does not observe it at once, we shall have Albertine discovering it some day, and teasing the poor child by saying she has weighed down the flooring by kneeling too much—it is just where she will kneel.'

'Is Albertine a tease?' I asked; and in my heart I was not sorry to hear it.

'Ah, yes indeed,' said Madame. 'She is full of spirits. But Virginie, too, has plenty of fun in her.'

My misgivings soon dispersed.

The two girls had not been forty-eight hours at Viremont before we were the best of friends, Virginie and I especially. For though Albertine was charming, and truly high-principled and reliable, there was not about her the quite indescribable fascination which her sister has always possessed for me. I have never known anyone like Virginie, and I am quite sure I never shall. Her character was the most childlike one in certain ways that you could imagine—absolutely single-minded, unselfish, and sunny—and yet joined to this a strength of principle like a rock, a resolution, determination, and courage, once she was convinced that a thing was *right*, such as would have made a martyr of her without a moment's flinching. I have often tried to describe her to you; and the anecdote of her childhood, which at last I am approaching—she was barely out of childhood—shows what she was even then.

Those were very happy days. Everything united to make them so. The weather was lovely, we were all well, even Monsieur's gout and Madame's occasional rheumatism having for the time taken to themselves wings and fled, while we girls were as brilliantly healthful and full of life as only young things can be. What fun we had! Games of hide-and-seek in the so-called garden—much of it better described as a wilderness, as I have said—races on the terrace; explorations now and then, on the one or two partially rainy days, of Madame's stores—from her own treasures of ancient brocades and scraps of precious lace and tapestry, to the 'rubbish', much of it really rubbish, though some of it quaint and interesting, hoarded for a century or two in the great 'grenier' which extended over a large part of the house under the rafters. I have by me now, in this very room where I write, some precious odds and ends which we extracted from the collection, and which my godmother told me I might take home with me to Scotland, if I thought it worth the trouble.

One day we had been running about the grounds till, breathless and tired, we were glad to sit down on the seat at the far end of the terrace. And, while there, we heard some one calling us.

'Albertine, Virginie, Jeannette,' said the voice.

'It is grandpapa,' said Virginie, starting up, and running in the direction indicated, Albertine and I following her more leisurely.

'Where have you been, my children?' said the old gentleman, as we got up to him. 'I have been seeking you—what are your plans for the afternoon? Your grandmother is going to pay some calls, and proposes that one of you should go with her, while I invite the other two to join me in a good walk—a long walk, I warn you—to Plaudry. What do you say to that?'

The two girls looked at me. As the stranger, they seemed to think it right that I should speak first.

'I should like the walk best,' I said with a smile. 'I have not been to Plaudry, and they say it is so pretty. And—perhaps Marraine would prefer one of you two to pay calls—I have already visited most of your neighbours with her before you came, and everyone was asking when you were coming.'

'Albertine, then,' said her grandfather, 'Yes, that will be best. And you two little ones shall come with me.'

The arrangement seemed to please all concerned, especially when Monsieur went on to say that the object of his expedition was to see Gervais the mason.

'Oh,' said Virginie, 'I am so glad. I want to thank him for all the interest he took in my dear little oratory. Grandmamma told me about it.'

Her eyes sparkled. I think I have omitted to say that Madame de Viremont had been well rewarded for her trouble by Virginie's delight in the little surprise prepared for her.

'I want him to see the arch of the window in the "cave",' said Monsieur. 'Some stones are loosened, one or two actually dropped out. Perhaps his knocking out of your little window, Virginie, has had to do with it. In any case, it must be looked to, without delay. Come round that way, and you shall see what I mean.'

He led us to the far side of the house. The window in question had been made in the out-jut I have described; but as it was below the level of the ground, a space had been cleared out in front of it, making a sort of tiny yard, and two or three steps led down to this little spot. It seems to have been used as a receptacle for odds and ends—flowerpots, a watering can, etc., were lying about. Monsieur went down the steps to show us the crumbling masonry. He must have had good eyes to see it, I thought, for only by pushing aside with his stick the thickly growing ivy, could he show us the loosened and falling stones. But then in a moment he explained.

'I saw it from the inside. I was showing the men where to place some wine I have just had sent in, in the wood. And the proper cellar is over-full—yes, it must certainly be seen to. Inside it looks very shaky.'

So we three walked to Plaudry that afternoon. It was a lovely walk, for Monsieur knew the shortest way, partly through the woods, by which we avoided the long, hot stretch of high-road. And when we reached our destination—a hamlet of only half a dozen cottages at most—by good luck Gervais was at home, though looking half ashamed to be caught idle, in spite of his evident pleasure at the visit.

He had not been very well lately, his good wife explained, and she had insisted on his taking a little rest. And though I had never seen him before, it seemed to me I could have discerned a worn look—the look of pain patiently borne—in the old man's quiet, gentle face and eyes.

'Gervais not well!' said Monsieur. 'Why, that is something new. What's been the matter, my friend?'

Oh, it was nothing—nothing at all. The old wife frightened herself for nothing, he said. A little rheumatism, no doubt—a pain near the heart. But it was better, it would pass. What was it Monsieur wanted? He would be quite ready to see to it by tomorrow.

Then Monsieur explained, and I could see that at once the old mason's interest was specially aroused. 'Ah yes, certainly,' he interjected. It must be seen to—he had had some misgivings, but had wished to avoid further expense. But all should be put right. And he was so glad that Mademoiselle was pleased with the little oratory, his whole face lighting up as he said it. Tomorrow by sunrise, or at least as soon as possible after, he would be at the château.

Then we turned to go home again, though not till Madame Gervais had fetched us a cup of milk, to refresh us after our walk; for they were well-to-do, in their way, and had a cow of their own, though the bare, dark kitchen, which in England would scarcely seem better than a stable, gave little evidence of any such prosperity. I said some words to that effect to my companions, and then I was sorry I had done so.

'Why, did you not see the armoire?' said Virginie. 'It is quite a beauty.'

'And the bed and bedding would put many such commodities in an English cottage to shame, I fancy,' added Monsieur, which I could not but allow was probably true.

Gervais kept his word. He was at his post in the 'cave' long before any of us were awake, and Virginie's morning devotions must have been disturbed by the knocking and hammering far below.

He was at it all day. Monsieur went down to speak to him once or twice, but Gervais had his peculiarities. He would not give an opinion as to the amount of repair necessary till he was sure. And that afternoon we all went for a long drive—to dine with friends, and return in the evening. When we came home, there was a message left for Monsieur by the old mason to the effect that he would come again 'tomorrow', and would then be able to explain all. Monsieur must not mind if he did not come early, as he would have to get something made at the forge—something iron, said the young footman who gave the message.

'Ah, just so,' said Monsieur. 'He has found it more serious than he expected, I fancy; but it will be all right, now it is in his hands.'

So the next morning there was no early knocking or tapping to be heard in the old cellar. Nor did Gervais return later, as he had promised.

'He must have been detained at the forge,' said Monsieur. 'No doubt he will come tomorrow.'

Tomorrow came, but with it no Gervais. And Monsieur de Viremont, who was old and sometimes a little irascible, began to feel annoyed. He went down to the cellar, to inspect the work.

'It is right enough,' he said, when he came upstairs to the room where we four ladies were sitting—there had been a change in the weather, and it was a stormily rainy day—'I see he has got out the loose stones, and made it all solid enough, but it looks unsightly and unfinished. It wants pointing, and—'

'What was it Alphonse said about an iron band or something?' said Madame. 'Perhaps Gervais is getting one made, and it has taken longer than he expected.'

'It is not necessary,' said the old gentleman. 'Gervais is over-cautious. No—a girder would be nonsense; but I do not like to see work left so untidy; and it is not his usual way.'

So little indeed was it the old mason's way, that when another day passed, and there was no news of Gervais, Monsieur determined to send in the morning to hunt him up.

'I would have walked over this afternoon myself,' he said, 'if the weather had been less terrible.'

For it really was terrible—one of those sudden storms to which, near the sea, we are always liable, even in summer—raging wind, fierce beating, dashing rain, that take away for the time all sensation of June or July.

But whatever the weather was, orders were given that night that one of the outdoor men was to go over to Plaudry first thing the next morning.

Monsieur had a bad night, a touch of gout, and he could not get to sleep till very late, or rather early. So Madame told us when we met at table for the eleven o'clock *big* breakfast.

'He only awoke an hour ago, and I wanted him to stay in bed all day,' she said. 'But he would not consent to do so. Ah! there he comes,' as our host at that moment entered the room with apologies for his tardiness.

The wind had gone down, though in the night it had been fiercer than ever; but it was still raining pitilessly.

'I do hope the storm is over,' said Virginie. 'Last night, when I was saying my prayers, it almost frightened me. I really thought I felt the walls rocking.'

'Nonsense, child!' said her grandfather, sharply. Incipient gout is not a sweetener of the temper. But Virginie's remark had reminded him of something.

'Has Jean Pierre come back from Plaudry?' he asked the servant behind his chair; 'and what message did he bring?'

Alphonse started. He had been entrusted with a message, though not the one expected, but had forgotten to give it.

'He did not go, Monsieur,' he said; hastily adding, before there was time for his master to begin to storm. 'There was no need. Old Gervais was here this morning—very early, before it was light almost; so Nicolas'—Nicolas was the bailiff—'said no one need go.'

'Oh—ah, well,' said Monsieur, mollified. 'Then tell Gervais I want to speak to him before he leaves.'

Then Alphonse looked slightly uneasy.

'He is gone already, unfortunately—before Monsieur's bell rang. He must have had but little to do—by eight o'clock, or before, he was gone.'

Monsieur de Viremont looked annoyed.

'Very strange,' he said, 'when he left word he would explain all to me. Did you see him? Did he say nothing?'

No, Alphonse had not seen him—he had only heard him knocking. But he would enquire more particularly if there was no message.

He came back in a few moments, looking perplexed. *No one*, it appeared, had really seen the mason; no one, at least, except a little lad, Denis by name—who worked in the garden—'the little fellow who sings in the choir', said Alphonse. He—Denis—had seen Gervais' face from the garden, at the window. And he had called out, 'Good morning,' but Gervais did not answer.

'And the work is completed? Has he perhaps left his tools? If so, he may be coming back again,' asked Monsieur.

Alphonse could not say. Impatient, the old gentleman rose from the table, and went off to make direct enquiry.

'Very odd, very odd indeed,' he said when he returned and sat down again. 'To all appearance, the work is exactly as it was when he left it three days ago. Not tidied up or finished. And yet the cook and all heard him knocking for two hours certainly, and the child, Denis, saw him.'

'I dare say he will be returning,' said Madame, soothingly. 'Let us wait till this evening.'

So they did; but no Gervais came back, and the rain went on falling, chill, drearily monotonous.

Just before dinner Monsieur summoned the bailiff.

'Someone must go first thing tomorrow,' he began at once, when Nicolas appeared, 'and tell Gervais sharply that I won't be played the fool with. What has come over the old fellow?'

'No, Monsieur, certainly not. Monsieur's orders must be treated with respect,' replied Nicolas, ignoring for the moment his master's last few words. 'But—' and then we noticed that he was looking pale. 'Someone has just called in from Plaudry—a neighbour—he thought we should like to know. Gervais is *dead*—he died last night. He has been ill these three days—badly ill; the heart, they say. And the weather has stopped people coming along the roads as much as usual, else we should have heard. Poor old Gervais—peace to his soul.' And Nicolas crossed himself.

'*Dead!*' Monsieur repeated.

'*Dead!*' we all echoed.

It seemed incredible. Monsieur, I know, wished he had not spoken so sharply.

'Virginie, Jeanette,' whispered Albertine. 'It must have been his ghost!'

But she would not have dared to say so to her grandfather.

'It is sad, very sad,' said Monsieur and Madame. Then a few directions were given to the bailiff, to offer any help she might be in want of, to the poor widow, and Nicolas was dismissed.

'It just shows what imagination will do,' said Monsieur; 'all these silly servants believing they heard him, when it was *impossible*.'

'Yes,' whispered Albertine again, 'and Denis Blanc, who saw him. And Denis, who is so truthful; a little saint indeed! You know, Virginie, the boy with the lovely voice.'

Virginie bent her head in assent, but said nothing. And the subject was not referred to again that evening.

But—.

The storm was over, next day was cloudless, seeming as if such things as wind and rain and weather fury had never visited this innocent-looking world before. Again we went off to a neighbouring château, returning late and tired, and we all slept soundly. Again an exquisite day. Monsieur was reading aloud to us in the salon that evening; it was nearly bedtime, when a sort of skirmish and rush— hushed, yet excited voices, weeping even—were heard outside.

Monsieur stopped. 'What is it?' he said. Then rising, he went to the door.

A small crowd of servants was gathered there, arguing, vociferating, yet with a curious hush over it all.

'What is it?' repeated the master sternly.

Then it broke out. They could stand it no longer; something must be done; though Monsieur had forbidden them to talk nonsense—it was not nonsense, only too true.

'*What?*' thundered the old gentleman.

About Gervais. He was there again—at the present moment. He had been there the night before, but no one had dared to tell. He had returned, no notice having been taken of his first warning. And he *would* return. There now, if every one would be perfectly still, even here, his knockings could be heard.

The speaker was the cook. And truly, as an uncanny silence momentarily replaced the muffled hubbub, far-off yet distinct taps, coming from below, were to be heard.

'Some trick,' said Monsieur. 'Let us go down, all of us together, and get to the bottom of this affair.'

He led the way; we women, and after us the crowd of terrified servants, following. Monsieur paused at the kitchen door.

'It is dark in the "cave",' he said.

'No, no' cried the cook. 'There is a beautiful moon. Not a light, pray Monsieur; he might not like it.'

All was silent.

We reached the cellar, and entered it a little way. Quite a distance off, so it seemed, was the arched window, the moonlight gleaming through it eerily, the straggling ivy outside taking strange black shapes; but no one to be seen, nothing to be heard.

Ah, what was that? The knocking again, unmistakable, distinct, *real*. And why did one side of the window grow dark, as if suddenly thrown into shadow? Was there *something* intercepting the moonlight? It seemed misty, or was it partly that we scarcely dared look?

Then, to our surprise, the grandfather's voice sounded out clearly.

'Virginie, my child,' he said, 'you are the youngest, the most guileless, perhaps the one who has least cause for fear. Would you dread to step forward and—*speak?* If so be it is a message from the poor fellow, let him tell it. Show every one that those who believe in the good God need not be afraid.'

Like a white angel, Virginie, in her light summer dress, glided forward, silent. She walked straight on; then, rather to our surprise, she crossed the floor, and stood almost out of sight in the dark corner, at the further side of the window. Then she spoke—

'Gervais, my poor Gervais,' she said. 'Is it you? I think I see you, but I cannot be sure. What is troubling you, my friend? What is keeping you from your rest?'

Then all was silent again. I should have said that as Virginie went forward, the knocking ceased—*so* silent that we could almost hear our hearts beat. And then—Virginie was speaking again, and *not repeating her questions!* When we realized this, it did seem awful. She was carrying on a conversation. *She had been answered.*

What she said I cannot recall. Her voice was lower now; it sounded almost dreamy. And in a moment or two she came back to us, straight to her grandfather.

'I will tell you all,' she said. 'Come upstairs—all will be quiet now,' she added, in a tone almost of command, to the awestruck servants. And upstairs she told.

'I do not know if he spoke,' she said, in answer to Albertine's eager enquiries. 'I cannot tell. I know what he wanted, that is enough. No; I did not *exactly* see him; but—he was there.'

And this was the message, simple enough. The wall was *not* safe, though he had done what could be done to the stonework. Iron girders must be fixed and that without delay. He had felt too ill to go to the forge that night as he had intended, and the unfinished work, the possible danger, was sorely on his mind.

'He thanked me,' said Virginie, simply. 'He feared that grandfather would think all the solid work was done, and that the wall only needed finishing for appearance.'

As, indeed, Monsieur de Viremont *had* thought.

Afterwards the old woman told us a little more. Gervais had been alternately delirious and unconscious these two or three days. He had talked about the work at Viremont, but she thought it raving, till just at the last he tried to whisper something, and she saw he was clear-headed again, about letting Monsieur know. She had meant to do so

when her own first pressure of grief and trouble was over. She never
knew that the warning had been forestalled.

That is all. And it was long ago, and there are thrillingly sensational
ghost-stories to be had by the score nowadays. It seems nothing. But I
have always thought it touching and impressive, knowing it to be true.

If I have wearied you by my old woman's garrulity, forgive it. It has
been a pleasure to me to recall those days.

Your ever affectionate,

JANET MARIE BETHUNE

9

HUME NISBET

The Phantom Model

A WAPPING ROMANCE

I

The Studio

'Rhoda is a very nice girl in her way, Algy, my boy, and poses wonderfully, considering the hundreds of times she has had to do it; but she isn't the model for that Beatrice of yours, and if you want to make a hit of it, you must go further afield, and hook a face not quite so familiar to the British Public.'

It was a large apartment, one of a set of studios in the artistic barrack off the Fulham Road, which the landlord, himself a theatrical Bohemian of the first class, has rushed up for the accommodation of youthful luminaries who are yet in the nebulous stage of their Art-course. Each of these hazy specks hopes to shine out a full-lustred star in good time; they have all a proper contempt also for those servile daubsters who consent to the indignity of having RA added to their own proper, or assumed, names. Most of them belong to the advanced school of Impressionists, and allow, with reservations, that Jimmy Whitetuft has genius, as they know that he is the most generous, as well as the most epigrammatical, of painters, while Rhoda, the model, also knows that he is the kindest and most chivalrous of patrons, who stands more of her caprices than most of her other masters do, allows her more frequent as well as longer rests in the two hours' sitting, and can always be depended upon for a half-crown on an emergency; good-natured, sardonic Jimmy Whitetuft, who can well appreciate the caprices of any woman, or butterfly of the hour, seeing that he has so many of them himself.

174

Rhoda Prettyman is occupied at the present moment in what she likes best, warming her young, lithe, Greek-like figure at the stove, while she puffs out vigorous wreaths of smoke from the cigarette she has picked up at the table, in the passing from the dais to the stove. She is perfect in face, hair, figure, and colour, not yet sixteen, and greatly in demand by artists and sculptors; a good girl and a merry one, who prefers bitter beer to champagne, a night in the pit to the ceremony of a private box, with a dozen or so of oysters afterwards at a little shop, rather than run her entertainer into the awful expense of a supper at the Criterion or Gatti's. Her father and mother having served as models before her, she has been accustomed to the disporting of her charms *à la vue* on raised daises from her tenderest years, and to the *patois* of the studios since she could lisp, so that she is as unconscious as a Solomon Island young lady in the bosom of her own family, and can patter 'Art' as fluently as any picture dealer in the land.

They are all smoking hard, while they criticize the unfinished Exhibition picture of their host, Algar Gray, during this rest time of the model; Rhoda has not been posing for that picture now, for at the present time the studio is devoted to a life-club, and Rhoda has been hired for this purpose by those hard-working students, who form the young school. Jimmy Whitetuft is the visitor who drops in to cut them up; a marvellous eye for colour and effect Jimmy has, and they are happy in his friendly censorship.

All round the room the easels are set up, with their canvases, in a half-moon range, and on these canvases Rhoda can see herself as in half-a-dozen mirrors, reflected in the same number of different styles as well as postures, for these students aim at originality. But the picture which now occupies their attention is a bishop, half-length, in the second working upon which the well-known features and figure of Rhoda are depicted in thirteenth-century costume as the Beatrice of Dante, and while the young painter looks at his stale design with discontented eyes, his friends act the part of Job's comforters.

'There isn't a professional model in London who can stand for Beatrice, if you want to make her live. They have all been in too many characters already. You must have something fresh.'

'Yes, I know,' muttered Algar Gray. 'But where the deuce shall I find her?'

'Go to the country. You may see something there,' suggested Jack Brunton, the landscapist. 'I always manage to pick up something fresh in the country.'

'The country be blowed for character,' growled Will Murray. 'Go to the East End of London, if you want a proper Beatrice; to the half-starved crew, with their big eyes and thin cheeks. That's the sort of thing to produce the spiritual longing, wistful look you want. I saw one the other day, near the Thames Tunnel, while I was on the prowl, who would have done exactly.'

'What was she?' asked Algar eagerly.

'A Ratcliff Highway stroller, I should say. At any rate, I met her in one of the lowest pubs, pouring down Irish whiskey by the tumbler, with never a wink, and using the homespun in a most delectable fashion. Her mate might have served for Semiramis, and she took four ale from the quart pot, but the other, the Beatrice, swallowed her dose neat, and as if it had been cold water from one of the springs of Paradise where, in olden times, she was wont to gather flowers.'

'Good Heavens! Will, you are atrocious. The sentiment of Dante would be killed by such a woman.'

'Realistic, dear boy, that's all. You will find very exquisite flowers sometimes even on a dust-heap, as well as where humanity grows thickest and rankest. We have all to go through the different stages of earthly experience, according to Blavatsky. This Beatrice may have been the original of Dante in the thirteenth century, now going through her Wapping experience. It seems nasty, yet it may be necessary.'

'What like was she?'

'What sort of an ideal had you when you first dreamt of that picture, Algy?'

'A tall, slender woman, of about twenty or twenty-two, graceful and refined, with pale face blue-veined and clear, with dark hair and eyes indifferent as to shade, yet out-looking—a soulful gaze from a classical, passive and passionless face.'

'That is exactly the Beatrice of the East End shanty and the Irish whiskey, the sort of holy after-death calm pervading her, the alabaster-lamp-like complexion lit up by pure spirits undiluted, the general dreamy, indifferent pose—it was all there when I first saw her, only a battle royal afterwards occurred between her and the Amazon over a sailor, during which the alabaster lamp flamed up and Semiramis came off second best; for commend me to your spiritual demons when claws and teeth are wanted. No matter, I have found your model for you; take a turn with me this evening and I'll perhaps be able to point her out to you, the after negotiations I leave in your own romantic hands.'

II

Dante in the Inferno

It is a considerable distance from the Fulham Road to Wapping even going by 'bus, but as the two artist friends went, it was still further and decidedly more picturesque.

They were both young men under thirty. Art is not so precocious as literature, and does not send quite so many early potatoes into the market, so that the age of thirty is considered young enough for a painter to have learnt his business sufficiently to be marketable from the picture-dealing point of view.

Will Murray was the younger of the two by a couple of years, but as he had been sent early to fish in the troubled waters of illustration, and forced to provide for himself while studying, he looked much the elder; of a more realistic and energetic turn, he did not indulge in dreams of painting any single *magnum opus*, with which he would burst upon an astonished and enthusiastic world, he could not afford to dream, for he had to work hard or go fasting, and so the height of his aspirations was to paint well enough to win a note of approval from his own particular school, and keep the pot boiling with black and white work.

Algar Gray was a dreamer on five hundred per year, the income beneficent Fortune had endowed him with by reason of his lucky birth; he did not require to work for his daily bread, and as he had about as much prospect of selling his paint-creations, or imitations, as the other members of this new school, he spent the time he was not painting in dreaming about a possible future.

It wasn't a higher ideal, this brooding over fame, than the circumscribed ideal of Will Murray; each member of that young school was too staunch to his principles, and idealized his art as represented by canvas and paints too highly to care one jot about the pecuniary side of it; they painted their pictures as the true poet writes his poems, because it was right in their eyes; they held exhibitions, and preached their canons to a blinded public; the blinded public did not purchase, or even admire; but all that did not matter to the exhibitors so long as they had enough left to pay for more canvases and frames.

Will Murray was keen sighted and blue-eyed, robust in body and for ever on the alert for fresh material to fill his sketch-book. Algar Gray was dark to swarthiness, with long, thin face, rich-toned, melancholy eyes, and slender figure; he did not jot down trifles as did his friend, he absorbed the general effect and seldom produced his sketching-block.

Having time on their hands and a glorious October evening before them, they walked to Fulham Wharf and, hiring a wherry there, resolved to go by the old water way to the Tower, and after that begin their search for the Spiritual, through the Inferno of the East.

There is no river in the world to be compared for majesty and the witchery of association, to the Thames; it impresses even the unreading and unimaginative watcher with a solemnity which he cannot account for, as it rolls under his feet and swirls past the buttresses of its many bridges; he may think, as he experiences the unusual effect, that it is the multiplicity of buildings which line its banks, or the crowd of sea-craft which floats upon its surface, or its own extensive spread. In reality he feels, although he cannot explain it, the countless memories which hang for ever like a spiritual fog over its rushing current.

This unseen fog closes in upon the two friends as they take up their oars and pull out into mid-stream; it is a human fog which depresses and prepares them for the scenes into which they must shortly add their humanity; there is no breaking away from it, for it reaches up to Oxford and down to Sheppey, the voiceless thrilling of past voices, the haunting chill of dead tragedies, the momentous hush of acted history.

It wafts towards them on the brown sails of the gliding barges where the solitary figures stand upright at the stern like so many Charons steering their hopeless freights; it shapes the fantastic clouds of dying day overhead, from the fumes of countless fires, and the breaths from countless lips, it is the overpowering absorption of a single soul composed of many parts; the soul of a great city, past and present, of a mighty nation with its crowded events, crushing down upon the heart of a responsive stream, and this is the mystic power of the pulsating, eternal Thames.

They bear down upon Westminster, the ghost-consecrated Abbey, and the history-crammed Hall, through the arches of the bridge with a rush as the tide swelters round them; the city is buried in a dusky gloom save where the lights begin to gleam and trail with lurid reflections past black velvety-looking hulls—a dusky city of golden gleams. St Paul's looms up like an immense bowl reversed, squat, un-English, and undignified in spite of its great size; they dart within the sombre shadows of the Bridge of Sighs, and pass the Tower of London, with the rising moon making the sky behind it luminous, and the crowd of shipping in front appear like a dense forest of withered pines, and then mooring their boat at the steps beyond, with a shuddering farewell look at the eel-like shadows and the glittering lights of that writhing river, with its burthen seen and invisible, they plunge into the purlieus of Wapping.

Through silent alleys where dark shadows fleeted past them like forest beasts on the prowl; through bustling market-places where bloaters predominated, into crammed gin-palaces where the gas flashed over faces whereon was stamped the indelible impression of a protest against creation; brushing tatters which were in gruesome harmony with the haggard or bloated features.

Will Murray was used to this medley and pushed on with a definite purpose, treating as burlesque what made the dreamer groan with impotent fury that so dire a poverty, so unspeakable a degradation, could laugh and seem hilarious even under the fugitive influence of Old Tom. They were not human beings these breathing and roaring masses, they were an appalling army of spectres grinning at an abashed Maker.

'Here we are at last, Algy,' observed Will, cheerily, as the pair pushed through the swinging doors of a crammed bar and approached the counter, 'and there is your Beatrice.'

III
The Picture

The impressionists of Fulham Road knew Algy Gray no more, after that first glimpse which he had of Beatrice. His studio was once again to let, for he had removed his baggage and tent eastward, so as to be near the woman who would not and could not come West.

His first impressions of her might have cured many a man less refined or sensitive;—a tall young woman with pallid face leaning against the bar and standing treat to some others of her kind; drinking furiously, while from her lips flowed a husky torrent of foulness, unrepeatable; she was in luck when he met her, and enjoying a holiday with some of her own sex, and therefore wanted no male interference for that night, so she repulsed his advances with frank brutality, and forced him to retire from her side baffled.

Yet, if she offended his refined ears, there was nothing about her to offend his artistic eyes; she had no ostrich feathers in her hat, and no discordancy about the colours of her shabby costume; it was plain and easy-fitting, showing the grace of her willowy shape; her features were statuesque, and as Will had said, alabaster-like in their pure pallor.

That night Algar Gray followed her about, from place to place, watching her beauty hungrily even while he wondered at the unholy thirst that possessed her, and which seemed to be sateless, a quenchless desire which gave her no rest, but drove her from bar to bar, while her money lasted; she appeared to him like a soulless being, on whom neither fatigue nor debauchery could take effect.

At length, as midnight neared, she turned to him with a half smile and beckoned him towards her; she had ignored him hitherto, although she knew he was hunting her down.

'I say, matey, I'm stumped up, so you can stand me some drink if you like.'

She laughed scornfully when she saw him take soda water for his share, it was a weakness which she could neither understand nor appreciate.

'You ain't Jacky the Terror, are you?' she enquired carelessly as she asked him for another drink.

'Certainly not, why do you ask?'

''Cos you stick so close to me. I thought perhaps you had spotted me out for the next one, not that I care much whether you are or not, now that my money is done.'

His heart thrilled at the passivity of her loneliness as he looked at her; she had accepted his companionship with indifference, unconscious of her own perfection, utterly apathetic to everything; she a woman that nothing could warm up.

She led him to the home which she rented, a single attic devoid of furniture, with the exception of a broken chair and dilapidated table, and a mattress which was spread out in the corner, a wretched nest for such a matchless Beatrice.

And as she reclined on the mattress and drank herself to sleep from the bottle which she had made him buy for her, he sat at the table, and while the tallow candle lasted, he watched her, and sketched her in his pocket-book, after which, when the candle had dropped to the bottom of the bottle which served as a candle stick, and the white moonlight fell through the broken window upon that pure white slumbering face, so still and death-like, he crept softly down the stairs, thralled with but one idea.

Next day when he came again she greeted him almost affectionately, for she remembered his lavishness the night before and was grateful for the refreshment which he sent out for her. Yes, she had no objections to let him paint her if he paid well for it, and came to her, but she wasn't going out of her beat for any man; so finding that there was another attic in the same house to let, he hired it, got the window altered to suit him and set to work on his picture.

The model, although untrained, was a patient enough sitter to Algar Gray when the mood took her, but she was very variable in her moods, and uncertain in her temper, as spirit-drunkards mostly are. Sometimes she was reticent and sullen, and would not be coaxed or bribed into obedience to his wishes, at other times she was lazy and would not stir from her own mattress, where she lay like a lovely savage, letting him admire her transparent skin, with the blue veins intersecting it, and a luminous glow pervading it, until his spirit melted within him, and he grew almost as purposeless as she was.

Under these conditions the picture did not advance very fast, for now November was upon them with its fogs. Very often on the days when she felt amiable enough to sit, he had no light to take advantage of her mood, while at other times she was either away drinking with her own kind or else sulking in her bleak den.

If he wondered at first how she could keep the purity of her complexion with the life she led or how she never appeared overcome with the quantity of spirits she consumed, he no longer did so since she had given him her confidence.

She was a child of the slums in spite of her refinement of face, figure and neatness of attire; who, six years before had been given up by the doctors for consumption, and informed that she had not four months of life left. Previous to this medical verdict she had worked at a match factory, and been fairly well conducted, but with the recklessness of her kind, who resemble sailors closely, she had pitched aside caution, resolved to make the most of her four months left, and so abandoned herself to the life she was still leading.

She had existed almost entirely upon raw spirits for the past six years, surprised herself that she had lived so long past her time, yet expecting death constantly; she was as one set apart by Death, and no power could reclaim her from that doom, a reckless, condemned prisoner, living under a very uncertain reprieve, and without an emotion or a desire left except the vain craving to deaden thought, and be able to die *game*, a craving which would not be satisfied.

Algar Gray, for the sake of an ideal, had linked himself to a soul already damned, which still held on to its fragile casement, a soul which was dragging him down to her own hell; her very cold indifference to him drew him after her, and enslaved him, her unholy transparent loveliness bewitched him, and the foulness of her lips and language no longer caused him a shudder, since it could not alter her exquisite lines or those pearly tints which defied his palette; and yet he did not love the woman; his whole desire was to transfer her perfection to his canvas before grim Death came to snatch her clay from the vileness of its surroundings.

IV

A Lost Soul

December and January had passed with clear, frosty skies, and the picture of Beatrice was at length ready for the Exhibition.

When a man devotes himself body and spirit to a single object, if he has training and aptitude, no matter how mediocre he may be in ordinary affairs, he will produce something so nearly akin to a work of genius as to deceive half the judges who think themselves competent to decide between genius and talent.

Algar Gray had studied drawing at a good training-school, and was acknowledged by competent critics to be a true colourist, and for the last three months he had lived for the picture which he had just completed, therefore the result was satisfactory even to him. Beatrice, the ideal love of Dante, looked out from his canvas in the one attic of this Wapping slum, while Beatrice, the model, lay dead on her old mattress in the other.

He had attempted to make her home more home-like and comfortable for her, but without success; what he ordered from the upholsterer she disposed of promptly to the brokers, laughing scornfully at his efforts to redeem her, and mocking coarsely at his remonstrances, as she always had done at his temperate habits. He was not of her kind, and she had no sympathy with him, or in any of his ways; she had tolerated him only for the money he was able to give her and so had burnt herself out of life without a kindly word or thought about him.

She had died as she wished to do, that is, she had passed away silently and in the darkness leaving him to discover what was left of her, in the chill of a winter morning, a corpse not whiter or less luminous than she had been in life, with the transparent neck and delicate arms, blue-veined and beautiful, and the face composed with the immortal air of quiet which it had always possessed.

She had lasted just long enough to enable him to put the finishing touches upon her replica, and now that the undertakers had taken away the matchless original, he thought that he might return to his own people, and take with him the object which he had coveted and won. The woman herself seemed nothing to him while she lay waiting upon her last removal in the room next to his, but now that it was empty, and only her image remained before him, he was strangely dissatisfied and restless.

He had caught the false appearance of purity which was about her, but all unaware to himself, this constant communication of the more natural part had been absorbed into his being, until now the picture looked like a body waiting for the return of its own mocking spirit, and for the first time, regretful wishes began to tug at his heartstrings; it was no longer the Beatrice of Dante that he wanted, but the Beatrice who had mockingly enslaved him with her vileness, and whom he had permitted to escape from him for an ideal, she who had never tempted him in life, was now tormenting him past endurance with hopeless longings.

He had gone out that afternoon with the intention of returning to his studio in the West End, and making arrangements for bringing his picture there, but after wandering aimlessly about the evil haunts where he had so often followed his late model, he found that he could not tear himself from that dismal round. A shadowy form seemed to glide before him from one gin-palace to another as she had done in life; the places where she had leaned against the bars seemed still to be occupied by her cold and mocking presence, no longer passive, but repulsing him as she had done in the early part of the first night, while he grew hungry and eager for her friendship.

She was before him on the pavement as he turned towards his attic; her husky, oath-clogged voice sounded in his ears as he passed an alley, and when he rushed forward to seize her, two other women fled from him out of the gloom with shrieks of fear. All the voices of these unfortunates are alike, and he had made a mistake.

The ice had given way on the morning of her death, and the streets were now slushy and wet, with a drizzling fog obscuring objects, so that only an instinct led him back to his temporary studio; he would draw down his blind and light his lamp, and spend the last evening of the slums in looking at his work.

It appeared almost a perfect piece of painting, and likely to attract much notice when it was exhibited. The dress which Beatrice had worn still lay over the back of the chair near the door, where she had carelessly flung it when last she took it off. He turned his back to the dress-covered chair and looked at the picture. Yes, it was the Beatrice whom Dante yearned over all his life—as she appeared to him at the bridge, with the same pure face and pathetic eyes, but not the Beatrice whom he, Algar Gray, passed over while she lived, and now longed for with such unutterable longing when it was too late.

He flung himself down before his *magnum opus*, and buried his face in his hands with passionate and hopeless regret.

Was that a husky laugh down in the court below, on the stairs, or in the room beside him?—her devil's laugh when she would go her own way in spite of his remonstrances.

He raised his head and looked behind him to where the dress had been lying crumpled and away from his picture. God of Heaven! his dead model had returned and now stood at the open door beckoning upon him to come to her, with her lovely transparent arm bare to the elbow, and once more dressed in the costume which she had cast aside.

He looked no more at his replica, but followed the mocking spirit down the stairs, into the fog-wrapped alley, and onwards where she led him.

Down towards Wapping Old Stairs, where the shapeless hulks of the ships and barges loomed out from the swirling, rushing black river like ghosts, as she was, who floated towards them, luring him downwards, amongst the slime, to the abyss from which her lost soul had been recalled by his evil longings.

10

VINCENT O'SULLIVAN

When I Was Dead

'And yet my heart
Will not confess he owes the malady
That doth my life besiege.'
All's Well that Ends Well

That was the worst of Ravenel Hall. The passages were long and gloomy, the rooms were musty and dull, even the pictures were sombre and their subjects dire. On an autumn evening, when the wind soughed and wailed through the trees in the park, and the dead leaves whistled and chattered, while the rain clamoured at the windows, small wonder that folks with gentle nerves went a-straying in their wits! An acute nervous system is a grievous burthen on the deck of a yacht under sunlit skies: at Ravenel the chain of nerves was prone to clash and jangle a funeral march. Nerves must be pampered in a tea-drinking community; and the ghost that your grandfather, with a skinful of port, could face and never tremble, sets you, in your sobriety, sweating and shivering; or, becoming scared (poor ghost!) of your bulged eyes and dropping jaw, he quenches expectation by not appearing at all. So I am left to conclude that it was tea which made my acquaintance afraid to stay at Ravenel. Even Wilvern gave over; and as he is in the Guards, and a polo player his nerves ought to be strong enough. On the night before he went I was explaining to him my theory, that if you place some drops of human blood near you, and then concentrate your thoughts, you will after a while see before you a man or a woman who will stay with you during long hours of the night, and even meet you at unexpected places during the day. I was explaining this theory, I repeat, when he interrupted me with words, senseless enough, which sent me fencing and parrying strangers,—on my guard.

'I say, Alistair, my dear chap!' he began, 'you ought to get out of this place and go up to Town and knock about a bit—you really ought, you know.'

'Yes,' I replied, 'and get poisoned at the hotels by bad food and at the clubs by bad talk, I suppose. No, thank you: and let me say that your care for my health enervates me.'

'Well, you can do as you like,' says he, rapping with his feet on the floor. 'I'm hanged if I stay here after tomorrow—I'll be staring mad if I do!'

He was my last visitor. Some weeks after his departure I was sitting in the library with my drops of blood by me. I had got my theory nearly perfect by this time; but there was one difficulty.

The figure which I had ever before me was the figure of an old woman with her hair divided in the middle, and her hair fell to her shoulders, white on one side and black on the other. She was a very complete old woman; but, alas! she was eyeless, and when I tried to construct the eyes she would shrivel and rot in my sight. But tonight I was thinking, thinking, as I had never thought before, and the eyes were just creeping into the head when I heard a terrible crash outside as if some heavy substance had fallen. Of a sudden the door was flung open and two maid-servants entered. They glanced at the rug under my chair, and at that they turned a sick white, cried on God, and huddled out.

'How dare you enter the library in this manner?' I demanded sternly. No answer came back from them, so I started in pursuit. I found all the servants in the house gathered in a knot at the end of the passage.

'Mrs Pebble,' I said smartly, to the housekeeper, 'I want those two women discharged tomorrow. It's an outrage! You ought to be more careful.'

But she was not attending to me. Her face was distorted with terror.

'Ah dear, ah dear!' she went. 'We had better all go to the library together,' says she to the others.

'Am I master of my own house, Mrs Pebble?' I enquired, bringing my knuckles down with a bang on the table.

None of them seemed to see me or hear me: I might as well have been shrieking in a desert. I followed them down the passage, and forbade them with strong words to enter the library. But they trooped past me, and stood with a clutter round the hearthrug. Then three or four of them began dragging and lifting, as if they were lifting a helpless body, and stumbled with their imaginary burthen over to a sofa. Old Soames, the butler, stood near.

'Poor young gentleman!' he said with a sob. 'I've knowed him since he was a baby. And to think of him being dead like this—and so young, too!'

I crossed the room. 'What's all this, Soames?' I cried, shaking him roughly by the shoulders. 'I'm not dead. I'm here—here!' As he did not stir I got a little scared. 'Soames, old friend!' I called, 'don't you know me? Don't you know the little boy you used to play with? Say I'm not dead, Soames, please, Soames!'

He stooped down and kissed the sofa. 'I think one of the men ought to ride over to the village for the doctor, Mr Soames,' says Mrs Pebble; and he shuffled out to give the order.

Now, this doctor was an ignorant dog, whom I had been forced to exclude from the house because he went about proclaiming his belief in a saving God, at the same time that he proclaimed himself a man of science. He, I was resolved, should never cross my threshold, and I followed Mrs Pebble through the house, screaming out prohibition. But I did not catch even a groan from her, not a nod of the head, nor a cast of the eye, to show that she had heard.

I met the doctor at the door of the library. 'Well,' I sneered, throwing my hand in his face, 'have you come to teach me some new prayers?'

He brushed by me as if he had not felt the blow, and knelt down by the sofa.

'Rupture of a vessel on the brain, I think,' he says to Soames and Mrs Pebble after a short moment. 'He has been dead some hours. Poor fellow! You had better telegraph for his sister, and I will send up the undertaker to arrange the body.'

'You liar!' I yelled. 'You whining liar! How have you the insolence to tell my servants that I am dead, when you see me here face to face?'

He was far in the passage, with Soames and Mrs Pebble at his heels, ere I had ended, and not one of the three turned round.

All that night I sat in the library. Strangely enough, I had no wish to sleep nor during the time that followed, had I any craving to eat. In the morning the men came, and although I ordered them out, they proceeded to minister about something I could not see. So all day I stayed in the library or wandered about the house, and at night the men came again bringing with them a coffin. Then, in my humour, thinking it shame that so fine a coffin should be empty I lay the night in it and slept a soft dreamless sleep—the softest sleep I have ever slept. And when the men came the next day I rested still, and the undertaker shaved me. A strange valet!

On the evening after that, I was coming downstairs, when I noted some luggage in the hall, and so learned that my sister had arrived. I had not seen this woman since her marriage, and I loathed her more than I loathed any creature in this ill-organized world. She was very beautiful, I think—tall, and dark, and straight as a ram-rod—and she had an unruly passion for scandal and dress. I suppose the reason I disliked her so intensely was, that she had a habit of making one aware of her presence when she was several yards off. At half-past nine o'clock my sister came down to the library in a very charming wrap, and I soon found that she was as insensible to my presence as the others. I trembled with rage to see her kneel down by the coffin— my coffin; but when she bent over to kiss the pillow I threw away control.

A knife which had been used to cut string was lying upon a table: I seized it and drove it into her neck. She fled from the room screaming.

'Come! come!' she cried, her voice quivering with anguish. 'The corpse is bleeding from the nose.'

Then I cursed her.

On the morning of the third day there was a heavy fall of snow. About eleven o'clock I observed that the house was filled with blacks and mutes and folk of the county, who came for the obsequies. I went into the library and sat still, and waited. Soon came the men, and they closed the lid of the coffin and bore it out on their shoulders. And yet I sat, feeling rather sadly that something of mine had been taken away: I could not quite think what. For half-an-hour perhaps—dreaming,

dreaming: and then I glided to the hall door. There was no trace left of the funeral; but after a while I sighted a black thread winding slowly across the white plain.

'I'm not dead!' I moaned, and rubbed my face in the pure snow and tossed it on my neck and hair. 'Sweet God, I am not dead.'

11

BERNARD CAPES

Dark Dignum

'I'd not go nigher, sir,' said my landlady's father.

I made out his warning through the shrill piping of the wind; and stopped and took in the plunging seascape from where I stood. The boom of the waves came up from a vast distance beneath; sky and the horizon of running water seemed hurrying upon us over the lip of the rearing cliff.

'It crumbles!' he cried. 'It crumbles near the edge like as frosted mortar. I've seen a noble sheep, sir, eighty pound of mutton, browsing here one moment, and seen it go down the next in a puff of white dust. Hark to that! Do you hear it?'

Through the tumult of the wind in that high place came a liquid vibrant sound, like the muffled stroke of iron on an anvil. I thought it the gobble of water in clanging caves deep down below.

'It might be a bell,' I said.

The old man chuckled joyously. He was my cicerone for the nonce; had come out of his chair by the inglenook to taste a little the salt of life. The north-easter flashed in the white cataracts of his eyes and woke a feeble activity in his scrannel limbs. When the wind blew loud, his daughter had told me, he was always restless, like an imprisoned seagull. He would be up and out. He would rise and flap his old draggled pinions, as if the great air fanned an expiring spark into flame.

'It *is* a bell!' he cried—'the bell of old St Dunstan's, that was swallowed by the waters in the dark times.'

'Ah,' I said. 'That is the legend hereabouts.'

'No legend, sir—no legend. Where be the tombstones of drownded mariners to prove it such? Not one to forty that they has in

191

other seaboard parishes. For why? Dunstan bell sounds its warning, and not a craft will put out.'

'There is the storm cone,' I suggested.

He did not hear me. He was punching with his staff at one of a number of little green mounds that lay about us.

'I could tell you a story of these,' he said. 'Do you know where we stand?'

'On the site of the old churchyard?'

'Ay, sir; though it still bore the name of the *new* yard in my first memory of it.'

'Is that so? And what is the story?'

He dwelt a minute, dense with introspection. Suddenly he sat himself down upon a mossy bulge in the turf, and waved me imperiously to a place beside him.

'The old order changeth,' he said. 'The only lasting foundations of men's works shall be godliness and law-biding. Long ago they builded a new church—here, high up on the cliffs, where the waters could not reach; and, lo! the waters wrought beneath and sapped the foundations, and the church fell into the sea.'

'So I understand,' I said.

'The godless are fools,' he chattered knowingly. 'Look here at these bents—thirty of 'em, may be. Tombstones, sir; perished like man his works, and the decayed stumps of them coated with salt grass.'

He pointed to the ragged edge of the cliff a score paces away.

'They raised it out there,' he said, 'and further—a temple of bonded stone. They thought to bribe the Lord to a partnership in their corruption, and He answered by casting down the fair mansion into the waves.'

I said, 'Who—who, my friend?'

'They that builded the church,' he answered.

'Well,' I said. 'It seems a certain foolishness to set the edifice so close to the margin.'

Again he chuckled.

'It was close, close, as you say; yet none so close as you might think nowadays. Time hath gnawed here like a rat on a cheese. But the foolishness appeared in setting the brave mansion between the winds and its own graveyard. Let the dead lie seawards, one had thought, and the church inland where we stand. So had the bell rung to this day; and only the charnel bones flaked piecemeal into the sea.'

'Certainly, to have done so would show the better providence.'

'Sir, I said the foolishness *appeared*. But, I tell you, there was foresight in the disposition—in neighbouring the building to the cliff path. *For so they could the easier enter unobserved, and store their kegs of Nantes brandy in the belly of the organ.*'

'They? Who were they?'

'Why, who—but two-thirds of all Dunburgh?'

'Smugglers?'

'It was a nest of 'em—traffickers in the eternal fire o' weekdays, and on the Sabbath, who so sanctimonious? But honesty comes not from the washing, like a clean shirt, nor can the piety of one day purge the evil of six. They built their church anigh the margin, forasmuch as it was handy, and that they thought, "Surely the Lord will not undermine His own?" A rare community o' blasphemers, fro' the parson that took his regular toll of the organ-loft, to him that sounded the keys and pulled out the joyous stops as if they was so many spigots to what lay behind.'

'Of when do you speak?'

'I speak of nigh a century and a half ago. I speak of the time o' the Seven Years War and of Exciseman Jones, that, twenty year after he were buried, took his revenge on the cliff side of the man that done him to death.'

'And who was that?'

'They called him Dark Dignum, sir—a great feat smuggler, and as wicked as he was bold.'

'Is your story about him?'

'Ay, it is; and of my grandfather, that were a boy when they laid, and was glad to lay, the exciseman deep as they could dig; for the sight of his sooty face in his coffin was worse than a bad dream.'

'Why was that?'

The old man edged closer to me, and spoke in a sibilant voice.

'He were murdered, sir, foully and horribly, for all they could never bring it home to the culprit.'

'Will you tell me about it?'

He was nothing loth. The wind, the place of perished tombs, the very wild-blown locks of this 'withered apple-john', were eerie accompaniments to the tale he piped in my ear:

193

'When my grandfather were a boy,' he said, 'there lighted in Dunburgh Exciseman Jones. P'r'aps the village had gained an ill reputation. P'r'aps Exciseman Jones's predecessor had failed to secure the confidence o' the exekitive. At any rate, the new man was little to the fancy of the village. He was a grim, sour-looking, brass-bound galloot; and incorruptible—which was the worst. The keg o' brandy left on his doorstep o' New Year's Eve had been better unspilled and run into the gutter; for it led him somehow to the identification of the innocent that done it, and he had him by the heels in a twinkling. The squire snorted at the man, and the parson looked askance; but Dark Dignum, he swore he'd be even with him, if he swung for it. They were hurt and surprised, that was the truth, over the scrupulosity of certain people; and feelin' ran high against Exciseman Jones.

'At that time Dark Dignum was a young man with a reputation above his years for profaneness and audacity. Ugly things were said about him; and amongst many wicked he was feared for his wickedness. Exciseman Jones had his eye on him; and that was bad for Exciseman Jones.

'Now one murky December night Exciseman Jones staggered home with a bloody long slice down his scalp, and the red drip from it spotting the cobble-stones.

' "Summut fell on him from a winder," said Dark Dignum, a little later, as he were drinkin' hisself hoarse in the Black Boy. "Summat fell on him retributive, as you might call it. For, would you believe it, the man had at the moment been threatenin' me? He did. He said, 'I know damn well about you, Dignum; and for all your damn ingenuity, I'll bring you with a crack to the ground yet!' " '

'What had happened? Nobody knew, sir. But Exciseman Jones was in his bed for a fortnight; and when he got on his legs again, it was pretty evident there was a hate between the two men that only bloodspillin' could satisfy.

'So far as is known, they never spoke to one another again. They played their game of death in silence—the lawful, cold, and unfathomable; the unlawful, swaggerin', and crool—and twenty year separated the first move and the last.

'This were the first, sir—as Dark Dignum leaked it out long after in his cups. This were the first; and it brought Exciseman Jones to his grave on the cliff here.

'It were a deep soft summer night; and the young smuggler sat by hisself in the long room of the Black Boy. Now, I tell you he were a fox-ship intriguer—grand, I should call him, in the aloneness of his villainy. He would play his dark games out of his own hand; and sure, of all his wickedness, this game must have seemed the sum.

'I say he sat by hisself; and I hear the listening ghost of him call me a liar. For there were another body present, though invisible to mortal eye; and that second party were Exciseman Jones, who was hidden up the chimney.

'How had he inveigled him there? Ah, they've met and worried that point out since. No other will ever know the truth this side the grave. But reports come to be whispered; and reports said as how Dignum had made an appointment with a bodiless master of a smack as never floated, to meet him in the Black Boy and arrange for to run a cargo as would never be shipped; and that somehow he managed to acquent Exciseman Jones o' this dissembling appointment, and to secure his presence in hidin' to witness it.

'That's conjecture; for Dignum never let on so far. But what *is* known for certain is that Exciseman Jones, who were as daring and determined as his enemy—p'r'aps more so—for some reason was in the chimney, on to a grating in which he had managed to lower hisself from the roof; and that he could, if given time, have scrambled up again with difficulty, but was debarred from going lower. And, further, this is known—that, as Dignum sat on, pretendin' to yawn and huggin' his black intent, a little soot plopped down the chimney and scattered on the coals of the laid fire beneath.

'At that—"Curse this waitin"! said he. "The room's as chill as a belfry", and he got to his feet, with a secret grin, and strolled to the hearthstone.

' "I wonder," said he, "will the landlord object if I ventur' upon a glint of fire for comfort's sake?" and he pulled out his flint and steel, struck a spark, and with no more feeling than he'd express in lighting a pipe, set the flame to the sticks.

'The trapt rat above never stirred or give tongue. My God! what a man! Sich a nature could afford to bide and bide—ay, for twenty year, if need be.

'Dignum would have enjoyed the sound of a cry; but he never got it. He listened with the grin fixed on his face; and of a sudden he heard a scrambling struggle, like as a dog with the colic jumping at a wall; and presently, as the sticks blazed and the smoke rose denser, a thick coughin', as of a consumptive man under bedclothes. Still no cry, or any appeal for mercy; no, not from the time he lit the fire till a horrible rattle came down, which was the last twitches of somethin' that choked and died on the sooty gratin' above.

'When all was quiet, Dignum he knocks with his foot on the floor and sits hisself down before the hearth, with a face like a pillow for innocence.

' "I were chilled and lit it," says he to the landlord. "You don't mind?"

' "Mind? Who would have ventur'd to cross Dark Dignum's fancies?"

'He give a boisterous laugh, and ordered in a double noggin of humming stuff.

' "Here," he says, when it comes, "is to the health of Exciseman Jones, that swore to bring me to the ground."

' "To the ground," mutters a thick voice from the chimney.

' "My God!" says the landlord—"there's something up there!"

'Something there was; and terrible to look upon when they brought it to light. The creature's struggles had ground the soot into its face, and its nails were black below the quick.

'Were those words the last of its death-throe, or an echo from beyond? Ah! we may question; but they were heard by two men.

'Dignum went free. What could they prove agen him? Not that he knew there was aught in the chimney when he lit the fire. The other would scarcely have acquent him of his plans. And Exciseman Jones was hurried into his grave alongside the church up here.

'And therein he lay for twenty year, despite that, not a twelvemonth after his coming, the sacrilegious house itself sunk roaring into the waters. For the Lord would have none of it, and, biding His time, struck through a fortnight of deluge, and hurled church and cliff into ruin. But the yard remained, and, nighest the seaward edge of it, Exciseman Jones slept in his fearful winding sheet and bided *his* time.

'It came when my grandfather were a young man of thirty, and mighty close and confidential with Dark Dignum. God forgive him! Doubtless he were led away by the older smuggler, that had a grace of villainy about him, 'tis said, and used Lord Chesterfield's printed letters for wadding to his bullets.

'By then he was a ramping, roaring devil; but, for all his bold hands were stained with crime, the memory of Exciseman Jones and of his promise dwelled with him and darkened him ever more and more, and never left him. So those that knew him said.

'Now all these years the cliff edge agen the graveyard, where it was broke off, was scabbing into the sea below. But still they used this way of ascent for their ungodly traffic; and over the ruin of the cliff they had drove a new path for to carry up their kegs.

'It was a cloudy night in March, with scud and a fitful moon, and there was a sloop in the offing, and under the shore a loaded boat that had just pulled in with muffled rowlocks. Out of this Dark Dignum was the first to sling hisself a brace of rundlets; and my grandfather followed with two more. They made softly for the cliff path—began the ascent—was half-way up.

'Whiz!—a stone of chalk went by them with a skirl, and slapped into the rubble below.

' "Some more of St Dunstan's gravel!" cried Dignum, pantin' out a reckless laugh under his load; and on they went again.

'Hwish!—a bigger lump came like a thunderbolt, and the wind of it took the bloody smuggler's hat and sent it swooping into the darkness like a bird.

' "Thunder!" said Dignum; "the cliff's breaking away!"

'The words was hardly out of his mouth, when there flew such a volley of chalk stones as made my grandfather, though none had touched him, fall upon the path where he stood, and begin to gabble out what he could call to mind of the prayers for the dying. He was in the midst of it, when he heard a scream come from his companion as froze the very marrow in his bones. He looked up, thinkin' his hour had come.

'My God! What a sight he saw! The moon had shone out of a sudden, and the light of it struck down on Dignum's face, and that was the colour of dirty parchment. And he looked higher, and give a sort of sob.

'For there, stickin' out of the cliff side, was half the body of Exciseman Jones, with its arms stretched abroad, *and it was clawin' out lumps of chalk and hurling them down at Dignum!*

'And even as he took this in through his terror, a great ball of white came hurtling, and went full on to Dignum's face with a splash—and he were spun down into the deep night below, a nameless thing.'

The old creature came to a stop, his eyes glinting with a febrile excitement.

'And so,' I said, 'Exciseman Jones was true to his word?'

The tension of memory was giving—the spring slowly uncoiling itself.

'Ay,' he said doubtfully. 'The cliff had flaked away by degrees to his very grave. They found his skelington stickin' out of the chalk.'

'His *skeleton*?' said I, with the emphasis of disappointment.

'The first, sir, the first. Ay, his was the first. There've been a many exposed since. The work of decay goes on, and the bones they fall into the sea. Sometimes, sailing off shore, you may see a shank or an arm protrudin' like a pigeon's leg from a pie. But the wind or the weather takes it and it goes. There's more to follow yet. Look at 'em! look at these bents! Every one a grave, with a skelington in it. The wear and tear from the edge will reach each one in turn, and then the last of the ungodly will have ceased from the earth.'

'And what became of your grandfather?'

'My grandfather? There were something happened made him renounce the devil. He died one of the elect. His youth were heedless and unregenerate; but, 'tis said, after he were turned thirty he never smiled agen. There was a reason. Did I ever tell you the story of Dark Dignum and Exciseman Jones?'

12

RICHARD MARSH

The Fifteenth Man

THE STORY OF A RUGBY MATCH

It was not until we were actually in the field, and were about to begin to play, that I learnt that the Brixham men had come one short. It seemed that one of their men had been playing in a match the week before—in a hard frost, if you please! and, getting pitched on to his head, had broken his skull nearly into two clean halves. That is the worst of playing in a frost; you are nearly sure to come to grief. Not to ordinary grief, either, but a regular cracker. It was hard lines on the Brixham team. Some men always are getting themselves smashed to pieces just as a big match is due! The man's name was Joyce, Frank Joyce. He played half-back for Brixham, and for the county too—so you may be sure Lance didn't care to lose him. Still, they couldn't go and drag the man out of the hospital with a hole in his head big enough to put your fist into. They had tried to get a man to take his place, but at the last moment the substitute had failed to show.

'If we can't beat them—fifteen to their fourteen!—I think we'd better go in for challenging girls' schools. Last year they beat us, but this year, as we've one man to the good, perhaps we might manage to pull it off.'

That's how Mason talked to us, as if *we* wanted them to win! Although they were only fourteen men, they could play. I don't think I ever saw a team who were stronger in their forwards. Lance, their captain, kicked off; Mason, our chief, returned. Then one of their men, getting the leather, tried a run. We downed him, a scrimmage was formed, then, before we knew it, they were rushing the ball across the field. When it did show, I was on it like a flash. I passed to Mason. But he was collared almost before he had a chance to start. There was another turn at scrimmaging, and lively work it was, especially for us who had the pleasure of looking on. So, when again I got a sight of it, I didn't lose much time. I had it up, and I was off. I didn't pass; I tried a run upon my own account. I thought that I was clear away. I had passed the forwards; I thought that I had passed the field, when, suddenly, someone sprang at me, out of the fog—it was a little thick, you know—caught me round the waist, lifted me off my feet, and dropped me on my back. That spoilt it! Before I had a chance of passing they were all on top of me. And again the ball was in the scrimmage.

When I returned to my place behind I looked to see who it was had collared me. The fellow, I told myself, was one of their half-backs. Yet, when I looked at their halves, I couldn't make up my mind which of them it was.

Try how we could—although we had the best of the play—we couldn't get across their line. Although I say it, we all put in some first-rate work. We never played better in our lives. We all had run after run, the passing was as accurate as if it had been mechanical, and yet we could not do the trick. Time after time, just as we were almost in, one of their men put a stop to our little game, and spoilt us. The funny part of the business was that, either owing to the fog, or to our stupidity, we could not make up our minds which of their men it was.

At last I spotted him. Mason had been held nearly on their goal line. They were playing their usual game of driving us back in the scrimmage, when the ball broke through. I took it. I passed to Mason. I thought he was behind, when—he was collared and thrown.

'Joyce!' I cried. 'Why, I thought that you weren't playing.'

'What are you talking about?' asked one of their men. 'Joyce isn't playing.'

I stared.

'Not playing! Why, it was he who collared Mason.'

'Stuff!'

I did not think the man was particularly civil. It was certainly an odd mistake which I had made. I was just behind Mason when he was collared, and I saw the face of the man who collared him. I could have sworn it was Frank Joyce!

'Who was that who downed you just now?' I asked of Mason, directly I had the chance.

'Their half-back.'

Their half-back! Their halves were Tom Wilson and Granger. How could I have mistaken either of them for Joyce?

A little later Giffard was puzzled.

'One of their fellows plays a thundering good game, but, do you know, I can't make out which one of them it is.'

'Do you mean the fellow who keeps collaring.'

'That's the man!'

The curious part of it was that I never saw the man except when he was collaring.

'The next time,' said Giffard, when, for about the sixth time, he had been on the point of scoring, 'if I don't get in, I'll know the reason why. I'll kill that man.'

It was all very well to talk about our killing him. It looked very much more like his killing us. Mason passed the word that if there was anything like a chance we were to drop. The chance came immediately afterwards. They muffed somehow in trying to pass. Blaine got the leather. He started to run.

'Drop,' yelled Mason.

In that fog, and from where Blaine was, dropping a goal was out of the question. He tried the next best thing—he tried to drop into touch. But the attempt was a failure. The kick was a bad one—the ball was as heavy as lead, so that there was not much kick in it—and as it was coming down one of their men, appearing right on the spot, caught it, dropped a drop which was a drop, sent the ball right over our heads, and as near as a toucher over the bar.

Just then the whistle sounded.

'Do you know,' declared Ingall, as we were crossing over, 'I believe they're playing fifteen men.'

Mason scoffed.

'Do you think, without giving us notice, they would play fifteen when they told us they were only playing fourteen?'

'Hanged if I don't count them!' persisted Ingall.

He did, and we all did. We faced round and reckoned them up. There were only fourteen, unless one was slinking out of sight somewhere in the dim recesses of the fog, which seemed scarcely probable. Still Ingall seemed dissatisfied.

'They're playing four three-quarters,' whispered Giffard, when the game restarted.

So they were—Wheeler, Pendleton, Marshall, and another. Who the fourth man was I couldn't make out. He was a big, strapping fellow, I could see that; but the play was so fast that more than that I couldn't see.

'Who is the fourth man?'

'Don't know; can't see his face. It's so confoundedly foggy!'

It was foggy; but still, of course, it was not foggy enough to render a man's features indistinguishable at the distance of only a few feet. All the same, somehow or other he managed to keep his face concealed from us. While Giffard and I had been whispering they had been packing in. The ball broke out our side. I had it. I tried to run. Instantly I saw that fourth three-quarter rush at me. As he came I saw his face. I was so amazed that I stopped dead. Putting his arms about me he held me as in a vice.

'Joyce!' I cried.

Before the word was out of my mouth half a dozen of their men had hold of the ball.

'Held! held!' they screamed.

'Down!' I gasped.

And it was down, with two or three of their men on top of me. They were packing the scrimmage before I had time to get fairly on my feet again.

'That was Joyce who collared me!' I exclaimed.

'Pack in! pack in!' shouted Mason from behind.

And they did pack in with a vengeance. Giffard had the ball. They were down on him; it was hammer and tongs. But through it all we stuck to the leather. They downed us, but not before we had passed it to a friend. Out of it came Giffard, sailing along as though he had not been swallowing mud in pailfuls. I thought he was clear—but no! He stopped short, and dropped the ball!—dropped it, as he stood there, from his two hands as though he were a baby! They asked no questions. They had it up; they were off with it, as though they meant to carry it home. They carried it, too, all the way—almost! It was in disagreeable propinquity to our goal by the time that it was held.

'Now then, Brixham, you've got it!'

That was what they cried.

'Steyning! Steyning! All together!'

That was what we answered. But though we did work all together, it was as much as we could manage.

'Where's Giffard?' bellowed Mason.

My impression was that he had remained like a signpost rooted to the ground. I had seen him standing motionless after he had dropped the ball, and even as the Brixham men rushed past him. But just then he put in an appearance.

'I protest!' he cried.

'What about?' asked Mason.

'What do they mean by pretending they're not playing Frank Joyce when all the time they are?'

'Oh, confound Frank Joyce! Play up, do. You've done your best to give them the game already. Steady, Steyning, steady. Left, there, left. Centre, steady!'

We were steady. We were more than steady. Steadiness alone would not have saved us. We all played forward. At last, somehow, we got the ball back into something like the middle of the field. Giffard kept whispering to me all the time, even in the hottest of the rush.

'What lies, pretending that they're not playing Joyce!' Here he had a discussion with the ball, mostly on his knees. 'Humbug about his being in the hospital!'

We had another chance. Out of the turmoil, Mason was flying off with a lead. It was the first clear start he had that day. When he has got that it is catch him who catch can! As he pelted off the fog, which kept coming and going, all at once grew thicker. He had passed all their men. Of ours, I was the nearest to him. It looked all world to a china orange that we were going to score at last, when, to my disgust, he reeled, seemed to give a sort of spring, and then fell right over on to his back! I did not understand how he had managed to do it, but I supposed that he had slipped in the mud. Before I could get within passing distance the Brixham men were on us, and the ball was down.

'I thought you'd done it that time.'

I said this to him as the scrimmage was being formed. He did not answer. He stood looking about him in a hazy sort of way, as though the further proceedings had no interest for him.

'What's the matter? Are you hurt?'

He turned to me.

'Where is he?' he asked.

'Where's who?'

I couldn't make him out. There was quite a curious look upon his face.

'Joyce!'

Somehow, as he said this, I felt a trifle queer. It was his face, or his tone, or something. 'Didn't you see him throw me?'

I didn't know what he meant. But before I could say so we had another little rough and tumble—one go up and the other go down. A hubbub arose. There was Ingall shouting.

'I protest! I don't think this sort of thing's fair play.'

'What sort of thing?'

'You said you weren't playing Joyce.'

'*Said* we weren't! We aren't.'

'Why, he just took the ball out of my hands! Joyce, where are you?'

'Yes, where is he?'

Then they laughed. Mason intervened.

'Excuse me, Lance; we've no objection to your playing Joyce, but why do you say you aren't?'

'I don't think you're well. I tell you that Frank Joyce is at this moment lying in Brixham hospital.'

'He just now collared me.'

I confess that when Mason said that I was a trifle staggered. I had distinctly seen that he had slipped and fallen. No one had been within a dozen yards of him at the time. Those Brixham men told him so—not too civilly.

'Do you fellows mean to say,' he roared, 'that Frank Joyce didn't just now pick me up and throw me?'

I struck in.

'I mean to say so. You slipped and fell. My dear fellow, no one was near you at the time.'

He sprang round at me.

'Well, that beats anything!'

'At the same time,' I added, 'it's all nonsense to talk about Joyce being in Brixham hospital, because, since half-time at any rate, he's been playing three-quarter.'

'Of course he has,' cried Ingall. 'Didn't I see him?'

'And didn't he collar me?' asked Giffard.

The Brixham men were silent. We looked at them, and they at us.

'You fellows are dreaming,' said Lance. 'It strikes me that you don't know Joyce when you see him.'

'That's good,' I cried, 'considering that he and I were five years at school together.'

'Suppose you point him out then?'

'Joyce!' I shouted. 'You aren't ashamed to show your face, I hope?'

'Joyce!' they replied, in mockery. 'You aren't bashful, Joyce?'

He was not there. Or we couldn't find him, at any rate. We scrutinized each member of the team; it was really absurd to suppose that I could mistake any of them for Joyce. There was not the slightest likeness.

Dryall appealed to the referee.

'Are you sure nobody's sneaked off the field?'

'Stuff!' he said. 'I've been following the game all the time, and know every man who's playing, and Joyce hasn't been upon the ground.'

'As for his playing three-quarter, Pendleton, Marshall, and I have been playing three-quarter all the afternoon, and I don't think that either of us is very much like Joyce.'

This was Tom Wilson.

'You've been playing four three-quarters since we crossed over.'

'Bosh!' said Wilson.

That was good, as though I hadn't seen the four with my own eyes.

'Play!' sang out the referee. 'Don't waste any more time.'

We were at it again. We might be mystified. There was something about the whole affair which was certainly mysterious to me. But we did not intend to be beaten.

'They're only playing three three-quarters now,' said Giffard.

So they were. That was plain enough. I wondered if the fourth man had joined the forwards. But why should they conceal the fact that they had been playing four?

One of their men tried a drop. Mason caught it, ran, was collared, passed—wide to the left—and I was off. The whole crowd was in the centre of the field. I put on the steam. Lance came at me. I dodged, he missed. Pendleton was bearing down upon me from the right. I outpaced him. I got a lead. Only Rivers, their back, was between the Brixham goal and me. He slipped just as he made his effort. I was past. It was only a dozen yards to the goal. Nothing would stop me now. I was telling myself that the only thing left was the shouting, when, right in front of me, stood—Joyce! Where he came from I have not the least idea. Out of nothing, it seemed to me. He stood there, cool as a cucumber, waiting—as it appeared—until I came within his reach. His sudden appearance baulked me. I stumbled. The ball slipped from beneath my arm. I saw him smile. Forgetting all about the ball, I made a dash at him. The instant I did so he was gone!

I felt a trifle mixed. I heard behind me the roar of voices. I knew that I had lost my chance. But, at the moment, that was not the trouble. Where had Joyce come from? Where had he gone?

'Now then, Steyning! All together, and you'll do it!'

I heard Mason's voice ring out above the hubbub.

'Brixham, Brixham!' shouted Lance. 'Play up!'

'Joyce or no Joyce,' I told myself, 'hang me if I won't do it yet!'

I got on side. Blaine had hold of the leather. They were on him like a cartload of bricks. He passed to Giffard.

'Don't run back!' I screamed.

They drove him back. He passed to me. They were on the ball as soon as I was. They sent me spinning. Somebody got hold of it. Just as he was off I made a grab at his leg. He went down on his face. The ball broke loose. I got on to my feet. They were indulging in what looked to me very much like hacking. We sent the leather through, and Lance was off! Their fellows backed him up in style. They kept us off until he had a start. He bore off to the right. Already he had shaken off our forwards. I saw Mason charge him. I saw that he sent Mason flying. I made for him. I caught him round the waist. He passed to Pendleton. Pendleton was downed. He lost the ball. Back it came to me, and I was off!

I was away before most of them knew what had become of the leather. Again there was only Rivers between the goal and me. He soon was out of the reckoning. The mud beat him. As he was making for me down he came upon his hands and knees. I had been running wide till then. When he came to grief I centred. Should I take the leather in, or drop?

'Drop!' shouted a voice behind.

That settled me. I was within easy range of the goal. I ought to manage the kick. I dropped—at least, I tried to. It was only a try, because, just as I had my toe against the ball, and was in the very act of kicking, Joyce stood right in front of me! He stood so close that, so to speak, he stood right on the ball. It fell dead, it didn't travel an inch. As I made my fruitless effort, and was still poised upon one leg, placing his hand against my chest, he pushed me over backwards. As I fell I saw him smile—just as I had seen him smile when he had baulked me just before.

I didn't feel like smiling. I felt still less like smiling when, as I yet lay sprawling, Rivers, pouncing on the ball, dropped it back into the centre of the field. He was still standing by me when I regained my feet. He volunteered an observation.

'Lucky for us you muffed that kick.'

'Where's Joyce?' I asked.

'Where's who?'

'Joyce.'

He stared at me.

'I don't know what you're driving at. I think you fellows must have got Joyce on the brain'.

He returned to his place in the field. I returned to mine. I had an affectionate greeting from Giffard.

'That's the second chance you've thrown away. Whatever made you muff that kick?'

'Giffard,' I asked, 'do you think I'm going mad?'

'I should think you've gone.'

I could not—it seems ridiculous, but I could not ask if he had seen Joyce. It was so evident that he had not. And yet, if I had seen him, he must have seen him too. As he suggested—I must have gone mad!

The play was getting pretty rough, the ground was getting pretty heavy. We had churned it into a regular quagmire. Sometimes we went above the ankle in liquid mud. As for the state that we were in!

One of theirs had the ball. Half a dozen of ours had hold of him.

'Held! held!' they yelled.

'It's not held,' he gasped.

They had him down, and sat on him. Then he owned that it was held.

'Let it through,' cried Mason, when the leather was in scrimmage.

Before our forwards had a chance they rushed it through. We picked it up; we carried it back. They rushed it through again. The tide of battle swayed, now to this side, now to that. Still we gained. Two or three short runs bore the ball within punting distance of their goal. We more than retained the advantage. Yard by yard we drove them back. It was a match against time. We looked like winning if there was only time enough. At last it seemed as though matters had approached something very like a settlement. Pendleton had the ball. Our men were on to him. To avoid being held he punted. But he was charged before he really had a chance. The punt was muddled. It was a catch for Mason. He made his mark—within twenty yards of their goal! There is no better drop-kick in England than Alec Mason. If from a free kick at that distance he couldn't top their bar, we might as well go home to bed.

Mason took his time. He judged the distance with his eye. Then, paying no attention to the Brixham forward, who had stood up to his mark, he dropped a good six feet on his own side of it. There was an instant's silence. Then they raised a yell; for as the ball left Mason's foot one of their men sprang at him, and, leaping upwards, caught the ball in the air. It was wonderfully done! Quick as lightning, before we had recovered from our surprise, he had dropped the ball back into the centre of the field.

'Now then, Brixham,' bellowed Lance.

And they came rushing on. They came on too! We were so disconcerted by Mason's total failure that they got the drop on us. They reached the leather before our back had time to return. It was all we could do to get upon the scene of action quickly enough to prevent their having the scrimmage all to themselves. Mason's collapse had put life into them as much as, for the moment, it had taken it out of us. They carried the ball through the scrimmage as though our forwards were not there.

'Now then, Steyning, you're not going to let them beat us!'

As Mason held his peace I took his place as fugleman.

But we could not stand against them—we could not—in scrimmage or out of it. All at once they seemed to be possessed. In an instant their back play improved a hundred per cent. One of their men, in particular, played like Old Nick himself. In the excitement—and they were an exciting sixty seconds—I could not make out which one of them it was; but he made things lively. He as good as played us single-handed; he was always on the ball; he seemed to lend their forwards irresistible impetus when it was in the scrimmage. And when it was out of it, wasn't he just upon the spot. He was ubiquitous—here, there, and everywhere. And at last he was off. Exactly how it happened is more than I can say, but I saw that he had the ball. I saw him dash away with it. I made for him. He brushed me aside as though I were a fly. I was about to start in hot pursuit when someone caught me by the arm. I turned—in a trifle of a rage. There was Mason at my side.

'Never mind that fellow. Listen to me.' These were funny words to come from the captain of one's team at the very crisis of the game. I both listened and looked. Something in the expression of his face quite startled me. 'Do you know who it was who spoilt my kick? It was either Joyce or—Joyce's ghost.'

Before I was able to ask him what it was he meant there arose a hullaballoo of shouting. I turned, just in time to see the fellow, who had run away with the leather, drop it, as sweetly as you please, just over our goal. They had won! And at that moment the whistle sounded—they had done it just on time!

The man who had done the trick turned round and faced us. He was wearing a worsted cap, such as brewers wear. Taking it off, he waved it over his head. As he did so there was not a man upon the field who did not see him clearly, who did not know who he was. He was Frank Joyce! He stood there for a moment before us all, and then was gone.

'Lance,' shouted the referee, 'here's a telegram for you.'

Lance was standing close to Mason and to me. A telegraph boy came pelting up. Lance took the yellow envelope which the boy held out to him. He opened it.

'Why! what!' Through the mud upon his face he went white, up to the roots of his hair. He turned to us with startled eyes. 'Joyce died in Brixham Hospital nearly an hour ago. The hospital people have telegraphed to say so.'

BIOGRAPHICAL NOTES

1

'An Engineer's Story' by Amelia [Ann] B[lanford] Edwards (1831–92). First published in *All the Year Round* (1866); reprinted in *Monsieur Maurice* (3 vols., 1873). Amelia Edwards became a published author at the age of 7 and went on to become a prolific and successful novelist and journalist. In the late 1850s she was on the staff of the *Saturday Review* and the *Morning Post* and in 1864 achieved major success with her novel *Barbara's History*. After a trip to the Middle East in 1873 she became passionately interested in ancient Egypt and helped found the Egypt Exploration Fund in 1882. She was also a supporter of the women's suffrage movement.

2

'Madam Crowl's Ghost' by J[oseph] S[heridan] Le Fanu (1814–73). First published in *All the Year Round* (31 Dec. 1870); later incorporated in 'A Strange Adventure in the Life of Miss Laura Mildmay' (in *Chronicles of Golden Friars*, 1871); reprinted as the title story in M. R. James's selection *Madam Crowl's Ghost, and Other Tales of Mystery* (1923). Le Fanu was born in Dublin, into an old Huguenot family, and was related to the dramatist Richard Brinsley Sheridan on his father's side. He was called to the Irish Bar in 1839 but never practised. Many of his stories and novels— including his most famous novel, *Uncle Silas* (1864)—were first published in the *Dublin University Magazine*, of which he was the proprietor from 1861 to 1870.

3

'Poor Pretty Bobby' by Rhoda Broughton (1840–1920). First published in *Temple Bar* (Dec. 1872); repr. in *Tales for Christmas Eve* (1873). Rhoda Broughton, who was related to J. S. Le Fanu, was amongst the most successful women novelists of the Victorian period. Her best-selling works included *Cometh Up As a Flower* (1867) and *Red as a Rose Is She* (1870). *Tales for Christmas Eve* (reissued and enlarged as *Twilight Stories* in 1879) was her only collection of ghost stories, in the writing of which she was encouraged by Le Fanu.

4

'The Ghostly Rental' by Henry James (1843–1916). Published in *Scribner's Monthly* (Sept. 1876); not reprinted during James's lifetime. Born in New York, James settled in Europe in 1875, by which time he was a regular contributor of reviews and short stories to American periodicals such as *Scribner's*. His first major novel,

Roderick Hudson, was published in the same year as 'The Ghostly Rental'. His celebrated ghost novella *The Turn of the Screw* was published in 1898. Several other supernatural tales are scattered amongst his short stories. They include 'The Romance of Certain Old Clothes' (1875), 'Sir Edmund Orme' (1891), 'Nona Vincent' (1892), 'The Altar of the Dead' (1895), and 'The Great Good Place' (1900). All James's ghost stories were collected by Leon Edel and published in 1948.

5

'The Lady's Walk' by Margaret Oliphant *née* Wilson (1828–97). Published in *Longman's Magazine* (Dec. 1882, Jan. 1883). Mrs Oliphant was one of the most prolific of all Victorian novelists, with over a hundred works of fiction to her credit. Her first novel, *Margaret Maitland* (published anonymously in 1849), was praised by Charlotte Brontë and was quickly followed by others, including her celebrated 'Chronicles of Carlingford' series, beginning with *Salem Chapel* in 1863. She was reportedly Queen Victoria's favourite novelist. She also wrote several 'Stories of the Seen and the Unseen', including the well-known 'The Open Door'.

6

'No. 11 Welham Square' by Sir Herbert Stephen (1857–1932). Published in the *Cornhill Magazine* (May 1885), with illustrations by George du Maurier. The son of the barrister and judge Sir James Fitzjames Stephen (1829–94), some of whose legal works he re-edited, Herbert Stephen was educated at Rugby and Trinity College, Cambridge. He was called to the Bar in 1881 and succeeded to his father's baronetcy in 1894. In his early days he contributed journalistic pieces to the *Saturday Review* and other periodicals and from 1889 to 1927 was Clerk of Assize on the Northern Circuit.

7

'The Khitmatgar' by B[ithia] M[ary] Croker *née* Sheppard (1860?–1921). From *To Let* (1893). Bithia Sheppard was born in Ireland but educated in England. After her marriage to an officer in the Royal Scots Guards she spent several years in India, which forms the background to much of her fiction. Her first novel, *Proper Pride*, was published in 1882. Anglo-Indian life was also described in *Pretty Miss Neville* (1883), whilst her native Ireland features in *Beyond the Pale* (1897).

8

'Old Gervais' by Mary Louisa Molesworth *née* Stewart (1839–1921). From *Studies and Stories* (1893). Mary Molesworth began publishing novels in 1869, initially under the pseudonym 'Ennis Graham'. Her adult fiction included *Not Without Thorns* (1873) and *Cicely* (1874). In 1876 she turned to children's fiction with what is probably her best-known work *Carrots*. Other works for children included *The*

Cuckoo Clock (1877) and *Christmas Tree Land* (1895). Her main collection of super-natural stories was *Uncanny Tales* (1896).

9

'The Phantom Model' by Hume Nisbet (1849–*c.*1920). From *The Haunted Station* (1894). Nisbet, born in Scotland, spent much of his youth in Australia, returning there in 1855 after a spell teaching art in Edinburgh. Several of his novels—for instance *Bail Up* (1890) and *A Bush Girl's Romance* (1894)—drew on his colonial experience. As well as his novels and short stories he also published poetry.

10

'When I Was Dead' by Vincent O'Sullivan (1872–1940). From *A Book of Bargains* (1896). O'Sullivan was born in America but educated in England. He was a minor *fin-de-siècle* figure, a friend of Oscar Wilde and Aubrey Beardsley, who wrote poetry (*The Houses of Sin*, 1897) as well as a small but well-crafted body of short stories with supernatural themes. His other fiction collections are *The Green Window* (1899) and *Human Affairs* (1907).

11

'Dark Dignum' by Bernard Capes (1854–1918). From *At a Winter's Fire* (1899). Capes was born in London and educated at the Catholic Beaumont College. He began work in a tea-broker's office and went on to study art at the Slade, after which he turned to publishing and journalism. Until his death from influenza at the age of 64 he poured out a flood of short stories, novels, articles, and reviews. He remains an important but underrated writer of supernatural fiction with a fertile but deeply pessimistic imagination. A collection of his tales of terror, selected and introduced by Hugh Lamb, was published in 1989 as *The Black Reaper*.

12

'The Fifteenth Man' by Richard Marsh (1857–1915). From *The Seen and the Unseen* (1900). Marsh is perhaps best remembered for his classic novel of the macabre, *The Beetle*, published in 1897 (the same year as Bram Stoker's *Dracula*). Marsh regularly contributed stories to monthly magazines such as the *Strand*. As well as *The Seen and the Unseen*, Marsh's tales of terror and the supernatural can be found in two other collections, *Marvels and Mysteries* (1900) and *Between the Dark and the Daylight* (1902). He was the grandfather of the distinguished ghost-story writer Robert Aickman (1914–81).